Guy Walters was a journalist on *The Times* for eight years, where he travelled around the world and reported on a wide variety of subjects. He is married with two children, and lives in Wiltshire. His other novels, *The Traitor*, *The Leader* and *The Occupation* are also available from Headline.

Also by Guy Walters

Non-fiction
The Voice of War (ed)

Fiction
The Traitor
The Leader
The Occupation

THE COLDITZ LEGACY

Guy Walters

headline

First published in 2005
by HEADLINE BOOK PUBLISHING

First published in paperback in 2006
by HEADLINE BOOK PUBLISHING

A HEADLINE paperback

1

ISBN 0 7553 2717 9 (Super A format)
ISBN 0 7553 3199 0 (A format)

Typeset in Goudy by Avon DataSet Ltd,
Bidford-on-Avon, Warwickshire

Printed and bound in Great Britain by
Mackays of Chatham plc, Chatham, Kent

HEADLINE BOOK PUBLISHING
A division of Hodder Headline
338 Euston Road
London NW1 3BH

www.headline.co.uk
www.hodderheadline.com

This book is for
ALICE

This book is for
ALICE

Prologue

East Germany, 1973

FRÄULEIN ERICA GARTNER threw her half-finished cigarette on to the damp cobbles, where it hissed briefly before expelling its last curl of smoke. The steepness of the hill meant that her lungs required air, and she regretted obeying the craving that had made her light up as she walked through the market square. She had done this climb five days a week for the past six years, and it had never got any easier. When the weather was very bad – which it often was – Fräulein Gartner found it hard to keep her balance, and on a few occasions she had slipped and dirtied her uniform. The ward sisters were always unsympathetic to her excuses, telling her she was clumsy, and nobody else seemed to fall over, did they?

This morning Fräulein Gartner knew she was going to slip. Last night's storm had made the cobbles particularly slippery, and the worn soles of

1

her shoes afforded her almost no grip. She held her arms slightly away from her body in an effort to secure more balance, an act of gentle gymnastics that drew the smirking attention of a couple of overcoated men, who were watching her through two smeary holes they had wiped on their fugged-up windscreen.

Fräulein Gartner stopped when she saw them, her progress arrested by sudden panic. She knew who they were – not their names, of course – but where they were from. It wasn't always so easy to spot Stasi men, but sometimes secret policemen weren't so secret. Perhaps it was deliberate. Perhaps they wanted people to know they were being watched.

But who were they watching? Fräulein Gartner wondered. Was it her? No, not now, not after so long. That was all in the past: they had forgiven her, had told her that such 'political errors' were normal for a girl of her age. They had taken the radio, sent her a receipt for it, and that had been that. Yet what had they said to her back then? 'Fräulein Gartner, one day we may need you to perform a service for us, and we will expect you to do it.' She remembered the man who told her, a young captain – quite handsome, in fact – with hair slicked back like a movie star from the West, one of the stars she was supposed never to have heard of. He had seemed friendly, but there was a certainty in his voice, a directness of tone, reinforced by the exact way in which he kept his fingertips pressed firmly together. Was now the time, this Thursday morning, when they would finally call upon her?

Fräulein Gartner looked up at the car, partly expecting to see the face of the captain. The men were still staring at her, still smiling. What at? Was there something funny about her? Or something funny about what they were going to do to her? She imagined them getting out of the car, seizing her by the arms and hustling her into the back, there to be driven to Leipzig to face the same captain in the same interrogation room. Was that what they found so funny?

She continued walking, doing her best not to let her eyes flit towards the car as she edged closer. She sensed that the men were still smiling – was that a laugh? She concentrated on the cobbles. Just keep going, ignore them, don't lose grip.

Eventually, and without slipping, she made it past the car. She visibly relaxed, her shoulders dropping down. So they weren't looking for her, after all. Perhaps they just happened to be parked there for no reason, or maybe they were looking for someone else. Who? No one sprang to mind; she hadn't heard that anyone was in trouble.

She carried on up the hill and, slightly breathless, arrived at the main gate to the hospital. It was gloomy, she thought, this old castle, dirty, huge and cold. Hardly a place to make people feel better, more a place to shut them away and forget about them. There were lots here, mostly men who had lost their minds in the war and spent days gazing out of windows across the damp countryside.

She presented her pass at the little office under the first arch. It was Frau Munt this morning, the usual Glatt cigarette wedged between her yellow teeth, the office reeking of countless other Glatts.

'Good morning,' said Fräulein Gartner, and Frau Munt grunted, raising an indifferent eye to a pass that had been presented to her month after month, year after year.

'Did you see the men in the car?' Fräulein Gartner asked.

'I did.'

'Why are they here? Are they looking for someone?'

'A new patient is coming,' said Frau Munt. 'From Berlin. Someone important, I hear. You'd do well to keep your nose down this morning.'

'Who's the patient?'

'How the hell should I know?' Frau Munt replied, and with that she stuck her fat head back into the pages of her thin magazine.

Fräulein Gartner put her pass back into her small handbag and walked into the main hospital courtyard. She strolled thoughtfully across it, ignoring the

4

looming great centuries-old edifice that surrounded her. A new patient? From Berlin? She expected it was a senior official – they had a few in here, and the staff were threatened with imprisonment if they mentioned their presence.

She reached the bottom of a small spiral staircase and waited for the set of footsteps coming down to materialise into the figure of Dr Petersen.

'Good morning, Fräulein Gartner!'

Dr Petersen was cheery and handsome, and she had a soft spot for him. It was pointless – the man was happily married with two teenage boys – but, still, she could not help it.

'Good morning, Doctor,' she replied, blushing.

'Horrible morning.'

'Yes, yes, it is.'

Petersen walked off into the courtyard, no doubt aware that her eyes were boring into his back. Fräulein Gartner let out a small, rueful sigh, and climbed the steps to the third floor. She stepped into a wide corridor, along which lay the entrances to eight wards.

The sister was walking towards her, anxiety on her face. 'I want everything to be perfect today,' she said. 'We've got a new patient from Berlin.'

'So I hear.'

The sister ignored her. 'We've been told to take great care of him, and I'd like him to be your responsibility, Nurse Gartner.'

Fräulein Gartner nodded. She hated patients like this. She far preferred the anonymous men, those with no names. No one expected them to make any progress, but when they did it was always most satisfying. But with the important patients, there was always some pressure on for a result, even if everyone knew it was impossible.

'When is he arriving, Sister?'

'At twelve o'clock.'

Fräulein Gartner spent her morning on her usual duties, and even managed to make old Hirschfeld smile. She had told him a joke she had recently heard, and at first she thought he had not understood: his face remained set in its usual blankness. But then his eyes crinkled, and his lips turned upwards, and he smiled a great smile, albeit one with only a few teeth in it.

At five minutes to twelve, the sister bustled up and down the corridor ensuring that everything was indeed perfect, and told Nurse Gartner to stand by the new patient's bed. He was a little late, but when he appeared he was escorted by two armed guards, whose presence was unusual but not entirely unexpected. The patient looked like a nice man, Fräulein Gartner thought, although he had a haunted expression on his face – one that she had seen all too often.

'Nurse,' said the sister, 'this is Herr Knopf. He will be under your personal care from now on.'

'Hello, Herr Knopf,' said Fräulein Gartner, smiling.

Herr Knopf smiled back weakly. He was in his fifties, she thought, although a lot of his hair was missing. He walked with a slight stoop, and when he got into bed, it was clear that it was a relief to be off his feet. The two guards left the room, along with the sister, and Fräulein Gartner was alone with her new patient. This was strange, she thought. She had been told nothing about Herr Knopf, not even what was wrong with him. Who was he? she wondered. He looked too nice to be a politician or a member of the Stasi. She didn't want to ask, because he might still wield an immense amount of power, which he could use to have her dismissed or locked up for asking prying questions.

Even if she had wanted to question him, it would not have been possible: within a couple of minutes he had fallen asleep. He was almost like a little boy now that his face had lost the haunted look.

The sleep-talking started a few minutes later, accompanied by much tossing and turning. It began as an indistinct mumble, but soon developed into a shout. Fräulein Gartner did not understand the words because they were not German. What were they? French? English?

'Put me down! You go over – you go!'

7

Fräulein Gartner rushed to the bed and held him. She did not want to shake him awake because that might frighten him. She stroked his forehead, and uttered some comforting phrases. The man's eyes snapped open, and he looked up at her quizzically. 'Where am I?' he asked in English.

'I'm sorry,' said Fräulein Gartner, 'I do not understand you. Can you speak German?'

The man blinked a few times, then nodded.

'Where am I?' he asked in German.

'You're in hospital,' she said. 'It's all right. Everything's all right.'

'Which hospital?'

'Why does it matter?'

'Which hospital?'

'Well, it's called Colditz.'

At that, the colour drained from Herr Knopf's face.

Chapter One

April 1941

HUGH HARTLEY GLANCED at his watch. Quarter to eleven. They would be here soon. A few thousand German troops were somewhere over there, just a few miles to the north, accompanied by God knew how many planes and tanks. How long would it take them? A few hours? A day? The Germans didn't keep a timetable, but they might as well have done. So far they had steamed through Greece in a matter of weeks, passing effortlessly through towns and villages. Some said they were unstoppable, a view to which Hartley secretly subscribed but never voiced, certainly not in front of the men.

The men. They were working hard and quickly, the underside of the bridge now bearing at least a dozen charges. That would stop them, thought Hartley, at least for a while. So far they hadn't fired a shot, let alone seen a German, but to blow up this bridge would make them feel as if they were getting their own back, especially after yesterday's Stuka attack. Some of the men bore wounds from the rocks that had been chipped up by the plane's machine-gun fire. A bandage wrapped round Corporal Stephenson's head revealed that he had been the worst hit, closely followed by Sergeant Franklin, whose upper arm was still oozing red and yellow. It was remarkable that nobody had been directly hit, torn to pieces, like some of the olive trees under which they had hidden.

Hartley's only casualty was his sunglasses, which had been crushed as he landed in a ditch. It was not for some ten minutes after the Stuka had departed that he had felt the jabbing pain in his left side – the sharp shards of lens piercing through shirt and skin. He had looked down, seen the blood, assumed for a panicky moment that he had been hit, then had pincered out a twisted mass of Christmas present from Sarah. He had thrown them back into the ditch, vowing that he would never tell her what had happened. 'Pinched in Athens,' he would say, 'some bloody urchin.'

'How are we doing, S'arnt Franklin?'

'Nearly there, sir.'

'How soon is "nearly"?'

Franklin shrugged his shoulders. 'Five minutes, sir, maybe ten.'

'Make it five,' said Hartley.

'Sir.'

Hartley squinted up into the blue, expecting to see another Stuka. The attack had unnerved him, its full enormity only now dawning on him. A man he had never met had tried to kill him yesterday. Yes, yes, he knew that that was what this was all about, what all his training had taught him, but there it was: a feeling of total dread. It was hard not showing it to the men, who were presumably trying to cope in the same way he was. Some had made light of it, even joked about it as they crammed into the one lorry that hadn't been hit, but no one had slept well last night. Young Private Bell had had a nightmare and had woken up screaming. Franklin had calmed him down in his brutal fashion, saying that if Private Bell didn't shut it right now, Franklin would stick his fist in his gob. That had done the trick, Hartley recalled.

Hartley estimated that the bridge had a hundred-foot span. A murky river flowed a couple of hundred feet below in no hurry to get to the sea. The banks were steep, and it would be impossible for the Germans to get their armour across with the bridge demolished. They would have to take a thirty-mile detour up and down the valley just to get back to the point where Hartley was standing. That should delay them by at least a day – or longer, if any of the infantry units managed to hold them up. There were some New Zealanders around here somewhere, good sorts, tough. Who knows? Perhaps they might finally stop them.

Another glance at the watch. Coming up for ten to. This was taking far too long. Hartley strode over to the side of the bridge. The men were busying themselves beneath it, attaching the detonator cord between the charges. They were doing a good job, had placed the explosives exactly where Hartley had told them – on the cross struts where the damage would be greatest: he had heard too many stories of the Germans repairing bridges in a few hours. Well, that wasn't going to happen with this one. They were going to blow the whole bloody thing into the sky. What was more, watching it would be fun.

'This is looking good, S'arnt Franklin.'

'Thank you, sir,' said Franklin, who was scrabbling up the slope with the detonator cable wrapped round a wooden reel.

Hartley leant down, held out his hand and heaved him up the last few feet.

'Thank you, sir.'

Hartley studied Franklin's arm. The bandage was disconcertingly filthy. Hartley had told Franklin that he didn't have to perform gymnastics under the bridge, but Franklin had insisted that he did his bit, as Hartley had known he would.

'How's your arm?'

Franklin briefly inspected it. 'It'll be all right, sir.'

'Not if you don't get it dressed it won't,' said Hartley. 'Get Miller to look at it after we've done this.'

'Yes, sir.'

'Good. I don't want you getting back to Derbyshire minus an arm.'

Franklin smiled. 'No, sir. My wife would be most unhappy.'

Hartley smiled back, allowing himself a second's thought about Sarah. He snapped himself out of it. 'Anyway, are we ready?' he asked.

'Yes, sir. Here's the cable.'

Hartley took it, then stepped backwards, feeding it out slowly from the reel. He was tempted to run with it, but he knew that that might nick the cable and cause it to fail. As it was, half of this bloody equipment was unreliable, no doubt stored in some damp quartermaster's stores in Croydon for the best part of ten years, then several weeks in a boat, a few months in a store outside Alexandria, more weeks in a boat, then rattled in a lorry along the worst roads the Greeks could offer.

The men, who looked in no better condition, now joined Franklin on the road. They were tired and their ten young faces had aged over the past few weeks. The rest of Hartley's unit, another twenty men, had been sent south to act as infantrymen rather than as sappers. Hartley had protested, but Major George had said it wasn't his decision, and that as far as he could work out it was nobody's decision, but there it was, Captain, so just get on with it, would you?

'Come on, get over here!' Hartley shouted, waving the men towards him.

'Quickly!' yelled Franklin.

The men ran, clearly having to coax their reluctant legs into action.

Hartley stopped unwinding the cable after fifty yards.

'Right,' he said, to no one in particular. 'This should do. Who's got the plunger?'

'Here, sir,' said Bell, passing him the small charger.

Hartley looked at the battered black box with disdain. The chances of it working were slim. With his pocket knife, he stripped away some of the cable's covering to reveal two strands of copper wire, which he now attached to the two terminals on the charger. Franklin watched him, the occasional bead of sweat dropping off his nose. Hartley had no problem with the sergeant's close attention – after all, the man was a far better engineer than he was.

'That look good to you, S'arnt?'

'Dandy, sir.'

Dandy? It was as if they were building a train set, thought Hartley. 'Well, the proof of the pudding is in the exploding.' He turned to the men. 'All right, we're live.'

The men crouched down. There was no doubting that all of them were gaining boyish excitement from this. Who wouldn't?

Hartley lifted the plunger. Please let the buggering thing work.

He pressed it down firmly and steeled himself for the explosion.

Nothing.

'Shit!' said Hartley.

He lifted up the plunger and brought it down again. 'Come on! What's wrong with this bloody thing?'

Franklin wiped his nose. 'Dirt, sir?'

'Your guess is as good as mine.'

Hartley pressed the plunger up and down several more times, his temper rising with the tempo. Don't lose your rag, he told himself. You know it'll work eventually. 'All right, Franklin, we'll have to take it apart. You do that while I check the charges and the cord. The men can stay put.'

'Sir!'

Hartley passed the plunger to Franklin and walked slowly along the length of the white cable. This was infuriating. Because of some ropy piece of kit, the Germans were going to have a *laissez-passer* across the river. For the want of a nail . . . Hartley studied the cable with care, brushing aside the occasional stone with the toe of his boot. It looked fine. The problem had to be with the damn plunger. He reached the bridge and half slid, half walked down the bank to the bridge's supports. Once again, as far as Hartley could tell, the cable was intact. It had to be the plunger.

Bent double, fingertips pressed to the ground so that he kept his balance, Hartley made his way back up the bank. Franklin was being assisted by Corporal Stephenson, both men kneeling over the dismembered plunger, a selection of tools on the ground beside them.

'Any joy?'

Franklin turned his head as Hartley approached him. He was smiling, thank God. 'Just a loose wire, sir. There's tons of dust and all sorts of crap in here. We're just giving it a clean, and then—'

'Good!' Hartley interrupted. 'But you don't have to make it spotless.'

'Yes, sir.'

Franklin continued to busy himself with the plunger. Hartley allowed himself another look at his watch. It was precisely eleven o'clock. So far, this had taken just over an hour – far too long. Many of the men were smoking, chatting idly in the sun. He knew he should be making them clean the lorry, but they deserved the break: they had worked hard. Was he too soft on them? Perhaps. Some of his fellow officers were real martinets. Hartley always suspected that the strictest were in some way the weakest, those whose authority came from the pips on their shoulders and not from within. It was hard, near impossible, to find the right balance.

Hartley did not hear the car immediately. He should have done, because the air was still and the sound was out of place.

'Sir!'

Hartley heard Franklin's shout at the same time as he heard the vehicle. With his left hand, he unbuttoned his holster hurriedly, and with the right he withdrew his revolver, all the time keeping his gaze fixed on the road on the other side of the bridge. 'Get back!' he shouted.

Hartley did not turn to check that his order was obeyed: he knew his men would need little encouragement to find whatever cover was available.

He pointed the revolver down the length of the bridge, listening to the increasing volume of the engine. It sounded close, very close, just round the bend before the bridge. The engine was screaming for its driver to change up a gear. Who the hell could it be? A German reconnaissance unit? No, they wouldn't be making so much noise.

Hartley noticed that the gun was shaking in his hand as he eased off the safety catch. His legs were weak, almost ready to buckle. This is pathetic, he told himself, but he couldn't control his muscles. He had to keep composed, not give in to his body, which was telling him to flee, to duck down the bank next to the bridge and hide.

The vehicle came into view, a trail of thick, sandy dust chasing behind it. Hartley's right index finger tightened over the trigger. As it started to cross the bridge, he could see the make of vehicle clearly – it was a jeep, a bloody jeep. Nevertheless, he kept his revolver pointing towards it, aiming at the driver's side of the windscreen. It could easily be a trap, some sort of German trick. The driver must be able to see him, he thought, so why the hell wasn't he slowing down?

Even if Hartley fired, he knew that his chance of hitting the driver was slight. He just had to hope the driver saw him and the gun, then slowed down. The jeep was now halfway across the bridge, with only fifty yards to go. Should he fire? What if it was a British soldier? Hartley strained his eyes to see the man through the windscreen, but the reflection made it opaque. The jeep roared on, engine still complaining. He had to fire: there was no choice. Whoever was driving it, enemy or not, was trouble.

Hartley took a brief aim at the left of the windscreen and squeezed the trigger. The revolver kicked up in his clenched hands, and the windscreen shattered. The driver was visible now – he was wearing a British uniform. Hartley could just about make out the wide-eyed, frantic look on his face. Suddenly, the jeep slowed violently, then swerved, crashing into the side of the bridge. Hartley held his breath as he watched it splinter through the flimsy wooden barrier.

'Oh, God,' he exhaled.

The jeep halted, its front wheels hanging over the side of the bridge. The driver was thrust forward, face and chest smashed into the steering-wheel. Hartley ran forward, pistol still at the ready. He could see that the man was a captain, but what was more important was his precarious position. He was motionless, his head lying drunkenly over the rim of the wheel.

Hartley shoved his revolver back into its holster. He ran round the jeep and attempted to open the driver's door, but it was wedged shut. He leant over the door and grabbed the man by the back of his tunic, pulling him as gently as he could. The man collapsed into the seat, his thin face a mass of cuts and bruises. A small amount of blood trickled from his mouth. Surely he hadn't killed him?

'Can you hear me?' Hartley shouted.

There was no reply.

Hartley looked back down the bridge towards the men. 'Miller!' he yelled.

The officer came to about fifteen minutes later. Corporal Miller told Hartley that, apart from the cuts, he was suffering from no more than some bad bruising on his chest. The bleeding had been caused by the loss of a tooth. His tunic was spotted with blood.

'Aha!' exclaimed Hartley. 'Here he comes!'

The man's eyes opened slowly and adjusted to the midday light.

Although he was relieved that the soldier was still alive, Hartley was furious with him. What the hell had he thought he was playing at, driving like that? He must be unhinged. Or scared. Then there was the small matter of the bridge, which still needed to be destroyed.

'Can you hear me?'

The man opened his mouth a little. 'Yes,' he croaked.

'What's your name?'

The man paused.

'Your *name*,' Hartley insisted.

'Royce,' said the man. 'Malcolm Royce.'

'Can you prove it?'

The man reached inside his tunic, but the movement caused him pain.

'All right,' said Hartley. 'I'll get it.'

Hartley unbuttoned the tunic, reached inside and pulled out a brown leather wallet. He flicked it open, and got out the man's identity card. Hartley frowned. Although the name and face matched, the man shouldn't have been carrying the card so near to the front line – it carried far too much information. He replaced it. There was a photograph of a woman in a WRNS uniform in the wallet too, and he took it out. She was stunning, he thought.

'Who's this?'

'Jackie. My sister.'

Hartley had expected it to be a sweetheart. 'Nice-looking, if I may say so.'

Royce's face did not register.

'Where're you and she from?' asked Hartley.

'Near Gillingham.'

'Which one?'

Royce didn't pause. 'Dorset, of course.'

Hartley slipped the photograph back into the wallet. If the man was a spy, he was well trained.

'You got an identity disc?'

Royce lifted a hand to his neck and tugged at a black leather bootlace. Hartley pulled out a small metal disc. Once more, Royce's identity was confirmed, and that he was blood group O. There were many more questions he wanted to ask, but this was not the time.

He stood up. 'Get him in the back of the lorry, would you, Miller?'

'Sir.'

Hartley walked over to where Franklin and Stephenson were waiting with the plunger.

'All right, S'arnt?'

'I think so, sir.'

'Good. Let's get a move on.'

Once more, Hartley informed the men that they were live. Franklin passed the plunger to Hartley.

'No, Sergeant, why don't you do it? You could do with a present to make up for your arm.'

Franklin grinned. 'You sure, sir?'

'No. But do it now before I change my mind.'

Franklin lifted the plunger's handle. 'Apologies to all those fine Greeks who built this bridge,' he said, then slammed down the handle.

There was a pause, and then an almighty blast filled the air. The bridge leapt a few feet, causing the jeep to dislodge and fall. The ground shook and, with a grinding sound, the bridge collapsed, replacing itself with a thick cloud of dust and debris. The men cheered. They deserved it, thought Hartley, after all they'd done.

But now it was time to go and find the next valley, the next bridge. He would talk to the new arrival in the lorry.

It was clear that every jolt caused Royce immense pain, despite Miller's dispensation of two large aspirins. Nevertheless, Hartley was determined to find out what had caused him to be driving so insanely fast in a jeep on his own.

'So, what happened, Royce?'

The two men sat in the lorry's cab. Private Bell was driving them down a succession of ludicrously sharp bends, on one side of which there were nearly sheer drops of a few hundred feet. Hartley had found that the best way to deal with any sort of incipient acrophobia was simply to look straight ahead.

Royce didn't reply.

'Come on, man,' said Hartley, 'don't tell me you've got amnesia.'

'I wish I had,' said Royce.

'Go on.'

'They were all killed.'

'Who?'

'My men. All of them.'

'How?'

Hartley turned to look at Royce: his face was expressionless.

'Two bloody great tanks. We were in a church and they destroyed it. Collapsed on top of us.'

'Jeeesus!' Bell exclaimed.

'Quiet, Private!' snapped Hartley.

Bell cleared his throat. 'Sorry, sir.'

'So how did you get out?'

Royce's eyes were glassy, moist. 'I was taking a leak. I didn't think it was right to pee in a church.'

Hartley nodded. 'I see. So, you decided to go outside even though there were tanks about?'

23

'I didn't know about the bloody tanks! For God's sake, man, what are you accusing me of?'

'Nothing. And, for heaven's sake, calm down, will you? It just seems an odd thing to do.'

'There's nothing *odd*, Captain Hartley, about not wishing to urinate in a church.'

'No, but there's something odd about abandoning your men.'

'I did not abandon my men! How dare you suggest—'

'I'm not suggesting anything,' Hartley interrupted. 'All I'm saying is that it looks strange.'

He sighed. There were too many parts of Royce's story that didn't make sense. Why was he the only survivor? Which men had been in the church? How had he got hold of the jeep? Royce was evidently one of two things: a spy or a coward. If he was a spy, he was both a very bad one and a very good one. Bad, because his story was atrociously fabricated, and good, because he was quickly able to say which county his Gillingham was in. But a spy would have gone into the field with a better cover story than the one he had, thought Hartley. No, he was clearly a coward, a deserter, perhaps. Maybe his unit was still engaging the Germans, and Royce had snapped, found a vehicle and driven away. The man was a deserter, and Hartley would hand him over to the first red-cap he could find. But God knew when that would be. Until then, it was best to keep the man calm, unsuspicious.

'I'd like to ask just one more question, if I may.'

Royce folded his arms. 'What?' he asked irritably.

'Why didn't you stop?'

'Stop where?'

'On the bridge. You must have seen my revolver.'

'I was panicking. I just wanted to get away from what I'd seen.'

Hartley nodded, but if Royce had looked into his eyes, he would have seen that he was unconvinced. Hartley played along with it. 'It must have been terrifying.'

'It was,' said Royce.

Had this been a different sort of conversation, a jocular exchange, Hartley would have waved his hand across Royce's face to snap him out of the stare. Whatever Royce was looking at, it wasn't the road.

'Are we stopping for lunch, sir?' It was Private Bell.

'Why? Do you know somewhere nice around here?' asked Hartley.

'A lovely little place called the White Hart,' said Bell. 'It's just a couple of miles down the road.'

'Good beer?'

'Ruddles, I hear.'

Hartley chuckled, and noticed that Royce's face was not registering even a hint of amusement. Sod him, frankly. 'All right, Bell, let's find some cover and have a brew.'

Bell beamed. 'Thank you, sir.'

Hartley turned to Royce. 'I don't suppose you brought any food with you?'

'Er . . . no. I'm afraid not.'

There was a surprise, thought Hartley. The sooner they got rid of him, the better.

It was clear that the men didn't care for Royce – and not only because his presence lightened their bowls a little. It was his attitude. Hartley heard the odd 'la-di-da' and 'Who the hell does he think he is?' as they ate a quick lunch in the shade of some pine trees. Royce made no effort to talk to them, and his expression was of either contempt, or distance, or a mixture of both. He offered no thanks when Barnes gave him a spare mug, neither did he acknowledge the soup that filled it. He sat on a rock a little apart from the men, and Hartley was in no mood to join him. Instead, he sat next to Franklin. 'What do you think of our new arrival, then, Franklin?'

Franklin finished chewing some stale bread. 'You want my honest opinion, Captain?'

'Yes.'

Franklin drew breath. 'I think he's a prick.'

Somewhere in the regulations, Hartley knew there was something about not allowing men to speak disrespectfully of officers.

'Well, that's certainly honest. Why?'

'Because he's a bloody coward.'

26

Hartley swigged some soup. He could only agree, but he thought it best not to share this. 'Maybe, Franklin. Or he's in shock.'

'I don't care. Shocked or not, he's still a coward.'

Hartley drained the soup. Whatever it was, it had tasted almost pleasant. He looked up through the thickness of the pine trees, the occasional gems of sunlight forming a kaleidoscopic pattern. The trees reminded him of the rushed honeymoon he and Sarah had had in Scotland last summer. They had lain under some pines, thinking it a romantic spot, only to find that their exposed legs and arms acted as bait for the midges.

'If only we'd blown the bridge a few minutes before,' said Franklin, 'he wouldn't be here.'

Briefly Hartley recalled his shot at the jeep. He was pleased – not smug – that he had done it. He had been nervous, all right, but he had stayed in control. He felt far better than he had after the Stuka. How would he have felt if he had killed Royce? Nothing? The man was a danger to his men and, like any good officer, it was his duty to protect them. If Royce had died, Hartley hazarded that he would even have been pleased. Was that awful? Sarah would say it was, but he wasn't sure she would be right.

'I want you to make sure that the men afford him the proper respect,' said Hartley.

Franklin looked at him over the rim of his mug.

His eyes told Hartley that Franklin knew his captain was only going through the motions. 'Of course, sir.'

'Good. Coward or no coward, he's still an officer.'

'Yes, sir.'

Hartley stood up. 'Tell the men we're off in five minutes. I don't fancy another Stuka having us for lunch.'

'Kalamata, that's where we're off to.'

'Where's that, then, Captain?'

'About as far south as we can go.'

'And what happens there?' asked Franklin.

'We're to wait.'

'For what?'

'I'd lay good money on a boat.'

The men stood in silence in the middle of the village's square while Lance Corporal Henderson packed away the radio. It was four hours later, and the journey down the valley had been uneventful. Royce had barely spoken, uttering only grunts in response to Hartley's questions. Hartley had tried to ask about his life in Britain, but Royce had said he didn't want to talk about it. Perhaps some other time.

'A boat where?' asked Miller.

'Even if I knew the answer,' Hartley replied, 'I certainly wouldn't tell you.'

'How far is it, this Calamity?'

Hartley rolled his eyes back. The pun was predict-

28

able, but he hadn't thought of it. Trust Bell. 'About a hundred kilometres – sixty-odd miles. All being well, we'll get there tomorrow night.'

'No more bridges, then?' asked Franklin.

'No. Our orders from Major George are to get south as fast as we can. But tonight we'll stay here.'

Hartley studied the faces of the villagers watching them. They had come through this village a month ago, on their way north, and had been welcomed as heroes. Bottles of wine and every imaginable delicacy had been presented to them, and from somewhere a Union flag had been produced and strung across the square. It was not in evidence today, and neither was there a rush to inundate them with gifts. The villagers were sombre, crestfallen. The British were leaving them to the mercy of the Germans. It would have been better had they not been there at all – at least then many lives would have been saved, many villages left intact. Hartley had heard such sentiments before, and he didn't need to hear them again. The Greeks' faces spoke loudly.

The one that spoke loudest belonged to George Liveris, the village's mayor. In his early forties with a splendid moustache, he was standing by the entrance to his shop, clutching his wife and two young daughters. Hartley walked up to them and removed his cap. 'I'm sorry, Mr Liveris,' he said. 'We really have tried as hard as we can.'

'I'm sure you have,' Liveris replied. 'We are very grateful for all your help. You British are brave people.'

'Well, it good of you to say so, but—'

'It is true. You are outnumbered, outgunned, and still you tried to fight. That is bravery, Captain.'

Hartley didn't respond. He didn't feel particularly brave. He looked down at the girls. They could be no more than eight or nine. By this time next year they would both be speaking German. Hartley wished there was something he could say to them, some consoling words, but none came. They were retreating, and that was that. It was shameful, abandoning these people. They had relied on the British, who had proved themselves incapable of helping them. Liveris was too much of gentleman to say so, but Hartley knew how he felt. 'I'm sorry to ask you, Mr Liveris, but my men and I, we need –'

'– Food and water.' Liveris completed his sentence. 'I have some for you. Not much, but enough. You and your men will be our guests tonight. You and the other officer can stay with my family, if you wish, and your men with my neighbours.'

'I'm very grateful. I can pay you for it.'

'I won't have it.'

'I wish you would accept, Mr Liveris. After all, this money will be of no use to me in a few days.'

Liveris looked down at the dirty crumpled notes in

Hartley's hand. 'It will be of no use to me either,' he said. 'I shall soon be using Reichsmarks.'

Hartley pushed the notes forward, but Liveris shook his head. 'You are still our guests, Captain Hartley.'

With the men billeted around the village, Hartley and Royce sat down in Liveris's dark kitchen. His wife was cooking a vast stew, and the room was filled with the aroma of herbs and woodsmoke from the fire. It felt homely, thought Hartley, but his appreciation of the setting was spoilt by Royce's presence, which was making him uneasy. So far, Royce had said nothing, but he looked disdainful.

The insult came sooner than Hartley had feared. Liveris had opened a bottle of retsina and had poured its contents into three large tumblers. 'Gentlemen,' he said, raising his glass, 'to victory.'

Hartley raised his glass. The toast was a good one, although both men knew it was an invocation that could not immediately be answered – perhaps not for a long time. Still, it had to be made. Royce, however, left his tumbler on the rough wooden table. 'Victory?' He snorted. 'What's the point? We may as well drink to surrender.'

Hartley put down his glass. Mrs Liveris stopped stirring her stew. Although she spoke no English, Royce's tone was universally recognisable.

31

'Don't talk like that, Royce.'

'Why not?'

'It's defeatist.'

'It's only the bloody truth. We're being defeated.'

Nobody said anything.

'Well, we are, aren't we? Or is this just another great victory like Dunkirk was?'

'Stop it, Royce.'

Royce glared at him. 'Aren't you the good boy, Captain? Loyal to the last, ready to go down with the sinking ship. We should never have been here in the first place.'

Hartley wanted to punch him, lay him out cold, but he kept calm. 'There's nothing wrong with loyalty,' he said. 'And even if we do have to leave Greece, the least we can do is promise the Greeks we'll come back.'

'What? And do another great job like we're doing at the moment?'

'I don't understand you, Royce. Do you think we should just give up and let the Germans take over the continent? Really?'

Royce paused. 'We should let these people fight their own battles. I've lost thirty men, thirty good men, and for what? To delay the Germans marching up to the Acropolis by – what? – five minutes? Ten?'

'It had to be tried, Royce. Not to have tried would have been despicable, cowardly.'

Royce leapt to his feet, sending his chair crashing back on to the stone floor. 'I'm no coward!'

Hartley resisted the urge to get up. He had no wish to argue with Royce in front of the Liverises, but this was too much. 'Is that so?' he said. 'If you were no coward you'd still be with your men, dead or alive.'

Royce's eyes grew wider. He looked insane, demented. 'Take that back!'

'No, I won't, because I mean it. And it's the truth.' Hartley knew he shouldn't have been speaking like this in front of their hosts, but he had been unable to stop himself.

'You have no idea what happened up there,' said Royce. 'No idea!'

'Then why don't you tell me?'

Royce glowered, then turned on his heel and stormed out. A few seconds later, they heard the front door slam shut. Hartley turned to Liveris. 'I'm sorry, Mr Liveris, he, um . . .'

Liveris held up his hands. 'You do not need to apologise.'

'He's been very badly, er, shocked by what's happened to him. All his men were killed in a church up the valley. He's in a bad state.'

Liveris nodded. 'You are all young men, Captain. Very young. This man has seen some terrible things, things that nobody should ever see.'

'That's no excuse to abandon your men.'

'Maybe he didn't. Maybe he is telling the truth.'

'Maybe,' said Hartley. A sudden wave of tiredness came over him. As with every day, it had been a long one.

'Shall we have that toast now?' asked Liveris.

'I think we should. Perhaps your wife would like to join in.'

After supper Mrs Liveris took Hartley upstairs to the girls' room. Two very basic beds, no more than four feet long, occupied most of the space. She indicated with her hands that the beds were very small, but Hartley replied with a thumbs-up, and pointed at his half-closed eyes to indicate that he was so tired it didn't matter. Liveris had told him that the girls would be sleeping in their parents' bed, despite Hartley's protests that he was happy to sleep on the floor.

After bidding Mrs Liveris good night, he removed his boots and lay on the bed, his legs dangling over the end. It occurred to him that he should have gone to look for Royce, but he was too tired and almost beyond caring. Let him run away, get lost. Good riddance. Hartley found himself half wishing that he had aimed for the other side of the windscreen that morning. That was unfair, he knew it was. What made him so confident that he would never behave as he suspected Royce had done? He had come close when the Stuka had attacked them, but he had stopped himself running. It sounded boyishly heroic, but he would stick with his men, come what may. He would rather die with them than run from them. Sarah would understand that – at least, he hoped she would.

A few minutes later Royce came into the room.

'Where did you go?' asked Hartley, sitting up.

'None of your business.'

Hartley slumped down again. He should have guessed that would be the response. Royce lay down on the other bed and Hartley turned to the wall. There was no point in talking to him, no point at all.

The scream was so high-pitched that Hartley thought at first it was a woman's. It tore into his dream, causing him to wake instantly. It was coming from Royce, who was sitting up in bed, his sweaty profile visible in the moonlight.

'Royce!' Hartley shouted.

Royce didn't turn and the screaming continued, no doubt waking the whole village. Hartley leant over the divide between the beds and shook him. 'Royce! Wake up! Royce!'

The screaming stopped, leaving Royce taking panicky gulps of air.

'You were having a nightmare,' said Hartley.

Royce looked terrified, his face like something out of *Son of Frankenstein*.

'It's all right, Royce, it was just a bad dream.'

Royce's breathing started to slow, to become less strained.

'What was it?'

Royce shook his head, as if to rid himself of what had been running through it. 'It was . . .'

'What?'

'It was what you thought hadn't happened.'

'The church?'

'Yes, Hartley, the church.'

Hartley lay back on the bed. He almost felt sorry for the man.

There must be thousands of them, thought Hartley, tens of thousands – British, New Zealanders, Australians, even Yugoslavs, all waiting to get on a boat for a ride to wherever the Royal Navy took them. The beach was littered with the debris of war – jerry-cans, burnt-out jeeps and lorries, charred wood, helmets, spent cartridges, rifles, bloodied bandages, cigarette packets, broken bottles, helmets, boots and blankets. What a sight to wake up to. Royce was right – it was another bloody Dunkirk.

Holding his wash-kit, Hartley jumped down from the back of the lorry and felt his feet sink into the sand. It was five o'clock in the morning, and the sun was rising down the coast to his left. The slowly increasing light was matched by the frequency of coughing coming from the assortment of bodies that lay amongst the debris. Occasional hawking and spitting could also be heard, along with 'Where's the bleeding Navy, then?'

Hartley scratched his jaw. He could do with a shave. The only source of water was the sea, and he trod warily past the awakening huddle of his men. They had all opted to sleep outside, the sand far more comfortable than the lorry floor. He and Royce had slept in the cab, which Hartley regretted, because once more he had been woken by screams.

He sat down next to the water's edge and removed his boots. The smell of his feet enveloped him briefly before it was wafted away on a light breeze. Swim. That's what he'd do. Why the hell not? He needed a decent wash. The dust from the roads had worked its way into every part of his body, making him feel desiccated. Hartley undressed, heard the odd wolf whistle and smiled. At least there was a sense of humour somewhere to be found.

The water was cool but not cold. Hartley plunged his head under, relishing the dark rush around it. For the few seconds he remained submerged, pretending he was anywhere but there, anywhere but in the middle of a disaster. He surfaced, then swam, enjoying the sudden burst of exercise after a day and a night cramped in the lorry. He trod water, looking back at the hill – or was it a mountain? – that overlooked the long beach. Under different circumstances he would have loved to climb it. It would make a perfect morning's exercise before a long lunch and a lazy afternoon. Hartley lay back in the water, allowing himself to be swept back and forth by the waves. The sun was brighter now, illuminating the mountain a brilliant yellow. Above it, he could make out birds circling its peak.

But they were not birds. They were aeroplanes, and almost certainly not those of the RAF. Hartley swam forward frantically. He had to warn the men. 'Air raid!' he shouted. 'Take cover!'

Nobody appeared to hear him.

'Stukas!' he shouted. 'Take cover!' His feet found the ground, and he surged forward through the surf, only vaguely self-conscious of his nakedness as he ran on to the beach. 'Air raid!'

Hartley stepped into his underpants and trousers quickly as he kept an eye on the Stukas. They were coming in fast, at least a dozen of them. He glanced up and down the beach: the realisation of what was about to happen was forcing hundreds of men to scramble towards the pathetically thin line of trees and scrub. They were at the Stukas' mercy.

His men were also starting to get up, early-morning grogginess disappearing as they gazed at the sky.

'Come on!' shouted Hartley. 'Get moving!'

The softness of the sand made it impossible to

run fast, and Hartley stumbled a few times as he led them up the beach. He found himself wondering where Royce had got to, then forgot him. He let the men run past, giving each a push on the back to force him forward. He didn't need to – they were running fast enough – but it gave him some sense of control. 'Move it! Come on, Barnes, bloody move it!'

He could hear the Stukas now, their distinctive wail as they dived. The sound filled him with a mixture of terror and hatred. About five hundred yards away, a lorry went up in flames. Hartley could see men on fire, hear their screams. He had to stop himself watching, had to get his men and himself under cover, such as it was.

After a few more yards, Hartley slid to the ground beneath a large, scratchy bush, joining Franklin and Stephenson. Nobody spoke, just watched, clutching their heads. The Stukas were working their way up and down the beach, methodically dropping bombs on to the more significant targets, such as lorries and armoured cars.

'Where are the fucking RAF?' Franklin shouted.

'Sodding Brylcreem boys,' said Stephenson.

Hartley felt the same. This was murder, slaughter. Just ahead they saw a couple of men running out of the sea. A few seconds later, they disintegrated, limbs snapped off and flung into the air.

Another explosion, a huge one, that shook the ground.

'That had to be an ammo lorry,' said Franklin. 'Let's hope the bastards don't get ours.'

Hartley glanced at their lorry. It seemed particularly vulnerable. He knew it would be hit – it was just a matter of time. The noise of the Stukas filled the air – it was impossible that one of them wouldn't give the lorry a pasting.

Dull thuds erupted all round the bush. Branches and leaves smashed into hundreds of fragments as though a massive chainsaw had sliced through them. This was it, thought Hartley. He was going to die. He would be ripped apart by the shrapnel, like those men on the beach. He thought of Sarah, their wedding day. He thought of looking into her eyes, and how he had wondered even then whether they would have children. Well, they wouldn't now, because he was about to be killed. This was the end of his life, here and now on this fucking beach. He closed his eyes, screwing them tight to shut out the horror, while the machine-gunning continued.

After a few seconds, the firing stopped. Hartley drew in shallow lungfuls of dirty air. It tasted foul, of smoke and dust.

'That was close,' he said.

He was alive, at least for the time being. He could rejoice, feel happy that that he had another few minutes to live. He turned to Franklin. 'That was close . . .'

Where Franklin's head had once been there was now a caved-in mess of blood, bandage, bone and brain. Hartley shut his eyes. 'Oh, God!'

He opened them again, in time to see a fly land on what might have been an ear.

'Stephenson!'

Nothing.

'Stephenson!' Hartley propped himself up so that he could see Stephenson over Franklin's body. 'Oh, please, God, no,' he mumbled. In the middle of Stephenson's back, punched through his uniform, was a smoking dark hole the size of a fist. Hartley's head slumped down.

The sound of the Stukas' engines dwindled, then finally dissolved into the blue. Hartley lay still, numb, in shock. He wanted never to get up, to lie still, sleep and forget. That was the easy option, he knew. It was what a bad officer would do, someone like Royce. Royce! What had happened to him? The last time he had seen him was when he had left the lorry to go for his swim. Hartley lifted his head. The lorry was still intact, miraculously. If it had been hit, Royce would have been obliterated. Of all the people to survive . . .

After half a minute, the shrieks of men in pain

spread along the beach. Hartley couldn't establish whether the shouts and moans had been there since the start of the action or whether his brain had shut them out. He could see movement now, men running to help wounded comrades. What could they do here, on this bloody beach? There was no hospital, and nowhere near enough medics to treat the wounded.

But they were doing something, and Hartley knew he had to as well. He got up, trying not to look at Franklin's corpse, caught a glimpse and retched. He vomited, and felt ashamed. The men might be watching, and would think him weak. He felt as if he was turning himself inside-out, and when there was nothing left to puke, he puked again.

'Are you OK, sir?'

Hartley waved Miller back with his hand. 'I'm fine. The men?'

'I don't know, sir. I've just got up.'

'Well, for heaven's sake, go and see.'

Two more had been killed: Privates Bell and Barnes. The remaining men found some blankets and laid the four corpses in a row. They gathered round, and Hartley said a short prayer. 'We should bury them immediately,' he said afterwards. 'Let's get them well off the beach – I don't want them being washed up in a few weeks. Corporal Miller, you're now the senior NCO. See to it, would you?'

'Yes, sir.'

'In the meantime, I'm going to try to find out who's in charge here.'

As Hartley walked past the lorry he heard a low moan coming from the cab. Royce. He opened the driver's door and looked inside. Royce was lying across the seats, sobbing. He was like a child. The poor bugger had completely gone round the bend, thought Hartley. Still, there was no time for sympathy. 'Royce!'

Royce didn't respond.

'Royce! Get up! C'mon! We need to find your unit. There should be someone from your lot around here somewhere.'

Slowly Royce brought up his head. His face was bright red and tear-stained. 'I don't want to die,' he whispered.

'None of us wants to die, Royce, but four of us just have.'

'Who?'

'Franklin, Stephenson, Barnes, Bell. All dead.'

'Christ.'

'Get out,' said Hartley.

Royce sat up.

'All right,' he said quietly. 'I'll do that. Get up. Yes. Good idea.'

Hartley fetched the rest of his clothes. Thankfully the tide had been going out, so they were still there. He lifted up his shirt to find that it now bore a bullet-hole. He was tempted to dwell on it, but snapped out of it. He had to control himself, not think about those who had just died. He could grieve when they were on the boat, which would take them away from this killing ground. He wasn't going to surrender to his fear, as Royce had.

He found Royce standing next to the lorry. 'You ready?'

Royce shrugged.

'Well, let's go into the village, then.'

'I'd rather stay here.'

'No, you bloody won't.'

If Hartley had expected to find some sort of organisation in Kalamata, he was wrong. All he and Royce could discover from Major George was that some boats were on their way, perhaps at nineish tonight, and that the Germans had closed in on the village. Hartley and his men were to sit tight and wait to be evacuated. Royce made some half-hearted questions about his regiment, but George advised him to stay with Hartley. There was no call for men to wander around on their own: it would create even more chaos – 'and, by God, we've got enough of that already.' George made a note of the dead men's names, and informed Hartley that this was a terrible business, it really was, but Hartley was doing a splendid job and he should keep it up.

Hartley found the men having a brew by the lorry. He told them the news.

'They'd better fucking be here,' was the consensual reply, along with another gripe about the RAF.

'What if we chance it ourselves?' asked Private Morris. 'Can't we just head up into the hills and hide?'

'And live off what?' asked Hartley. 'The goats?'

'I heard goat's quite tasty, sir.'

Slight laughter.

'No. You're all to stay here. The navy'll come, don't you worry.' Hartley hoped he sounded more convincing than he felt.

There was a silence.

'Cup of tea, sir?'

'Now, there's a good idea.'

Hartley sat down and waited for his tea. Royce walked back to the lorry, and climbed into the cab.

'Is he all right, sir?' asked Miller.

Hartley shook his head. 'I don't think so,' he replied. 'He's either cracked or he's about to.'

'After this morning, maybe we were wrong to be so harsh,' said Miller. 'I mean, I'm pretty much near to cracking up myself.'

'No, you're not, Miller. We're all shocked, but we're getting on with it. With Royce, it's something else, something deeper.'

'Like what?'

'I'm not a trick-cyclist, Miller.'

'A what?'

'A head-shrinker, psychiatrist.'

Miller smiled. 'Here's your tea, sir.'

Hartley took the cup gratefully. Then his attention was grabbed by a shout further down the beach.

'Air raid!'

There were seven more that day, which must have killed scores, perhaps hundreds, of men. Hartley's unit was comparatively lucky, but by the third raid its numbers had shrunk to four as the remainder had decided to ignore his order and fled inland. There was nothing he could have done to stop them because they had disappeared during the raid. In the lulls, he could hear gunfire in the surrounding hills and from Kalamata.

'Sounds like Jerry's being given a pasting,' said Miller, hopefully.

It was the early evening. Hartley, Royce and the remaining four members of the unit were sitting by a fire constructed from driftwood and diesel. It stank, but the mesmerising flicker of the flames was welcome, hypnotic after the horror of the day's events.

'Let's hope so,' said Hartley.

He felt drained, weary, ready to give up. He wanted to sleep, but every time he shut his eyes he saw bodies, dismembered limbs, Franklin's head. He would have nightmares, perhaps as bad as Royce's, and he didn't want to face them, because he knew they would be as bad as the raids themselves, perhaps worse. Was this what had happened to Royce? Had the horror done for him, or was it the memory of it? There was a difference, he was sure. If he could cauterise the memories, burn them out of his brain, they would trouble him no more.

'Sir?'

'What is it, Miller?'

'I think I can see something out to sea, sir. Ships, sir.'

Miller's words didn't immediately register. Ships? What ships?

'Look, sir! It's the navy!'

Hartley narrowed his eyes and gazed out to the horizon. A few miles off he could see at least a dozen black silhouettes. 'Those are ships all right,' he said, slowly standing up. 'I don't believe it! My God, Miller, you're right! It's the bloody navy!'

A cheer went up along the beach, and grew louder as the news spread. Officers and men leapt up and ran to the surf.

'The navy!' Miller shouted. 'I love the bloody navy! I'm going to marry a sailor, you mark my words!'

Hartley couldn't help but join the throng as it stumbled, ran, limped and walked down the beach. Some men waded into the water up to their chests, taut white arms beckoning the ships towards them. Hartley shut his eyes in relief. They were leaving this wretched place. Soon they would be back in Alex, or maybe in Cairo, drinking a beer at Shepheard's. He would write to Sarah, tell her he was well, that he would see her soon. He still felt guilty that they were abandoning the Greeks, but for the next five minutes, he didn't care, just sang and yelled along with the rest.

'We made it, sir!' said Miller. 'We bloody made it!'

'I bloody hope so, Miller.'

'Well, what's to stop 'em, sir?'

Hartley looked at the sky. It was disconcertingly empty.

'Fingers crossed.'

The excitement died down. The ships were seemingly in no hurry to reach the shore, and there was speculation that they might even have weighed anchor.

'Fucking navy!'

'Stopping for dinner, are we?'

'Bleeding ponces!'

Hartley glanced at his watch. It was eight o'clock and it would soon be dark.

'Miller!'

'Sir?'

'We won't be going tonight. There's no way the navy's going to get thousands of men off this beach when it's dark. They'll do it first thing, that's my guess.'

'But, sir!'

'It wasn't my idea, Miller, it's just what's going to happen. Now, let's get ourselves under some proper cover for our last night, eh?'

Miller nodded. 'Yes, sir.'

Just as Hartley turned away from the surf, balls of orange flame and smoke erupted from the town, followed quickly by the sound of the explosions, then a distant rumble from the hills.

'Fuck.' Hartley cursed under his breath. Artillery. The Germans were going to blow them to pieces.

The shelling lasted for half an hour, and after it had finished, the rumour of surrender spread quickly along the ever-dimming beach. Hartley noticed it was not just the wounded who were crying, but the unharmed as well, those for whom the frustration of seeing the navy so close was too much. Unusually, Royce had quietened. Hartley thought he knew why, and told Royce as much as they lay behind a sand dune. 'You want to be taken prisoner, don't you?'

Royce sighed.

'Well, you do, don't you? I'm sure you wouldn't mind sitting out the rest of the war in a POW camp.'

'I resent that, Hartley.'

'Well, despite the barrage, you seem a lot happier now that Jerry's on our doorstep.'

'Listen, Hartley, why don't you put a sock in it? You act like you're a deputy head-boy, all keen and eager to prove what a decent chap you are to your men.'

'I'd rather be accused of that than cowardice.'

'I'm not a coward!'

'I rather think you are.'

'Fuck you!'

Royce pushed himself to his feet and began frantically to unbutton his holster. Jesus Christ! thought Hartley. He really has gone insane – he's going to shoot me!

Hartley jumped up and launched himself at Royce, sending both of them tumbling against the dune. Royce had managed to pull out his revolver, and was using it as a club, trying to smash it on the back of Hartley's head. Hartley did his best to restrain the man, but Royce was immensely strong, and finally smashed the butt on to his crown.

The blow infuriated Hartley rather than knocking him out. He drew on a reserve of aggression he had never known he had and punched Royce's right ear. Royce responded with another blow to Hartley's skull, but Hartley avoided the full impact and the gun glanced off the side of his head.

'Hartley!'

Hartley didn't hear Major George.

'*Hartley!* Stop this!'

Suddenly he felt himself pulled back by his collar and choked. Then he was thrown aside. The major and a sergeant were standing over him.

'What the hell is all this about, Hartley?'

Hartley tried to collect himself. He was about to say, 'Royce started it,' but instead cleared his throat. 'I, er, there's no reason, sir.'

'And where are your men, for Christ's sake?'

'I regret to say that some of them have left the beach, sir.'

'Well, you'd better find them, hadn't you? Unless you want to get them killed.'

Hartley's brow furrowed. 'Get them killed, sir?'

'Haven't you heard, Hartley?'

'Heard what, sir?'

'We're surrendering at five thirty tomorrow morning. If the Germans find any of our men roaming around the Greek countryside they'll shoot them as partisans.'

'Surrendering, sir? But what about the navy?'

'The navy have to go. We don't know why.'

'Bastards,' Royce hissed.

It was the first thing Royce had said with which Hartley agreed. Bastards indeed.

Chapter Two

HE HAD NEVER thought he would hear the words, and they seemed such a cliché – they had become almost meaningless with constant repetition. Even the young lieutenant who spoke to them in broken English seemed weary at having to say them, a tired actor in a play that had long since exceeded its run.

'For you . . . the war is over.' There was a slight smile on the man's lips. 'Place all your weapons, including your pocket knives, over here.'

Hartley unbuttoned his holster and removed his revolver. So this was it: he really was surrendering. While he still had his gun, he retained an element of power, of military dignity. But without it he would be just another man who depended on his enemy to feed and house him. It was like being an invalid looked after by a nurse who hated him. Contemptuously Hartley threw his revolver on to the pile.

'Your knife, Captain.'

'I don't have one.'

This was a lie: he had a small lock knife hidden in his underpants.

'You will be searched, Captain.'

'Fine.'

Hartley had noticed that the searches were perfunctory. The Germans had an enormous number of men to process: they had no time to carry out a thorough search on thousands.

'Your name, rank and serial number?'

Hartley told him.

'Your regiment?'

Hartley opened his mouth, then shut it.

'Your regiment!'

'I don't have to tell you that.'

The lieutenant stared at him. He had a solid, unshaven jaw, and he was covered with dirt. His eyes were barely visible through the grime of battle. 'You are making life hard for yourself, Captain Hartley.'

'So be it.'

Resigned, the lieutenant nodded Hartley forward to a corporal who proceeded to pat him down. Behind him, he could hear Royce having the same conversation with the lieutenant. No doubt he would reveal everything. Thankfully, the corporal's search was minimal. No doubt the man shared Hartley's distaste for the task.

'And your regiment?' the lieutenant asked.

'My regiment?' Royce replied.

'Yes, Captain, your regiment.'

'Well, I'm not telling you.'

This was a surprise, thought Hartley. He turned to see Royce standing defiantly, hands on hips.

'We know which regiment you're from so why don't you tell me?'

'Warum sagst du es mir nacht?' Royce asked.

Royce spoke German! He'd kept that quiet. Hartley did too, so he understood the exchange that followed.

'Speaking German is not going to help you,' the lieutenant snapped. 'Your regiment!'

Royce muttered something, which enraged the lieutenant.

'Who the hell do you British think you are? You are the losers, not the victors!'

Royce shrugged. 'Can I go now?' he said, pointing towards Hartley.

'No!' And with that, the German hit Royce's face with the back of his hand. Royce's response was immediate: he returned the blow.

'Royce!' Hartley shouted, and – evading the clutches of the corporal – ran towards the two men. He was not the only one to do so. Within a few seconds a mêlée ensued, in which Royce, the lieutenant, the corporal and two more German NCOs took part. Punches and kicks were aimed randomly. Despite his best attempts, Hartley was unable to disengage Royce from the lieutenant, who was suffering a succession of beatings from the Englishman. The scuffle did not last long: Hartley and Royce were soon knocked to the floor, rifles aimed at their chests.

Hartley wanted to cry out, 'Don't shoot!' but he knew how pathetic it would sound. He felt more angry than afraid, annoyed that Royce had hit the lieutenant. 'For Pete's sake, man! Why the hell did you do that?'

'Silence!' the lieutenant shouted, wiping his bleeding nostrils with the back of a dirty fist.

Hartley was aware of a large crowd assembling around them. However, his attention was arrested by the face of the young German NCO pointing his rifle at him. Like his lieutenant, the man was battle-hardened. His own men, Hartley thought, still looked like boys. This man had probably fought in Poland and France as well as Greece. It must be his third campaign, and he had probably killed many men. The deaths showed in his cold, unblinking eyes. Not a bad face, but its owner would show no mercy. What chance did they have against a people like this?

'Get up!' shouted the lieutenant.

Hartley and Royce did as they were ordered.

'Hands up!'

Now what? thought Hartley. Were they going to be shot? Surely not. Had this been the SS, then they almost certainly would have been.

The lieutenant was clearly frustrated. He looked

up, then down, as though he might have expected a course of action to be delivered from above. Hartley guessed that he wanted to punish them, but doubtless he had to weigh that up against getting his job done quickly and efficiently. Besides, in the eyes of his superiors it would not reflect well on him if it was known that one of the surrendering *Englanders* had seen fit to hit him.

He walked right up to them and shouted at them from no more than a foot away, 'I should have you shot!'

Saliva splattered them, followed by the early-morning stench of the man's guts. Hartley gazed at the ground – he had no wish to inflame the lieutenant's temper any further by making eye-contact with him. Besides, most of the man's attention was reserved for Royce. Hartley prayed that Royce would keep cool.

'But we do not have time to arrange an execution.'

Hartley felt his shoulders sag in relief.

'Instead, I am going to do this.'

Hartley looked up in time to see a large fist heading towards his face. Excruciating pain, then darkness.

He came to slowly. His vision was blurred and he felt groggy, as though he had been drugged. His right cheekbone ached furiously, and he was trying to work out what he was looking at.

Legs in British battledress. It was dark wherever he

was, and they were rocking, but only a little. Despite all the legs, there was little sound. He became aware that it was suffocatingly hot. Where was he? What had happened to him? The fist. Royce. Royce hitting the lieutenant. The fucking idiot. The cold, hard eyes of the NCO.

'Are you all right there?'

Hartley didn't recognise the voice.

'Can you hear me, old chap?'

Who was it? All he could see were the bloody legs. He tried to push himself up, but he collapsed.

'Just stay there, old man, no need to get up. Not yet at least.'

Hartley shook his head, trying to rid it of the pain. He felt his cheek. It was badly bruised and caked with something like mud. He started to scratch it off, but that hurt even more.

'I'd leave it, if I were you. We'll get a doc to fix it up when we get there.'

Get where? The room rocked more now, the movement increasing in violence and frequency. Of course. He was on a train. He opened his mouth to speak, but no words came out. His throat was arid. He tried again, and managed to croak, 'Where are we going?' he asked. His eyes were still trying to find the voice's owner.

'Germany, I expect.'

'Germany?'

'That's it, old man. The *Reich*. To spend the rest of the war in some wretched cage.'

'Have you got any water?'

'Water? Good God, no! You don't think Jerry would be so kind as to give us *water*, do you?'

'What is this?' Hartley asked.

'What's what, old man?'

Hartley wished he would stop calling him 'old man'. 'What are we in?'

'A cattle truck on a train. Not exactly first class, but there you go.'

A cattle truck. It was inhumane, barbaric. 'How long have we been in here?'

'I'd tell you, but they took my watch. I'd say about an hour.'

'And do you know—'

'No. None of us has a clue, old boy. Two more hours, two more weeks. Who knows?'

'This is appalling. How are we supposed to go to the—'

'Some of us have started an, uh, informal latrine in a corner. D'you need to go?'

'Not yet.'

There was a brief pause.

'By the way,' said the voice, 'that was quite a fracas you had with the Jerry officer. Your friend's around here somewhere. He was knocked about a bit – quite a lot worse than you, I'm afraid.'

'He's not my friend.'

'Really? You certainly leapt to his defence.'

Hartley recalled the moment. The voice was right – he had helped Royce. Not that he'd deserved help. Bloody fool, talking back to the German like that. And in German too. What had he been trying to prove?

'How is he?' Hartley found himself asking.

'Broken nose looks like.'

Once more Hartley tried to get up. This time he was partially successful.

'Here, old chap, let me help.'

A pair of pale hands stretched out of the gloom and hauled Hartley to his feet. The vacuum created by his standing was immediately filled by those jostling for a little more room. 'Thanks,' he said.

The voice had come from beneath a thin moustache, which belonged to a man in his early forties. His shoulders revealed that he was a major. 'Sorry – thank you, *sir*,' said Hartley.

'Quite all right, Captain. How are you feeling?'

'I'll be all right. Where's my – my *friend*?'

It felt awkward using the word. Royce was most emphatically not his friend, yet he felt he could not leave him be.

'Somewhere over there,' said the major, jerking his head towards the door. 'We thought we'd put him where there was at least a little air.'

Hartley looked over the shoulders and heads of his fellow occupants. They were all officers. How were the men being transported? Worse than this? There must be at least a hundred of them in here, and there was just enough room perhaps to stretch out one's elbows, but little more. 'I should go and see him.'

'Good luck getting through, old boy.'

Hartley tapped on the shoulder of an officer in front of him. 'Excuse me, can I get past? I need to see my, um, friend.'

With a tut, the man allowed Hartley to squeeze past. It was a process he had to repeat at least ten more times, met with sighs and 'if you must'. He found Royce stretched out near the vast sliding door. His face was badly swollen, but a gleam in his puffy eye sockets revealed he was awake. A lieutenant was leaning over him.

'How is he?' Hartley asked, bending down.

The lieutenant was wearing the uniform of the Royal Army Medical Corps. 'Do you know him?'

'Not really, but we've been together for the past couple of days. We got involved in some sort of fight back in Kalamata . . .'

'So I heard, sir.' The lieutenant's tone was disapproving. 'Well,' he continued, 'his nose is never going to look particularly pretty. He's lucky not to have a fractured jaw, but he won't be speaking for a while. He could probably do with a dentist as well. I suspect at least two ribs are broken, but they'll mend if he gets some rest. I've done my best to bind him up, but I only have a few scraps of bandage left.'

'Well done, Lieutenant,' said Hartley. 'Thank you.'

'And how are you, sir? How's that eye?'

'All right, I think.'

'Let's have a look.'

The lieutenant motioned for Hartley to put his face next to a gap in the truck's wooden slats. The brightness of the incoming light almost made his eyes water. 'It just looks like a bad bruise and a nasty cut. It'll need a stitch at some point.'

'Can you do it now?'

'Not a chance while we're on the train. Just try to keep it clean for the time being.'

Hartley nodded.

'And don't touch it,' the lieutenant added. 'I've seen too many small wounds grow nasty over the past week. Wherever it is we're going, I don't suppose we'll get the finest medical facilities.'

'It'll be all right,' said Hartley. 'Nothing to worry about.'

The lieutenant looked back at Royce. 'All right,' he said. 'I've got some other men to look at, so you'll need to take care of him. Make sure he doesn't try to get up.'

'Have you got any water for him?'

The lieutenant flashed him a cold stare. 'None of us have any water, Captain.'

That disapproving tone again – the man was one of nature's prefects. Hartley knelt down next to Royce. 'Royce,' he said, 'can you hear me?'

Royce nodded.

'How are you feeling?'

A sound husked out of Royce's bloodied mouth. It resembled 'Not bad.' Hartley felt sorry for the poor bastard. He really had been knocked about. He was tempted to think that the man deserved it, and felt guilty for it. Royce had been brave in standing up to the German like that. Foolhardy, a little unhinged perhaps, but brave nevertheless.

An hour later they were collapsing. If there was room, they would have fallen to the floor, but instead they just fainted into each other. Those who hadn't succumbed were banging their hands against the sides of the truck, and demanding water. Eventually their cries grew weaker, and they fell silent.

Hartley had never felt so thirsty, or anticipated how painful it would be. His throat became increasingly sore, and the inside of his skull throbbed with an intense headache. Images of ice-cold water ran through his mind. Surely the Germans weren't going to let them die in here. What was the point of that? Wouldn't it have been easier just to shoot them all?

Or was this the coward's way of dealing with them –
simply to shut them away, send them up the track
and let them become somebody else's problem?

Now and then Royce groaned. Hartley had
reassured him that there would be water soon, and
that he was not to worry. He spoke to him as he
would have spoken to a child, his tone gentle and
slightly raised in pitch. The reassurance was as much
for his own benefit as it was for Royce's, although
there was nothing to suggest that they would be
fine. There was every chance that men were dying
around them, although it was impossible to tell.
Men did not die in such conditions with a scream or
a yell, they just slipped away silently, unnoticed.
Would that happen to Royce? Perhaps Hartley would
close his eyes and open them a few seconds later to
find that Royce's chest was no longer rising and
falling feebly. No matter what he thought of Royce
he did not deserve to die.

'Out!'

For a few seconds, there was no movement. Men
lay in twisted heaps, sprawled over each other.

'Out! Move! You have five minutes!'

Those who could do so lifted their heads and
squinted into the sudden invasion of daylight. As
Hartley's eyes adjusted, he made out a concrete
platform and some dusty bushes. A German, rifle

held defensively across his chest, was standing in front of him. He was older than the soldiers back at Kalamata, perhaps in his late thirties.

'This is disgraceful,' Hartley husked.

The soldier ignored him. 'Out!' he shouted again. 'There is water.'

The effect was immediate. Along with several others, Hartley got to his feet. Those who had not collapsed stirred those who had, and soon men were struggling upright. Royce was doing his best to get up. 'Come on, Royce,' he said. 'I'll help you down.'

Royce mumbled something.

'Get out of the way, man.'

Hartley turned to see a fellow captain standing behind him.

'Can't you see you're blocking the way, damnit?' said the officer.

'Then help me get him down,' said Hartley.

The captain glowered at him, but nodded reluctantly. After they had stepped out of the truck, the two men lifted Royce down and set him gently on his feet. Royce did his best to stand, but crumpled to the ground. Hartley looked for the other captain to lift him again, but he had already hurried off down the platform towards a large crowd. Hartley assumed that that was where the water was. 'Listen, Royce, I'm going to have to leave you here while I get us some water. All right?'

Royce lifted his right forearm in acknowledgement, and Hartley ran down the platform where, to his surprise, a more or less orderly queue was assembling. Somewhere up ahead, he could hear a gruff English voice barking at them, telling them there was enough for everyone and that if they didn't wait in a proper fashion that would be it.

It took Hartley fifteen minutes to reach the front of the queue. A British lieutenant-colonel and two majors were standing next to a milk churn, dispensing water into a small selection of enamel mugs. At least a dozen Germans surrounded them. 'One mug each, then put it back.'

Hartley swallowed the water, yearning for more.

'I need to take some back to my truck—' Hartley began.

'We all do, laddie,' said the lieutenant-colonel.

'But, sir, I have a friend there who can't walk.'

'What's wrong with him?'

'He was beaten up, sir.'

'By whom?'

'A German lieutenant back at Kalamata.'

'Ah, yes – I heard about that. All right, you can take a mug with you.'

Hartley handed his back to one of the majors, who refilled it. He ignored the envious stares that drilled into him as he nursed it down the platform. He found

Royce sitting up, leaning against an empty plant pot. 'I've got you some water, Royce.'

'Thank you.'

Hartley lifted the mug to Royce's cracked, bloodied lips, then slowly poured the water between them. Royce made to grab it, but Hartley stopped him. 'No, let me do it. You'll only spill it.' It was like giving him communion, Hartley thought.

By the time the train stopped at seven o'clock the following morning, there had been two deaths in their truck. Hartley estimated that, with eight, there would have been sixteen deaths that night. He wanted to scream at their guards, but he lacked the strength. All he could think about was water – water and food. Even when they were removing the bodies, his thoughts were concerned with sustenance. He found it disgusting, depraved even, that he could be so selfish, that he seemed to lack any form of sympathy. He tried to feel sorry for the dead men and their families, but he couldn't. He wanted water. Was that asking these bastards too much?

The smell inside the truck was atrocious. Many were suffering from loose bowels, and only those next to the makeshift latrine had been able to defecate with some degree of dignity. The others had had to go where they stood, sometimes on to the boots of the men next to them. Although initially there were mutters of protest, resignation and acceptance soon took over. Hartley thanked his stars that his bowels hadn't been afflicted, although Royce's had.

After the dead had been removed, the guards ordered them out. Once again, Royce was unable to get down on his own, and Hartley was assisted by the medical lieutenant who had tended Royce earlier. They stepped on to another platform, this one in better condition than the one where they had received yesterday's water. Royce stood and, with an arm round Hartley's shoulders, dragged himself along. 'Where are we?' he asked.

'I have no idea.'

They were at a station of sorts, albeit nothing more than a low, crumbling shack. Two metal poles next to the building suggested that it had once borne a sign, which must have been removed by either the British in a bid to confuse the invaders, or the Germans to disorient their captives. It mattered little to Hartley. He was just glad to have got out of the train.

Escape. The word came from nowhere. Escape. There it was again, tempting him, taunting him. Why hadn't he thought of it before? Wouldn't it be easy to run away in the confusion of prisoners and guards that was thronging the platform? Quickly Hartley looked about him. A few houses were dotted around the station – perhaps if he could get to one, the occupants would shelter him. And then what? Where would he go? A seagull flew overhead, advertising its presence with its shrill call. So they were near the sea. He could steal a boat. It had to be worth a try. Anything was better than sitting around being maltreated by the Germans in some wretched camp. A sudden wave of lightheadedness almost caused him to collapse.

'Are you . . . OK?' muttered Royce.

Hartley didn't reply: his heart was beating furiously, and he felt nauseous. Even as he struggled to compose himself, he knew he couldn't escape in this state. He had to get his strength up. He could barely walk now, let alone run. He would be shot as soon as he broke away from the other prisoners.

And then there was the small matter of what would happen to Royce. He felt responsible for him, no matter how much he disliked him.

Hartley squatted over the trench. The smell was overpowering, but he had no choice but to endure it as he had for the past week – or was it two? He had dysentery, along with the majority of the camp's population. At least seven others were squatting beside him, all of whom Hartley had seen at the trench only fifteen minutes before. Each man looked straight ahead, not wishing to catch a glimpse of the repellent scene being played out next to him.

Hartley finished and pulled up his trousers, his underpants long since discarded. The next part of the routine was to wait for a few seconds: far too often he needed to squat once more. Hartley paused. His insides felt painfully unstable, but he would manage the fifty feet to the camp's single tap in the middle of the parade ground. Next to it, a few medical officers had improvised what amounted to a field hospital from a ragged German tent, in which the sick could clean themselves and receive rudimentary treatment. There were a few drugs, and they were reserved for the worst cases.

The camp, in a former Greek Army barracks, was only marginally better than the train, Hartley thought, as he walked gingerly. At least five hundred British officers were crammed into a building designed to house around a third of that number. It was infested with rats and all manner of arthropod, and the latrines were beyond repair. There were around two hundred beds, of which only half had mattresses that heaved with fleas. Most chose to sleep outside, preferring the rough ground to bites.

'How are you today, sir?'

It was the young medical lieutenant, whom Hartley now knew as Kyle.

'Bearing up,' Hartley replied.

'Good,' Kyle replied. His attention had already wandered.

'Is there some water I can use?'

'Hmm?'

'Some *water*, Kyle.'

'Oh, yes – over there. We've rigged up a sort of shower. It works rather well.'

'Thank you.'

'One thing before you go, sir. Your friend Royce, how is he? I haven't seen him around.'

'On the mend, I think,' Hartley replied. 'His face has gone down. Still complains about his ribs, though.'

'That's hardly surprising. Is he keeping clean?'

'I'm not sure. He stays inside practically all day. I suspect he's a little . . . queer in the head.'

'That's not surprising either. Quite a few seem to be losing the plot.'

The two men stood in silence. The word 'escape' came into Hartley's mind once more, as it had many times. If he didn't leave, he, too, would lose it. Even planning to leave would achieve something: it would occupy his mind.

After he had washed, Hartley went to find Royce. He stepped into the main building, and was instantly struck by the oppressive heat, the smell of decay. When they had arrived, the colonel had ordered the building to be cleaned every day, but the Germans had supplied only modest materials and it had proved impossible to shift the worst of the dirt, some of which Hartley estimated was decades old. No wonder they all had the shits, he thought.

He walked down a wide corridor, along which lay several officers in different states of undress. Although discipline was largely maintained, the condition of uniforms was not. Trousers had been turned into shorts, and shirtsleeves had been co-opted as dressings. Hartley nodded at the occasional face he recognised, and told himself he would never lie festering here.

He stepped into a long dormitory, which contained some forty beds. He flapped his shirt front a few times in a vain attempt to cool himself. The ceiling fans remained resolutely motionless, their inertia mocking the sweating men beneath them. Hartley walked down the beds until he came to Royce, who was asleep. His face was a lot better, although by no means restored to normal.

Hartley nudged him awake. 'Royce!'

'Huh?'

'Wake up.'

'What?'

'Wake up.'

'Why?'

'Because I want to tell you something.'

Royce propped himself up on his elbows, and winced.

'Your ribs?' asked Hartley.

'Better than they were. But my bowels are killing me. The doctor says they're bad.'

'I know the feeling,' said Hartley. 'Anyway, can you get up?'

'Why?'

'Because I want to talk to you.'

'Why can't you talk to me here?'

Hartley lowered his voice and leant closer to him. 'Because it's confidential.'

Royce looked perplexed.

'Well, can you get up or not?' Hartley asked.

'I'll need a hand.'

After a few minutes of manhandling and stumbling, the two men stepped out into the midday sun.

'You could do with some air,' said Hartley.

'That's not why you brought me out here.'

'Come on, sit here,' Hartley said, and helped Royce to the ground.

'So, come on, then,' said Royce. 'Out with it.'

Hartley sat down. He could feel his bowels complaining, but they would have to wait. 'We should get out of here,' he said.

'What?'

'We should escape. We're going to die if we stay here.'

'But I'm no condition to get out . . .'

'No, but you soon will be.'

'But if we get caught we'll be shot!'

'As I said, we'll die anyway if we stay here. How many of us are dying each week? Two, maybe three. In about a year we'll all be dead. We can't just sit here, waiting for it to happen.'

'Don't be ridiculous! We're not all going to die.'

'Ask Lieutenant Kyle or any of the medical officers. They'd say exactly the same thing.'

'I'd prefer to take my chances here than run around the Greek countryside being chased by half the German Army.'

'Well, I wouldn't. I'd rather try to get home. And it's our duty.'

'Spoken like the perfect officer.'

'Spoken like the true coward.'

'Fuck you.'

Hartley was taken aback momentarily. Royce had spoken calmly, his tone ill-masking an edgy threat. He stood up and rubbed his palms together to clean them. 'Well, I'll leave you to die, then,' he said, straining to control his temper. 'You can just lie in your own filth, covered with fleas, until you die the sordid death you deserve.'

'It's my choice, Hartley. You go and get on with your heroics.'

Hartley walked away, seething. He'd find someone else or, better still, go alone.

*

Hartley spent the next few days working out how he might escape. The problem seemed insuperable. Although the prisoners had the run of the main building and the courtyard, the gate was heavily guarded, and no prisoners were allowed in or out. The walls were too high to scale, and even if they could have been climbed, a machine-gun was perched on each corner and would cut an escaper to pieces.

It occurred to Hartley that a tunnel might be attempted, but he decided that had to be a last resort. It was too time-consuming, and would require a lot of effort by many men. As most of the men were too weak to walk, the chance of them labouring underground with table knives and forks was minimal. Besides, he wanted to get out quickly. A tunnel would take several weeks to build, perhaps months.

The solution came to him the next time he was talking to Lieutenant Kyle. Hartley had just washed, and had asked about the state of the men's health.

'Well,' said Kyle, 'believe it or not, I think it's going to get better.'

'How?'

'The Germans have agreed to a request by the colonel that our worst cases should receive proper treatment.'

'Where?'

'Apparently there's a hospital of sorts in the town.'

'So who're the lucky ones?'

'They're not lucky, Captain. They're very sick men.'

A typically humourless response.

'What do you know about the hospital?' Hartley asked. 'Will it be well guarded?'

'Haven't the foggiest. Why?'

Hartley was about to answer when he stopped himself. If he told Kyle what he was thinking, the man would have a fit and moan about how the treatment of the patients might be put at risk.

'If you're thinking that those men will be able to escape,' said Kyle, 'you've got another think coming. Most will be too sick even to walk.'

Hartley nodded. He'd have a word with the colonel.

'*Escape?* Are you out of your mind, Hartley?'

The colonel was incandescent with fury, more so than Hartley had suspected he would be.

'Not at all, sir.'

'But where on earth would you go?'

'Back to England, sir.'

The colonel snorted – as colonels do, thought Hartley. This one was in the Hussars, and he came complete with a colonel's moustache and the worst sort of colonel's pomposity. He looked at the major next to him, another bloody Hussar.

'Well,' said the colonel, 'I admire your pluck, but

have you thought about how you're going to achieve this magnificent enterprise?'

'Yes, sir.'

'Then would you care to enlighten us?'

'Certainly, sir.'

Hartley nervously cleared his throat. 'As you know, the very sick are being taken to the hospital in town. I'd like to pose as one of those men, and escape either en route to the hospital, or from the hospital itself, which I'm assuming will not be as heavily guarded as it is here.'

The colonel nodded. 'Carry on.'

'I'd head into the countryside where I would hopefully find some locals willing to help me.'

'And if they don't?'

'Then I shall just have to do my best.'

The colonel chewed it over. The major did too, but more agitatedly.

'Colonel,' said the major, 'may I make an observation?'

'Of course.'

'If this man escapes, the Germans will be livid. It's highly likely they'll stop us using the hospital. That would be a disaster for the sick.'

The colonel studied Hartley. 'What do you say to that, eh? It's a good point.'

'It is, sir. But I believe it's also our duty to escape, and that we should seize any opportunity that comes our way. I'm sure the sick men would agree with me, sir.'

'Not necessarily, Hartley.'

Damn him, thought Hartley. Damn his pompous, stick-in-the-mud attitude. No wonder they were losing the war with men like him in command. 'Well, we could always ask them,' he said.

'Don't be flippant, man!'

'Sir.'

The colonel went red in the face. After a little while, the colour subsided. 'However, you do have a point,' he said gruffly.

'Sir?'

'You're quite right that it's our duty to escape.' He exhaled, as if he was reluctant to say what was coming. 'Here's what I'll do. I'll think about it, Hartley, for twenty-four hours. And I want you to think about it as well. I can see that you're a young man in a hurry, but I must urge caution. If you're still keen tomorrow, we shall talk again. But, remember, this is not something from the *Boy's Own* magazine, d'y' hear?'

'Of course, sir.'

'All right, dismissed.'

Hartley did ponder the colonel's words, but not for long. His thoughts were interrupted by his refusal to be blackmailed and by the news that Royce was one of the few going to hospital. Kyle told him

78

that without proper medical attention, Royce might well die. It almost seemed unfair that he was going to hospital and Hartley wasn't – as if the whole thing was a wasted opportunity. He knew he was being unreasonable, but that was how he felt.

When he went to see the colonel the following day, his resolve had strengthened.

'Well, Captain Hartley, have you thought about your madcap plan?'

'I have, sir.'

'And?'

'I'd still like to go through with it, sir.'

'Very well.'

Hartley's heart leapt.

'All right,' said the colonel. 'I, too, have been thinking about your plan, and I happen to share your opinion that it's your duty to escape. But I have a duty also to ensure that the men stay alive, Captain.'

His heart sank. 'I quite understand that, sir.'

'But, and this is a big but,' the colonel continued, 'I'm in no position to stop you escaping, Hartley. You may not have my full blessing, but you certainly have my blind eye.'

'Thank you, sir.'

'Not at all. If you escape, we shall deny that we knew about it. Hopefully, the Germans will believe us.'

'And what shall I tell the medical officer, sir?'

'Who? Kyle?'

'Yes, sir.'

'Tell him about what?'

Hartley tried to hide his exasperation. 'Shall I tell him I have your sanction to pretend to be sick?'

'There's no need.'

Hartley frowned.

'He's a lieutenant, isn't he? And you're a captain. Just tell him what's what. Got it?'

'Thank you, sir.'

The colonel wasn't too bad after all, Hartley thought. Pompous, but fair.

Predictably Kyle was outraged, but knew it was best to follow orders, and allowed Hartley to lie on a patched-up stretcher next to the dozen or so invalids. Hartley did his best to pretend he was genuinely ill – an act that no one in the camp would have had much trouble in pulling off. Many had lost a stone or two and, despite the sun, their skin bore the pallor associated with a lack of decent nourishment. After a wait of fifteen minutes, Hartley was lifted by two German NCOs. This was it, he thought. He was on his way.

His optimism was dashed by the presence of two officers at the gate. They were wearing white coats over their uniforms. Damn, thought Hartley. Doctors.

'And what is wrong with this man?'

The question was addressed to Kyle.

'Dysentery,' he replied. Hartley heard resignation in Kyle's voice and hoped it didn't transmit to the German.

'They all seem to have dysentery, Lieutenant Kyle.'

'Well, Major, they all drink the same water.'

The German doctor peered at Hartley over half-moon spectacles. Doctors looked the same wherever you went, Hartley thought. 'How long have you had this?' he asked.

'Ever since we got here,' Hartley replied. He coughed for good measure.

'Is he keeping food down?' The doctor addressed Kyle now.

'Hardly,' said Kyle, unconvincingly. He was a bad liar.

The doctor studied Hartley's face intently, as if he was going to diagnose him by looking at his skin. He breathed out, nostrils flaring. Hartley didn't meet his eyes: he feared his own would give him away.

'Yes,' said the doctor, eventually. 'This man had better go. If he is as sick as you say he is.'

'He *is* sick,' said Kyle. At last! thought Hartley. He was starting to sound believable.

'Next!'

The ride to the hospital was short. Hartley would have liked to see where he was going, but he couldn't get off his stretcher to look out of the ambulance's window without alerting even the most dopey guard, and the one sitting next to him was anything but that. The man's face was friendly, approachable, and Hartley accidentally half smiled at him, a gesture that was reciprocated.

'This is not good,' the guard said.

'What is not good?'

'You.'

'Well, yes, I am sick.'

'Not that. The way you British are in the camp. It is very bad.'

Hartley struggled to elucidate what the man was trying to say. 'The conditions?'

'Yes. Conditions. They are very bad. Soon you will all be sick.'

'I know,' said Hartley.

'If I am prisoner in England, I would not want these conditions.'

'Well, let me assure you,' said Hartley, reminding himself not to become too animated, 'we wouldn't treat our prisoners like that.'

The man smiled. 'You English are very . . . very decent.'

'Thank you,' said Hartley.

The guard grinned. 'Which is why you will lose the war.'

There had to be a sting in the tail. He let his head slump back on to the stretcher.

*

For a few minutes, Hartley wondered whether the drip would do him harm, then realised that of course it wouldn't. He watched as the needle slid into his vein, the plume of blood billowing into the clear solution, then disappearing whence it came. The matron smiled. 'You will be well soon,' she said.

Hartley smiled back. Another friendly face, not unattractive but neutral, bland. She wore her hair in the typically Teutonic way, with two plaits plastered over her head. She looked a little tired.

'Danke, Kindemädchen,' he replied.

'Sprechen Sie Deutsch?' she asked.

'Yes,' he replied, in German. 'I used to visit a lot before the war. I learnt it in school.'

'Where did you go?'

'Bavaria. My father liked climbing mountains, and he made all of us go with him.'

'You liked climbing mountains as well?'

'Not really. My mother hated it, though.'

She let out a giggle. 'Your poor mother.'

'My father was a real dictator.'

A cloud passed over the matron's face.

'I'm sorry,' he said, although an inner voice told him he had no need to apologise.

'No matter,' she said. 'You sleep now. I shall bring your lunch at half past twelve.'

'Thank you.'

83

The matron's mouth smiled, but the rest of her face did not.

Sleep was the last thing Hartley would do. He sat up and looked around the ward. The walls were white – or had once been white. The paint was old and tired, and in places bare masonry was visible. A large picture window drowned the room in fresh Greek light, giving the room an appearance of the sterility and health it lacked. Hartley craned his head further up, and was delighted to find that he could see the sea.

He was not alone: all thirteen of the sick men were in the ward. A man he knew as Peters lay on one side of him, and Royce was on the other. Hartley had not spoken to him since their contretemps; neither did he wish to.

'Clever of you,' Royce murmured.

Hartley ignored him.

'Clever of you, I said.'

'Clever what?'

'To use that word, "dictator".'

Hartley let out a snort of amusement.

'I know why you're here,' said Royce. 'You want to escape.'

'Maybe.'

'If you do that, they'll throw us all back into the camp.'

'I doubt it,' said Hartley. 'Anyway, Royce, it's none of your fucking business.'

Hartley had been dying to use that word to Royce, whose only response was to turn over, which suited Hartley because he wanted to think about how the hell he was going to get out of there. He knew he would have to be patient and study the hospital's routine. One thing gave him a burst of hope: so far he had not seen a single soldier.

Half an hour after dusk. The matron normally did her rounds at about eight o'clock, which took her ten minutes, and then there was quiet. He would wait for it to get almost dark, then slip out as if he was on his way to the lavatory. It would arouse no suspicion, because most of them did that all day and all night. However, this time he would be fully dressed. He knew his uniform was hardly an ideal escape outfit, but with luck he would be able to get rid of it as soon as he found help. The escape would start in the lavatory. It had a small window that overlooked a courtyard. Three sides were formed by the hospital itself, but the fourth was an eight-foot wall that separated the hospital from the street. It would be a bugger to climb, but that, as far as he could tell, was the easiest way out.

Hartley glanced at the clock above the window. It was five to eight – the matron would be here soon.

He did his best to conceal his nerves from Peters and Royce, especially Royce. Was this lunacy? What if he didn't find anyone to help him? Would he be shot? He had no proper clothes, no map, no food, no money. All he had were his wits and a good sense of direction – hardly enough to get him all the way to Dover. Sanity told him he should call it off. Perhaps the colonel was right: he was just a young man in a hurry. What difference would his escape make? None, most likely.

But the temptation was too strong to resist. He had to try, not just because it was his duty and that by escaping he would tie up Germans who might otherwise be fighting, but because it was a personal challenge. He had done nothing in this war, not even fired a shot – the one at Royce's jeep hardly counted – and he wanted to prove to himself that he was worthy of his uniform and of some standard he had set for himself, as his father had done when he challenged himself to climb a mountain within a certain time. Was he doing this to impress his father? Surely not. But if he was, so be it. There was nothing wrong with that. If he could get away with it, he would be a better man for it. If he failed, he would still be a better man. Not to try would be despicable.

The matron appeared. She walked slowly round the beds, talking to each man in turn. Hartley's relationship with her had never progressed after their first exchange, but she was positively in love with Royce. The way he flirted with her! He was all but trying to seduce her, despite his frailty.

'Ah, Matron,' Royce was saying, 'how nice to see you.'

'Captain Royce, how are you this evening?'

'All the better for seeing you.'

It was almost comic, but the woman fell for it. Well, let them have their fun.

'And you, Captain Hartley?' Her tone was a degree warmer than glacial.

Hartley nodded and said, 'All right.'

The matron checked his notes. 'I think we can let you go back to the camp soon,' she said. 'We shall talk to Dr Müller about it tomorrow morning.'

'As you wish,' said Hartley.

A few minutes later she had completed her round. After she had shut the door, Royce lay listening to the chatter of the other men. Thankfully, he had kept his mouth shut about Hartley's escape plan, and Hartley hadn't told them. Even if they were decent sorts, what was the point of trusting people with information they did not need? Those who told others their secrets wanted the listeners to like them, Hartley thought. It was an easy way to establish intimacy.

The clock showed twenty-five past eight. Time to go. There was no point in waiting any longer.

'Oh, shit,' he moaned.

The ward would not doubt that this was a reference to his bowels. Such language often preceded a dash out of the ward to the lavatory, and Hartley was on his way there now. Some of the men might notice he was fully clothed, even wearing his boots. Too bad. He couldn't hide them. He hurried along, and flung open the door into the corridor. The lavatory was five yards further down, and he walked quickly, clutching his stomach.

'Captain Hartley!'

He turned. The matron was behind him. Where the devil had she sprung from? 'Sorry, Matron. I can't stop!'

'But why are you dressed?'

He muttered something about feeling cold, then opened the lavatory door. The room was anything but antiseptic. In fact, Hartley hadn't seen a cleaner in there since they had arrived; the patients had had to keep the place clean as best as they could.

He opened a cubicle door and locked it behind him. He was breathing heavily, starting to panic. He told himself to get a grip, think things through. Now what? Abandon it? Or press on? Once again, the debate was between caution borne of reason, and something more gung-ho. Would she raise the alarm because she had seen him in his uniform? Perhaps. But even if she did, he would have a head start on any pursuers. If he was going to act, he had to do so now.

A side effect of his nervousness was the sudden looseness he felt in his bowels.

'Oh, shit,' he murmured. This time he meant it. He struggled to contain it, but knew he had to go. Although he was better off than the rest of the men in the hospital, he was in far from good shape, hardly in a condition to escape.

As he sat down, he heard the lavatory door open.

'Captain Hartley?'

It was the matron.

'Yes?'

'Are you all right? You were in your clothes.'

'I was a little cold.'

'Well, when you've finished in there, I shall take your temperature. You may have a fever.'

'All right.'

Hartley heard her shut the door. He pondered his next step. Surely it was madness to go now, especially while she was waiting for him. He opened the cubicle door, walked to the cracked washbasin and rinsed his hands in a trickle of cold water. A broken mirror reflected his uncertainty. He looked at the window. It was so tempting. All he had to do was open it and drop the few feet to the courtyard. Come on, man, just do it.

He looked at the door, straining his ears. Nothing. The matron would have gone back to her office where she would be waiting for him. Well, she'd have a long wait.

Twenty seconds later, Hartley was standing on the courtyard's dirty cobbles. He panted in the half-light, letting himself grow accustomed to his new surroundings. Keep moving, he told himself. Keep bloody moving. He walked briskly across the courtyard – some thirty feet – to the wall. Christ, it was huge. How in God's name was he going to get over it? Then he saw the absurdity of his situation. Here he was, a twenty-three-year-old Englishman, in the middle of a hospital courtyard in occupied Greece, and he couldn't even get past the first obstacle. The chance of him making the thousands of miles home seemed non-existent.

He stepped up to the wall and tried to reach up to the top of it. He couldn't, no matter how hard he tried. He looked for places along the brickwork where he might gain a foothold, but there were none. The wall was frustratingly well built. Why couldn't it have been the normal ramshackle affair he was used to seeing, with missing bricks that would have allowed him to climb up with ease?

Feeling that hundreds of eyes were upon him, looking through the chinks in the hospital's blackout curtains, Hartley tried to heave himself up at a point where there was a gap in the rendering, but it was hopeless. Some bloody escaper he was proving. He might as well have stuck it out at the camp. He couldn't even climb back into the lavatory because the window was higher than this wall.

'Do you want a hand?'

Hartley's heart jumped up to his neck. It was Royce.

'Mind if I come along too?' he said, his broad grin visible in the dim light.

Hartley's desire to get over the wall was so strong that he couldn't refuse him. Perhaps it was some kind of trick. Maybe Royce was teasing him in some way. After all, wasn't he ill? What sort of shape was he in to escape?

Nevertheless Hartley placed his foot in Royce's cupped hands and propelled himself up the wall. Even with Royce's assistance, the manoeuvre required a lot of effort: he was weak, his strength sapped by weeks of bad food and little or no exercise.

He sat on top of the wall, catching his breath and glancing up and down the street for signs of life, but there was only a scrawny cat. This would be easier than he'd thought.

'Help me up!' Royce hissed.

Hartley leant down and dragged him up the wall. The two men sat briefly next to each other, then jumped down. They landed quietly, and paused. Hartley was filled with a mixture of elation at the thought of freedom and perplexity at Royce's presence.

To his left, the road led down into the town. To the right, it ran up to the hills.

'This way,' he said, and started to walk quickly. After a few paces, Royce came up alongside him.

'Where are we going?' he asked.

'To the hills.'

'What happens there?'

'I don't bloody know!'

They made good progress. With every step they took, Hartley's exhilaration grew. Within a few minutes, they had left the town. So far, they had not seen a single German. They might have been having an after-dinner stroll, before a nightcap and bed. This was not what escaping was meant to be like, Hartley thought. It felt bizarrely normal. Where were the soldiers hunting them down? Where was the scrambling down cliffs? Where were the bullets smacking the air over their heads?

After another five minutes, they left the road and sat behind a rock to catch their breath. It had been only a short walk, but Hartley was already exhausted. 'How come you're here, Royce?' he asked.

'Let's call it a change of heart.'

'A rather dramatic one.'

'I know. I've been thinking about what you said, and realised you were right. It is our duty to escape.'

'When did you decide this?'

'Oh, it's been brewing for a while. When I saw you leave the ward, I knew you were going, and I thought, sod it, I've got to try as well. I'd never forgive myself if I hadn't.'

Silence.

'Royce?'

'Yes?'

'What really happened at the church where you said your men were killed?'

Royce looked up to the stars. 'I'll tell you, but not now. But I promise I'll tell you.'

Hartley stood up. The man had evaded the question once more, but in doing so he had revealed that his original story had indeed been a lie. Hartley felt uncomfortable to be travelling with a liar, but now he had no choice. 'Come on, let's go.'

Royce stood up unsteadily. 'Where are we going?' he asked.

'I really haven't a clue. All I want is to get as far from the town as possible.'

'Were you intending to get any sleep tonight?'

'At some point, yes. In a barn, maybe.'

'And then what?'

'Make contact with a local. See if we can get some help.'

They found their barn an hour later. It was a small wooden affair, built just off the side of the road and a few yards from a farmhouse, whose occupants Hartley would talk to in the morning. There was no point in disturbing them now – they would only be frightened by a knock in the middle of the night.

The two men settled down on some hay. It stank, but it was better than sleeping outside. The night was colder than Hartley had expected, and he was grateful for the warmth in the barn. As they settled down, Royce spoke. 'I'm sorry for the way I've been behaving,' he said.

Hartley didn't reply.

'What happened back at the church . . . it was too horrible.'

'What was?'

'I can't tell you now.'

Hartley wanted desperately to know, but he needed sleep.

'All right,' he said. 'Let's sleep now.'

They were awoken by a torrent of high-pitched Greek. Hartley squinted at the leathery face of a middle-aged farmer's wife, who was bawling at them in a way that left them in no doubt they were most unwelcome. Hartley stood up slowly and held out his hands towards her. She was carrying a milk churn, but it might as well have been a machine-gun.

'Good morning,' he said, in pidgin Greek. 'We are British soldiers.'

That met with another outpouring of Greek. Royce stood up too, and added, 'British, not Germans. British, not Germans.'

That did nothing to allay the woman's fears. She dropped the churn and ran.

'Now what?' Royce asked.

'We should let her bring back her husband.'

'But what if he doesn't like us?'

'I shall apologise and we'll be on our way.'

'Do you think that'll work?'

'I've no idea.'

While they waited, Hartley felt a pain in his stomach. He was famished, but for the time being he had to forget about food. If he played his cards right, they might get some from the farmer.

Footsteps approached the barn.

'Here he comes,' said Royce.

Hartley struggled to remember the Greek for 'I am very sorry' and 'Do you have food and clothes?' They had all been issued Greek phrase-books before they came out, but they had been useless, intended for tourists. Instead of useful, military-related vocabulary, they contained phrases like 'How many steps are there up to the Acropolis?' and 'Where is the nearest restaurant?', neither of which would be of much use now.

The barn door swung open, and a shiny black boot appeared. Greek farmers did not wear shiny black boots, Hartley thought. German officers did. He was right. The boot indeed belonged to a German officer: a captain, who was nervously pointing his Luger at them. 'Hands up!' he shouted, voice trembling.

Chapter Three

Mid-May

FIVE DAYS LATER, at seven o'clock on a damp
Monday morning in Saxony, a train drew up at a
small town in Germany. The usual assortment of
travellers was on board – soldiers on leave, middle-
aged businessmen, nurses – but it was far from full.
The town was quiet, hardly the sort of place to attract
visitors; it was a town people travelled from rather
than to. There were plenty of towns like it between
Dresden and Leipzig, decent places with decent
people, who lived off the green and fertile land
watered by the mighty river Mulde that flowed
through it.

Also on board that train were two men who knew
nothing about the town apart from its name, which
had been revealed to them on a rather tatty signboard
that hung above the platform.

'Colditz,' said Hartley. 'Ever heard of it?'

'No,' said Royce, who had wrapped his arms round himself in an attempt to keep warm and, Hartley fancied, to protect himself from the world. Since they had been captured – it seemed like a long time ago – they had been shouted at, kicked, punched, pushed and manhandled from the Greek sunshine to this misty station. It was little wonder that Royce looked so defensive. Hartley felt the same, but he didn't let it show.

'Right, this is it. Off!'

Hartley stood up, knee joints cracking. He let out a grunt and stretched his arms as far as he could within the confines of the compartment. They had arrived in Leipzig in the middle of the night, and had caught a train at five o'clock to bring them here. It had hardly been the best night's sleep, and his body ached. He looked at their guard – one of two who had escorted them from the Czech border. The man seemed as tired as Hartley was, perhaps more so – he hadn't been allowed to sleep.

They stepped off the train. Hartley had expected the other travellers to take some interest in them, but he and Royce were ignored as if they were an everyday sight. Perhaps they were, thought Hartley. Perhaps a lot of POWs came in on this train. He and Royce had no idea where they were going, except that it was a *Sonderlager*, a special camp, in the words of one German officer, for 'naughty boys'. Was it a concentration camp? Hartley had asked. No, it was not a KZ and, no, not everybody got locked up in a KZ. It was a prisoner-of-war camp, a maximum-security prisoner-of-war camp. A nice place to spend the rest of the war, the officer had added, with a superior grin that had made Hartley want to knock his teeth out.

The ticket collector ignored them too, but gave the two guards a nod of recognition as they passed him. Hartley hadn't expected a welcoming fanfare, but after so many days' travelling, this was so anticlimactic. They were everyday items of little consequence. It added to Hartley's sense of entrapment, which had grown since they had been captured. An entire company of German mountain troops had been camped a hundred yards from the farmhouse. Hartley could hardly blame the woman for handing them in: she would have been shot if the Germans had found them there – and they most probably would have. For the last five days, Hartley had cursed himself for not reconnoitring the area – he had allowed the desire for sleep to get the better of him. His escaping days – or, rather, hours – were over. Some bloody story to tell his grandchildren.

They walked out of the station on to a cobbled road. A few horses and carts were waiting to be loaded, the animals' breath steaming in the cold air. They were thin, Hartley noted, emaciated, not quite on their last legs but had it been peacetime they would have been pensioned off long ago.

'March!'

As if, thought Hartley. That was all the other guard had said – 'march'. And all Hartley and Royce had ever done was to ignore the command. There was no way he would take orders from some puffed-up runt of an NCO.

'Left, right, left, right!'

Hartley almost laughed, but he was too tired. Instead of marching, they walked – or, rather, shambled. The street was wide, lined with large nineteenth-century apartment buildings. Again, nobody looked down at them as they walked. Besides, it was not the type of morning for throwing open the windows and letting in the air.

After three hundred yards, they turned off and followed the road as it snaked to the left. Hartley could hear running water – a weir, most likely. It reminded him of school, the weir just past the bridge; occasionally a boy had plunged down when he lost control of his sculler. He had rather enjoyed rowing, and hadn't been too bad at it. He had even made the third eight, which was something of an achievement.

'Good God.' Royce was staring at the sky.

Hartley followed his eyes, and there, its grey-white face blending into the mist, was an enormous castle. It loured over them, thought Hartley. Its face was pockmarked by small black windows, its roofs pitched and steep, and it dominated the town. It was as if the houses quivered and cowered in its presence, each begging not to be struck down by a bolt issuing from its thick, dirty walls.

'That is your new home,' said the friendlier of the guards. 'I hope you like it.'

'What's it called?'

'Colditz Castle, of course. Now, keep walking.'

Hartley and Royce did so. Hartley felt as if he was being sucked in by the building, and hardly noticed when they crossed the river. The castle was ugly, brutal, an architectural mess of spires, extensions, differently angled roofs. It looked grim, sinister, as if no laughter had ever been heard within its walls.

A few minutes later, they were walking through a sloping market square. A delicious smell wafted out of a little bakery, but Hartley kept his eyes fixed on the looming mass. It was like a grey battleship, towering above them. It was the grey of the winter sea, an unforgiving grey that never warmed. Once they were inside, Hartley wondered whether they would ever get out, whether he would ever again smell freshly baked bread – indeed, whether he would ever again walk so far in a straight line.

'What do you think?' he asked Royce.

Royce said nothing.

'It's a big bugger, isn't it?' said Hartley.

'It's evil.'

'Evil?'

'Yes. There's something evil about it. I don't like it. I don't want to go into it. It will kill me, I know it.'

'Come on, man, it's not going to kill you. It's just a big old castle. It doesn't have teeth.'

Royce was shaking his head. 'I'm never going to leave here. I'll die here.'

Hartley noticed that what little colour Royce had had in his cheeks had vanished. 'You look as if you've seen a ghost . . . Royce? Royce!'

Hartley ran forward to catch Royce, who was collapsing. His body crumpled, as if a puppeteer had let go of his strings.

'Royce! Can you hear me?'

Clearly Royce had fainted. His eyes stared blankly ahead. Hartley struggled a little under his weight, and lowered him as gently as he could on to the wet cobbles.

'Royce!' For a few seconds, Hartley cradled Royce's head in his arms. 'Water!' he snapped at the guards. 'Go and get some water, and some food!' He was probably famished, thought Hartley, as Royce's eyelids flickered. He was coming to. 'Royce, can you hear me?'

He didn't reply, but his eyes darted crazily from side to side, up and down. 'What?' he said eventually.

'You've fainted,' said Hartley. 'Just stay there for a bit.'

'The castle,' said Royce.

'That's right, we're going to the castle.'

Royce started breathing quickly, panting like a dog.

'Calm down, man!' said Hartley.

It was no good. Royce was clearly having some sort of fit or seizure.

'For heaven's sake!' said Hartley, frustrated.

One of the guards arrived with a mug of water and a slice of bread. Hartley attempted to pour some water into Royce's mouth, which made him choke. He lifted him, and Royce coughed the water out of his lungs. It calmed him somewhat.

'Royce, are you all right? Whatever's got into you?'

Royce shook his head a couple of times, as if trying to dispel something from within it. 'I don't know,' he said, coughing again. 'Something just came over me.'

'What did?'

Royce turned to him. His face bore an expression that Hartley had never seen before, not on Royce or on anyone else. He was still staring, as he had been when he had fainted, and it was as if he was looking through Hartley, through the buildings behind him, over the fields and rivers to somewhere impossibly distant.

'What happened?'

'It was ... strange. I saw a long white corridor. Lots of black doors to the left. Not doors, just openings. And then a man, who was me. Lying in a

103

big white bed. He showed me his arm, which was covered with spots.'

'It was just a dream, Royce, from when you fainted. It happened to me once when I was knocked out on the rugby pitch. I saw a little man on a golden horse and cart trundling down a tunnel to a little white light. It gave me the creeps for a long time, I don't know why. But it was only a dream. Ignore it.'

'It wasn't a dream.'

'Of course it was. Here, have this.'

Hartley passed him the bread and water. Royce wolfed the bread.

'Is he all right?' asked one of the guards.

'Yes,' said Hartley. 'Give him a minute.'

Some passers-by stopped to gawk, but the guards shooed them away.

'I think he was just overtired and hungry,' said Hartley.

'We must go on,' said the guard.

'I won't!' Royce shouted.

'For heaven's sake, Royce, shut up!'

'I can't go in there!'

'You've got to.'

Royce stood up. 'I'm not going into that place.'

'For Christ's sake, Royce! You have no choice. This isn't some bloody hotel we're going to – pull yourself together!'

Royce let his hands fall to his sides. He had finally

seen sense, Hartley thought. The poor bloke was cracking up. And he was probably right – the castle would kill him in a way. 'Come on, man, let's just go.'

'*Schnell*,' said the guard.

They began to walk on.

The hill to the castle was a little steep, and the men slipped once or twice on the cobbles. As they neared the castle, it grew ever more impressive, ever more awesome. They approached a small gatehouse, where two sentries stood in front of a large wooden gate that filled the arch. Their escort conferred briefly with them, and the gate was opened with a predictable creak.

Ahead, a bridge led to another arch, this time in the castle itself. The sides were about three feet high, Hartley noticed, and at the end on the right, just before the arch, there was a small picket gate. They walked over the bridge, which spanned a dried-out moat. To the left they could see the town, and to the right a path led along the moat. What a place, thought Hartley. No wonder it had been used to house 'naughty boys'.

Above the arch an ornate coat-of-arms briefly caught his attention. In fact, it was two coats-of-arms, supported by a couple of magnificent creatures that Hartley took to be lions. A sentry stood under the arch, manning another gate. How, in God's name, could anybody escape from here? Hartley wondered, as the sentry inspected the papers carried by the escort.

'Goodbye,' said the friendlier guard.

Hartley was taken aback. 'Yes, er, goodbye.' He was about to add, 'Thank you,' because that was what you said, but stopped himself. The guard saluted. Hartley decided that saluting back would do no harm and did so. Royce did not follow suit: he was staring through the arch towards the interior of the place he fancied would be the death of him.

A door slammed nearby, and a German officer in his late forties was walking towards them. The sentry snapped to attention.

'Good morning,' said the officer. 'I am Major Carl Rensburg, the security officer, and I am hoping you are Captains Hartley and Royce. Correct?'

Hartley and Royce both stated their names and saluted. The salute was returned. Hartley was gratified to see that Rensburg used a conventional military salute rather than a Heil Hitler. His English was impeccable.

'In case you're wondering why I speak English so well,' said Rensburg, 'I should tell you that I taught in England before the war. At Wycombe Abbey school. Do you know it?'

'Know it?' said Hartley. 'My wife went there.'

Rensburg smiled. 'What's her name? Perhaps I taught her.'

Hartley paused. Was this some kind of trick – a trap to elucidate information? No – it couldn't be. Name, rank and number could go hang for a minute – this was just too intriguing. 'Her name is, or rather was, Sarah Howell. Do you—'

'Sarah Howell? With dark hair? She was one of my best pupils. You have done well there, Captain Hartley.'

'I can't quite believe this,' said Hartley.

'Neither can I,' said Rensburg. 'Sarah Howell – well, well. She spoke good German by the time I had finished with her. And you, Captain, do you speak German?'

Hartley almost walked into it. 'No,' he lied, '*sprechen Sie Deutsch* and *ein bier* are about my lot.'

'Ah, well, perhaps you can learn while you're here. Or maybe French? Polish, even – not that that'll be of much use soon.'

Hartley smiled weakly. What had turned a schoolmaster into a gaoler? This was an unmentioned effect of the war, he thought, landing people in impossible and unlikely places. He thought of Sarah, wondered where she was, what she was doing. Perhaps she was having breakfast in the flat, or maybe she was still asleep. He would write to her today, tell her his news, leaving out the unpleasantness of the dysentery. She seemed a long way off, not just in distance but in his thoughts. He felt guilty for having

107

not thought of her enough, as though he had been disloyal.

'How about you, Captain Royce, are you a linguist?'

Royce muttered, 'No.'

'Come come, Captain! Things aren't that bad. You're alive, aren't you? You could have been shot when you were in Greece, so you should count yourself lucky that you are our guest.'

Royce said nothing.

'I'm afraid he fainted a few minutes ago,' said Hartley. 'I think he should lie down.'

'Fainted?'

'Yes. Hungry and tired, I suspect. We're both getting over dysentery.'

Rensburg's face, once jolly, turned serious. 'You were badly treated in Greece?'

'Somewhat,' said Hartley.

'Well, that won't happen here, I promise. We shall get you looked at as soon as possible, Captain Royce.'

Royce nodded.

'Right,' said Rensburg. 'Step this way, please.'

By now a couple more sentries had joined them, and Rensburg led them down the short tunnel into a massive courtyard. Hartley estimated that at least two hundred windows looked down at them from two vast grey-brown buildings.

'This is the Kommandantur, gentlemen,' said Rensburg, uttering the words as if he was a tour guide. 'This is where we live, and there are at least four hundred of us.'

Four hundred, thought Hartley, and wondered whether that was a lie. This really was maximum security. He looked round as they walked the twenty yards to yet another arch, another gate, another sentry. To the right was a sloping lawn, which led up from the courtyard to one of the Kommandantur buildings. There was another arch too, a large one, under which a covered lorry was driving, no doubt ready to disgorge even more guards. The clattering of pots and pans echoed from a newer building, which Hartley assumed to be the kitchens.

Their footsteps echoed off the sides of the next tunnel, which Hartley estimated to be around ten yards long. Staircases twisted away from small doors cut into the side, leading God knew where.

'Nearly there,' said Rensburg. The man was infuriatingly cheerful.

They emerged into the damp daylight, and walked another fifteen yards up a shallow slope that curved gently to the right. Another sentry nodded them through. Ahead was a tower, which Hartley suspected they were making for. However, they were led to the right, to another arch with the now familiar guarded gate. Hartley noticed Rensburg show the guard a small disc, whereupon the man opened the gate.

Rensburg held out his hand. He was beaming.

'Gentlemen, your new home. If you step through, I shall leave you to get on with it.'

Hartley swallowed. He felt like a new boy at school. He knew now that he was going to become the lowest of the low. The same would go for Royce and, to Hartley's annoyance, they would always be thought of as a pair, no matter how long they stayed there. Hartley and Royce, the heroic escapers from Greece, the shortest escape attempt in history.

He turned to Royce, who looked as if he was about to faint again. Oh, God, please don't, thought Hartley. What a first impression that would make, walking in here and falling flat on your face. He, too, would be tarred with it, and Hartley knew that it was selfishness rather than sympathy that made him will Royce to remain on his feet. 'All right, Royce?'

'I think so,' he said hoarsely.

The two men stepped into another courtyard. This one was much smaller than the Kommandantur, much more claustrophobic. All Hartley could see were dirty grey walls, and tiny windows. It was like stepping into the bottom of a well, and Hartley and Royce instinctively lifted their heads, craning for a snatch of sky. There it was, the same colour as the walls and cobblestones. It was funny how you wanted to see the sky, and always looked for it wherever you found yourself. It was the only thing that was constant about the war, thought Hartley, that, the moon and the stars.

The courtyard was empty. Not a sound could be heard, apart from the dying echo of the door slamming behind them.

'They're going to shoot us,' said Royce. 'I tell you, we're going to die! It's all been some sort of—'

'Rubbish! It's seven in the morning. They're probably all still asleep or having breakfast. You'll see.'

Hartley advanced slowly into the courtyard, walking up a slight slope. He looked for a face at a window, any sign of life. He was almost tempted to call out, but thought that would be a little cocky.

'Hello, down there!'

Hartley's eyes scanned for where the voice had come from.

'Up here!'

Royce pointed to a window two floors above an archway set in a tower at the top right corner of the courtyard. There, a long face with large teeth beamed down at them.

'You must be Hartley and Royce. Welcome to Schloss Colditz.'

'Hello!' Hartley shouted.

'Where were you both at school?'

Hartley told him, as did Royce.

'Excellent! We've got quite a few of your chaps here, especially yours, you on the left.'

That was Hartley. 'Who?' By now a few more faces were appearing at windows round the courtyard.

'Gosh, let me see – Bob Beauchamp. Irby. Charles Huntington. Little Welshman called Ben Thomas. Know them?'

Hartley smiled. 'I do indeed.'

'I was at the other place, so I tend to give your lot a miss. By the way, I'm Ings-Chambers.'

Hartley felt both reassured and slightly thrown off centre. Although he had left school only five years ago, his memories of it had been overshadowed by the events of the past few years. Cambridge, coming down, joining up, training, more training, getting married, boat to Egypt, boat to Greece. It was bizarre to end up in Germany talking about school.

'Wait there,' said Ings-Chambers. 'I'm going to bring the colonel down.'

Hartley waved back and the face disappeared.

'*Bonjour, Anglais!*'

More faces at more windows.

'Welcome to Oflag Four C!' came a voice that sounded German, but Hartley realised was in fact Dutch.

'*Ça va?*'

The men were smiling, and some waved caps out of the windows.

'You see, Royce, this seems a pretty friendly place. Come on, it's like school.'

'I didn't like school,' said Royce.

Hartley could only laugh. Well, there was a surprise.

'We've got a man out at the moment,' said Colonel Kerr-Smiley, a hint of pride in his voice.

Hartley took a sip of the watery tea the colonel had offered him. A slice of stale black bread, topped with a thin layer of what was supposed to be blackberry jam, accompanied it. Under normal circumstances, Hartley would have let such a breakfast pass, but this morning he was starving.

'How did he get out, sir?' Hartley asked.

Kerr-Smiley walked to the window of his small room. It overlooked the castle's park, a tantalising glimpse of the world outside. 'It was a snap escape,' he said. 'Some old mattresses were being loaded on to the lorry in the courtyard by some French workers. We found our smallest chap, a little Scot called James Keith, stuffed him into a mattress and got the Frogs to load him on to the lorry. Off he went! We haven't heard a word since.'

'Do the Germans know?'

'God, yes. When Keith didn't appear at roll-call, all hell broke loose. They can't for the life of them work out how he got away. Anyway, I hope he makes it, not just for his sake but for our morale. We've got to beat the French.'

'Beat the French, sir?'

'Of course! So far, they've made a home run back to Switzerland. Chap called Dubois. We can't let them win – it'd be a disgrace!'

Hartley smiled. This was all rather jolly, he thought. It really was like school, but in place of different houses, they had nationalities, and for the beaks they had Goons. Did the other nationalities behave like this? He doubted it. They wouldn't have been educated in the same way, so the castle couldn't be passed off as a public school.

'How about the Poles, sir?'

'Oh, they're always trying. Good chaps, but nutcases. Forever jumping all over the roofs, risking their necks. No discipline! But for them escaping's a much more heartfelt business. They've lost their country, remember.'

'And the Dutch?'

'I'm rather fond of them. Bit like us, in many ways, although their English is probably better. They speak German too, as well as any Jerry, which is a boon for them. And they're very good at locks. God knows why, but there it is.'

Hartley cleared his throat. 'You should know, sir, that both Captain Royce and I speak German.'

Kerr-Smiley raised an eyebrow. 'Do you now? Well, that's interesting. Make sure you tell Major Wilds.'

'Major Wilds?'

'He's the escape officer. Each nationality has an escape officer, whose job is to evaluate escape plans, liaise with the other nationalities and make sure there are no conflicts of interest. As you can imagine, he's a busy man. In fact, we've got something big on at the moment, so you might find him a little distracted.'

Hartley wanted to know what the 'something big' was, but he knew better than to ask.

'I know what you're both thinking,' said Kerr-Smiley, 'but don't worry – you'll find out soon enough. Any other particular talents, either of you?'

Hartley and Royce exchanged a glance. Hartley noticed that Royce still looked washed out.

'None that I can think of, sir,' said Hartley.

'I don't suppose you can sew or anything like that?'

Hartley shifted uneasily in his seat. 'Well, actually, sir, I can.'

'A rare thing! Excellent. We need someone who can sew well. Are you any good?'

'Not bad, sir. What's this for? Making disguises, that sort of thing?'

Kerr-Smiley snorted. 'Heavens, no! It's for the play! We need someone to make up ballerinas' tutus for Lieutenant Beauchamp and Captain Irby.'

Hartley couldn't have been more flabbergasted. His mouth hung open.

'Captain Edginton's in charge. Fancies himself as a director. He's another of your lot.'

'What's the play about, sir?'

'Oh, I don't know. The usual nonsense about savages and schoolmasters. See Edginton, he'll tell you all about it. I think he even wrote it.'

'Yes, sir.'

'Now, then, I don't want to keep you.'

Hartley and Royce took the colonel's words to mean that they should leave. They both stood smartly to attention and saluted. Kerr-Smiley saluted back. He glanced at Royce's plate, which still contained half of his slice of bread.

'What's the matter with you, man?' he asked, eyes bulging with incredulity.

'I'm sorry, sir, I'm not feeling very well,' Royce replied. 'I think I've still got whatever I had in Greece.'

'I see,' said the colonel. 'Get down to the sickbay then. Captain Barnett should be there – he'll sort you out.'

'Yes, sir.'

'We've had quite a bit of this,' said Kerr-Smiley, 'chaps coming from Greece and Africa with the most terrible complaints. The Colditz diet normally sorts them out.'

'What does it consist of, sir?' asked Hartley.

'Well, you'd better like watery soup.'

The occupants of their room were still having breakfast when they walked in. There were four of them, seated round a small wooden table, upon which was placed a variety of chipped enamel bowls, plates and mugs, none of whose contents looked particularly appetising.

'Aha! The new boys!'

The speaker, who was tall and blond, stood up and grinned. 'Good God, Hardly, what the hell are you doing here?'

'Hello, Huntercombe,' Hartley replied. In fact, the man's name was Huntington, but a history master at school had insisted for no apparent reason that he should be called Huntercombe, and Huntercombe he had remained. Hartley had metamorphosed into Hardly.

'Christ, man,' said Huntington, 'you look bloody awful! What happened to you?'

'The trots, I'm afraid. Greek diet. Captain Royce here is still pretty bad.'

'Eeeurgh,' said Huntington. 'Nasty business. See the doc.'

'I will,' said Royce.

Huntington clapped his hands. 'Now, then introductions. Your new friends are Captain Edgar Bettridge, Lieutenant John Biddulph and Lieutenant Mark Davis. Say hello, everybody.'

It was evidently a little early in the morning for Huntington's ebullience, and the three men murmured soporifically.

'I'm afraid you're a bit late for breakfast,' Huntington went on 'but there are your beds.' He pointed to two iron bedsteads with thin striped mattresses and a single grey blanket. 'We've wangled you a cupboard where you can put your stuff, not that you've got much,' Huntington continued.

'Thanks,' said Hartley. 'So, we sleep and eat in here?'

'That's it.'

Hartley took in the room. It was about twenty-five feet long by fifteen wide, with a single window that shared the same view as the colonel's. Hartley went across to it and looked out past the bars. Below and to the right, through trees that were starting to leaf, he could see a park enclosed by a barbed-wire fence. A wall ran around it, and above it, just on the skyline, he could just make out the roof of a small cottage. Hartley turned back into the room. It was pretty Spartan and smelt of damp, fused with old uniforms and rancid boots. He could hear doors slamming down corridors, alien voices, dull footsteps above them. 'Pretty palatial,' he said.

Hartley was asleep when the alarm bell rang. His body and mind were exhausted after a week on the move, and within a minute of lying down to get a feel of his mattress, he had drifted off, to the amusement of his room-mates.

118

'Come on, new boy, up you get,' said Huntington.

Hartley sat up, rubbing his eyes. 'What is it? A fire alarm?'

'Nein, Kamerad, das ist ein Appel!' said Huntington.

'Roll-call, eh? How many of these do we get every day?'

'Three. This is the first. Half past eight in the morning.'

Hartley looked to the bed on his left. 'Where's Royce?'

'Gone to the san.'

Hartley swung his legs out of bed. 'Best place for him,' he said. 'He's been feeling pretty ropey for weeks now.'

He walked out of the room with the others. It felt good to be doing something with them, even if it was at the behest of their captors. He felt as if he was becoming part of things. They walked down the long, dim corridor, collecting other British officers as they went. Many faces seemed familiar, not because he had met them before but because they were of a type he had grown up with. They could have been on their way to morning chapel, he thought. All they lacked were exercise books under their arms. Some were so young that they could have left school only a couple of years ago.

They reached the top of a narrow, winding stone

staircase and clattered down it. Hartley almost lost his footing a couple of times.

'You'll get the hang of it within a few days,' said Huntington, above the hubbub.

'I'll probably have broken my neck before then.'

Hartley was astounded by how many men were packed into the small courtyard. There must have been hundreds. The atmosphere was lively, complete with an old tennis ball being thrown from one side of the courtyard to the other.

'Welcome to *Appel*,' said Huntington.

'How long does it take?'

Huntington shrugged. 'As long as we want it to. If it's cold, we're pretty well behaved and the count is over quickly. Otherwise it can take up to two hours.'

'Two hours? Isn't that a waste of time?'

'Well, not really. We've got time to waste, so we might as well waste the Germans' too. There's no point in making life easy for them.'

Hartley stood next to Huntington in the fourth row of a rough phalanx of British officers. To their right stood the French, their uniforms much smarter than those of the British, who were unashamedly scruffy and wore a mixture of unmilitary dress, ranging from cricket jerseys to greatcoats, boiler-suits, even the odd kilt. 'Where does everyone get these clothes from?' he asked.

'They're sent from home,' Huntington replied, 'via the Red Cross. They do the same for the Jerries imprisoned in Britain. Just don't expect anything by the end of the week, that's all. Three to six months is the average waiting time. Book your winter woollies now.'

The volume of noise in the courtyard dropped as the men's attention was drawn to the gate. Hartley craned his neck and saw Rensburg enter with two junior officers and a handful of NCOs.

'Rensburg,' said Huntington. 'Have you met him?'

'I have. Of all things, he was my wife's German teacher.'

'You're pulling my leg.'

'I'm afraid not. What's he like? He seems all right.'

'Yes, but nobody becomes security officer at a place like this without good reason. He's an oily tick, a real snake. Typical teacher, now you come to mention. Did your wife ever talk about him?'

'No. I shall have to write and ask her.'

Hartley looked back at Rensburg just in time to see his cap knocked off by the tennis ball. For a moment there was silence, and then the courtyard erupted with multilingual jeers and laughter.

'Oh, good shot!' shouted Huntington.

'Where did it come from?' Hartley asked.

'Not the French . . . I'd say it was the Poles.'

'Silence!'

Rensburg's command rang round the courtyard. The desired effect was by no means immediate.

'Silence!'

His face had gone bright red, his earlier friendly demeanour eradicated. Hartley noticed that a couple of the NCOs had unslung their rifles from their shoulders. The courtyard was plunged into silence.

'Who threw that?' shouted Rensburg.

'As if anyone's going to admit to it,' whispered Huntington, out of the corner of his mouth. 'Two weeks in solitary minimum, perhaps a month.'

Rensburg entered into a brief discussion with his fellow officers, who were pointing towards the other side of the courtyard from the British.

'Almost certainly the Poles,' said Huntington.

'Does this happen a lot?' Hartley whispered.

'No. You're in luck.'

Rensburg walked out of sight, presumably towards the Polish contingent. Hartley stood on tiptoe to watch him speaking to a senior Polish officer, who was either genuinely mystified or doing a good job of pretending. Eventually Rensburg stormed back to address the entire camp population.

'You will stand here until the culprit hands himself in. I do not care how long it takes. I have all the time in the world.'

'Here we go,' said Huntington.

It was getting more and more like school, thought Hartley.

After half an hour, it started to rain. A collective groan went up, and Rensburg smiled. An NCO appeared with an umbrella and held it over his head. Laughter broke out, and redoubled when it became clear that the NCO's arm was tiring.

'*Silence!*' shouted Rensburg.

After another few minutes, Hartley became aware of a commotion at the other side of the courtyard as the guilty Pole handed himself in. The British contingent clapped, hands high in the air, the French and the Dutch joining in.

'It's Kwasnieski,' said Huntington. 'The only Pole I know who plays cricket.'

Hartley watched the man being led away. He was grinning because he knew he had raised the prisoners' morale a notch. The knocking off of Rensburg's cap would be the talk of the castle for days to come. After he had disappeared through the arch, the count was carried out with the minimum of fuss. The prisoners had had their fun, and now it was time to go in.

'What do we do now?' asked Hartley.

'Get dry,' said Huntington, 'and then you can catch up on your kip if you want.'

'Do you know when I can meet Wilds?'

'You're an eager beaver, aren't you?' said Huntington. 'It's either that or making a tutu.'

Hartley found Major Wilds lying on his bed, an unlit pipe wedged between his teeth. He was reading a dog-eared book, legs crossed at the ankles. There were three other beds in the room, which Hartley noticed was far more luxurious than his own, with a gramophone and even a couple of watercolours on the wall. Wilds was a picture of serenity, not at all as he had expected.

'Excuse me, sir,' said Hartley, 'may I introduce myself?'

Wilds turned away from his book and stared at Hartley, indifferent but not unfriendly. He raised his eyebrows, and his neatly trimmed moustache moved up and down as he chewed on his pipe. Hartley's father had told him that pipe-smokers were slow thinkers, a theory that had been proved correct on numerous occasions. However, Hartley knew it was unlikely that Wilds was stupid. After all, he was the escape officer.

'I'm Hartley, sir, Captain Hugh Hartley, Royal Engineers.'

Wilds didn't say anything, but grimaced in a way that said, 'What of it?' He would be a hard man to convince.

'The colonel suggested I came to see you, sir.'

Again, no reply. But there was a slight opening of the eyes, which Hartley took to mean 'Did he now?'

'I told him I was a German speaker, sir, and he said you might be interested.'

Wilds nodded slowly. If Hartley had thought that piece of information was enough to make Wilds say something, he was wrong.

'I've just arrived, sir. I escaped from my camp in Greece, but I was recaptured.' Obviously, thought Hartley. Shut up, you fool.

Wilds removed the pipe from his mouth and, as Hartley thought he was about to speak, promptly shoved it back in, which was almost rude.

'So, I'm here, sir, to offer my help. If you need it. I'm sure I could do just about anything you asked me to.'

Another slow nod, and then, to Hartley's relief, a smile.

Wilds took the pipe out of his mouth. 'You're very eager, aren't you?'

'I've been accused of that in the past.'

'Nothing wrong with it. Makes a change. A lot of men in here don't want to escape.'

Hartley frowned. 'Really, sir?'

'Oh, yes. Some have already made quite a few attempts, and are reconciled to never managing it. They're happy to help with the ancillary stuff – forging, tailoring, et cetera, et cetera . . .'

Hartley noticed how precisely he articulated 'et cetera'.

'Others,' Wilds continued, 'have decided that they've had enough of fighting, and although they might have escaped from other camps in the past, they've no wish to risk their necks doing so again. And then, of course, there are those who find themselves physically unsuited to the dangerous and gymnastic process of getting out of a place like this. Running around on high roofs and wriggling through tunnels isn't everyone's cup of tea.'

'Yes, sir. I can see this place is no picnic.'

'There is another group, of course – those who find incarceration has a certain deleterious impact on their psyche.'

The man must have been an academic in his former life.

'Such men,' said Wilds, 'become withdrawn, introspective. For them, the pain of being away from their families is too much. Perhaps it's just claustrophobia and routine that has got to them. Or maybe they were cracking up anyway. Who knows? Such men are best left alone.'

Hartley thought of Royce. 'Do you think it's best to leave them alone, sir? What about talking to them?'

'No. The French try talking, but I don't think it's to our taste, do you?'

Hartley disagreed, but he kept his mouth shut.

'So, an eager thing like you is most welcome.'

Hartley did his best not to sigh too loudly with relief.

'At the moment,' said Wilds, 'we've got something big happening. You'll understand why I won't tell you, although I'm sure you'll find out via the grapevine sooner or later. It'll be a good test for your sniffing skills. Anyway, in the meantime, if you come up with anything, let me know and we'll discuss it.'

'Er, yes, sir.'

'What's the matter?'

'Nothing, sir.'

'You didn't expect me to give you a ticket, did you? A scrap of paper, saying, "This allows the bearer one escape"?'

'No, sir, of course not!'

In truth, Hartley had been expecting something, but didn't want to show it. So far everything had seemed far too comfortable, as if it really was school; where activities were served up for you. If he wanted to escape, he'd have to come up with his own ideas, like everyone else.

'Well, thanks for seeing me, Hartley. I hope you settle in well.'

Hartley saluted. 'Thank you, sir.'

Wilds nodded and put his pipe back into his mouth. Hartley wondered if he ever had any tobacco to put in it.

*

The sickbay was on the other side of the courtyard
from the British quarters. As he walked across,
Hartley tried to adopt the nonchalant hands-in-pockets
gait of the 'old-timers', but he knew he'd be spotted as
a fraud. His face would be too open, too enquiring,
too alert. Some old-timers were watching him now,
sitting in the small patch of sun that settled near the
chapel door. Presumably the only sun that ever
reached into here, Hartley thought. No wonder they
were all so pale.

He walked down some shallow steps into the
sickbay, where he was met by a French army captain.

'Bonjour,' said the captain.

'Bonjour,' said Hartley.

'Qui est vennez a voir?'

'Pardon?'

The Frenchman looked impatient, resigned. No
doubt Hartley was not the first non-French speaking
Englishman who had crossed his path.

'Whom would you like to see?'

'Captain Royce. I'm a friend of his.'

The Frenchman gave a shrug. 'You do not need to
be a friend of someone to come in here.'

Cheeky sod, thought Hartley.

'Is he here, then?'

'Of course. Come in.'

Hartley stepped past the Frenchman and into the

sickbay. It was dark and the ceiling was low. Some light penetrated through the small windows, but not enough to make a man feel better. There were at least twelve beds, and Royce lay half-way down on the right. Hartley made his way towards him, acknowledging the inquisitive glances of the other patients.

'Hello there. How are you feeling?'

Royce looked at him blankly. 'I don't know.'

'You don't know?'

'I don't know. I don't feel anything. I don't feel good. I don't feel bad.'

Hartley looked around for the Frenchman. 'Has he been given something?'

'Of course not!' was the indignant reply. 'We have nothing to give.'

'I wish I could have something,' said Royce. 'I just want to get out of this place. Something to knock me out would be good.'

'We all want to get out of this place, Royce.'

'Not like me you don't,' said Royce, and turned over.

Hartley thought of Wilds's words. Maybe it was better just to leave Royce, rather than try to talk to him. Maybe he really had cracked. 'All right, Royce. I'll go now. I'll come and see you later, if you like.'

'As you wish.'

Hartley studied Royce's back. He wanted to feel

angry with him, but he just felt pity. The man was ill in some way, although he had no idea what it might be. Perhaps it didn't have a name. Whatever it was, it couldn't be treated here.

'See you later,' said Hartley.

Royce grunted.

As Hartley left, the French doctor fell in behind him. 'What?' asked Hartley, irritated.

The Frenchman's face was grim. 'Your friend needs a different sort of hospital from this,' he said quietly.

'I agree. What do you think is wrong with him?'

'I do not know. I am no psychiatrist, but he obviously has some sort of condition. I do not think he has dysentery any more. In fact, I think he is physically well. Who knows? If he has truly gone mad, he can go home.'

'Go home?'

'Back to England. They send the mental cases home.'

Lost in thought, Hartley walked slowly up to the courtyard. He ignored the looks of the sun-worshippers by the chapel and ambled to the right. For the first time since his arrival, the reality of his incarceration struck him. It was turning into a pleasant day, and normally he would have gone for a walk, but he couldn't. He looked at the entrance gate, which stood resolutely closed. That, and a few yards of cobbles, was all that separated him from freedom. He fancied the idea of walking through it one day when the gate was open, in his British uniform, just sauntering past the guards. He wondered how far he would get. Perhaps they would be so shocked at his brazenness that they would let him go. Hartley smiled to himself. How many other men had had the same thought? Probably all of them.

He thought of Royce, lying there losing his mind. What if the Frenchman had told the truth? It would be easy enough to pretend you were mad to get home, wouldn't it? Royce might even be doing just that. He dismissed the thought. Royce had been unhinged since he had met him on the bridge in Greece, genuinely cracked. Thank God, thought Hartley, that Royce wasn't his responsibility any more. Even so, he didn't feel comfortable just abandoning the man to the ministrations of the French doctor. He would keep an eye on him, check him a couple of times a day.

Hartley spent the rest of the morning exploring the castle. In the theatre he was accosted by Captain Edginton. He sported a purple cravat under his tunic, which Hartley thought made him look like a pansy.

'Aha!' said Edginton, as he walked in. 'Are you one of the new boys?'

'I am,' said Hartley, and introduced himself.

Edginton got straight down to business. 'Now, the colonel tells me you're a dab hand with a needle and thread. Is that right?'

'Well, I wouldn't say a dab hand, but I do know a little—'

'Splendid!' Edginton interrupted. 'Come here.' He led Hartley to a tea chest that stood next to the stage. 'In here,' he was fumbling through the contents, 'we've got all our costumes. What I'm looking for is some . . . Ah, here it is.' He produced a a large sheet of off-white cotton. 'The Germans have given us this. It's a bit knackered, but it'll do. We need it made into a couple of tutus, if you can.'

'Er, I'm not sure—'

'And, if there's enough material, two bras. They shouldn't be too difficult, just a couple of circles and bits of cotton to hold them in place.'

Hartley heard laughter coming from the stage. A lieutenant, who had hitherto been painting a Norman church and some trees on a vast sheet of wood, was walking towards him. 'Is this our dressmaker, Humph?' he asked.

'It is indeed,' said Edginton.

'Well, you'd better make them flattering. Good God, Hartley! What the hell are you doing here?'

Robert Beauchamp had been in the house next to Hartley's at school. 'Hello, Bob. I could ask the same of you.'

'Oh, that's easy. I was captured after tunnelling out of Laufen.'

'How long have you been here?'

'Too long. Next month it'll be a year and a half.'

'Have you tried—'

'Oh, yes, many times. In fact, some of us are having a crack pretty soon. Did Wilds tell you about it?'

'No, he said it was hush-hush.'

'Well, fair enough. But let's just say we've been doing some digging in the canteen.' He flashed Hartley a wink.

'When are you going?' Hartley asked.

'Any day now. Just waiting for the right weather. Edginton here is very keen for me to finish his scenery before I go.'

'That's not true,' said Edginton. 'Besides, you'll only be gone a day or two so you can finish it when you get back.'

Beauchamp took the comment in good humour, and flicked wet paint from his brush over Edginton's front.

'My cravat!'

Now Beauchamp aimed directly at it, and succeeded in splattering it with drops of leaf-green paint.

'A vast improvement,' said Hartley.

'You arse!' said Edginton, as he inspected the damage. 'This means a lot to me. My girlfriend gave it me before I left.'

'Aaaah,' said Beauchamp. 'Anyway, I didn't know you had a girlfriend. Always thought you were . . . you know . . .'

Edginton grabbed Beauchamp in a headlock and aimed punches at his stomach.

'Before I let you carry on,' said Hartley, 'do you have needle and thread?'

'In the chest,' Edginton grunted, as he wrestled with Beauchamp.

Hartley searched and found them. 'Can I interrupt you two?'

'Fire away,' said Beauchamp, who was now getting the better of Edginton.

'Why don't you use all this stuff for escaping?' Hartley asked.

The fighters paused.

'Oh, that's easy,' said Beauchamp. 'We're not allowed to. The Germans let us have it on parole.'

'How very decent of you,' said Hartley.

'Well, we've got to play by the rules, old boy.' And Beauchamp kneed Edginton in the groin.

'So, your first night in Colditz,' said Huntington.

'I forgot to pack my pyjamas,' said Hartley.

'I bet you remembered your teddy, though.'

'Damn! Left him in Greece.'

Hartley lay down fully dressed on his bed. It would

be wrong to say that he liked it here, he thought, but he had missed the camaraderie of young men like himself, from similar backgrounds. The castle was cramped and austere, but they had done much to make it homely and almost comfortable. The atmosphere was friendly, and even the Germans, despite this morning's fracas with Rensburg, seemed no less human than the average schoolmaster. It was clear that they were only doing their job, and they didn't appear to be fanatical Nazis. The thing Hartley pined for was food – and female company. As he was yet to receive a Red Cross parcel, he would have to rely on the others' generosity for the time being. Their supper had been meagre – some watery soup, as the colonel had warned, a slice of bread, and a morsel of corned beef that smelt dangerously off but was more or less edible. Hartley's stomach rumbled, and although he felt that he should be thinking about something other than food he couldn't help but be distracted by the pangs.

'Do you want to borrow a book?' asked Bettridge, from another corner of the room.

'Yes, please,' said Hartley. 'What have you got?'

'Let me see,' said Bettridge. 'Thackeray. Dickens. Dickens. Dickens. Wodehouse. Dickens. Another Thackeray. And *Learn Accountancy*.'

'*Learn Accountancy*?'

'That's right, I'm studying to become an

accountant,' said Bettridge. 'When we're out of here, that's what I'm going to do.'

'But who teaches you?'

'The book does. A couple of others and I are doing a correspondence course. We'll be sent our exams from London some time over the summer.'

'He is joking, isn't he?' Hartley asked Huntington.

'Oh, no. Quite a lot of them are studying, one way or another. Some chap's even working towards the bar. Maybe you should take up something. I'm brushing up my French with a major called Lamentier.'

'But, forgive me for asking, what about *escaping*?'

The room fell silent. Hartley knew that his question had been gauche, but he'd had to ask it.

'Well,' said Huntington, eventually, 'we can't try to escape at every minute of the day and you've got to keep your brain occupied.'

'I see,' said Hartley. Was the room full of shirkers? He hoped not.

'So, which book would you like?' asked Bettridge.

'What Dickens have you got?'

'*Copperfield. Two Cities. Bleak House.*'

'*Bleak House*, then.'

Hartley was woken at two o'clock in the morning.

'Hartley!' a voice whispered in his ear. 'Wake up!'

It was Huntington, and Hartley could tell that something was wrong. 'What is it?'

'Get up and come with me.'

Hartley threw off his blanket and followed Huntington out of the room, across the corridor and into another room. At least seven or eight officers were standing at the window, looking down into the courtyard.

'Here he is,' said Huntington.

'Hartley, come to the window.'

Hartley rushed forward and narrowly avoided tripping over a chair.

'Look out here.' Someone pushed his face against the bars.

Hartley wondered if this was some new boys' initiation ceremony.

'Down there!'

Hartley looked sixty feet below into the courtyard. It was floodlit and he could see a group of Germans. They were clearly agitated, making a lot of noise. They were pointing at someone on the ground, wearing a British uniform.

'Is that your friend Royce?'

Hartley squinted. 'It might be. I can't see his face. Why? What's happened?'

'It looks like he's fallen off a roof,' said the man next to him.

'Off a *roof*? How the hell did he get there?'

'We've no idea. Look! The Germans are moving. Is it him?'

Hartley could see the man's face now, and even from that height, he knew it was Royce. He was staring blankly as he had this morning after his seizure. 'Oh, my God,' he said quietly. 'He's . . .'

'Dead?'

Hartley wanted to run down to the courtyard, but Huntington stopped him. 'Steady,' he said. 'They'll shoot you if you go out there.'

'But I must help him!'

'Stay here.'

Hartley watched as Royce was lifted on to a stretcher. His limbs flopped uselessly, and his face was still. There were white faces now at every window overlooking the courtyard – an audience of ghosts haunting the scene. What, in God's name, had happened to him? From his position, he had dropped from the gutter that ran up to the right of the bell tower. It would be madness to climb that. Suicidal.

Suicide. That had to be it. Somehow he had got out of the sickbay, climbed up inside the bell tower and jumped out of a window. The poor bugger. He'd been right when he'd said he would never leave the castle. Well, he would, but as a dead man.

'I think he's killed himself,' said Hartley.

'Killed himself?' someone echoed.

'Yes,' said Hartley. 'I haven't known him long, but he seems a little unhinged.'

'Enough to do this?' Huntington asked.

'Perhaps,' said Hartley.

The Germans lifted Royce and hurried out of the courtyard. At last, thought Hartley, Royce was free.

Chapter Four

NOBODY SLEPT WELL that night, least of all Hartley. They discussed how Royce had got out of the sickbay, as it was locked every night. It was a shame, said Biddulph, that such a seemingly good escaper had died, a real waste. Hartley thought the comment in poor taste. He could only think of Royce's dead stare. It chilled him. He had to be dead. Hartley felt as if Royce had been staring at him accusingly: 'Why didn't you do more to help me?' his eyes had asked.

Why hadn't he? If he had known Royce was seriously unwell, he would have insisted that he receive some psychiatric treatment. But he hadn't. He had thought Royce was in a funk. And even if he had demanded that the Germans treat him, would they have done so? Probably not. Pretending to be mad was presumably one of the oldest tricks in the book, and German doctors would able to sniff out a genuine case from a phoney one.

Anyway, thought Hartley, he wasn't my

responsibility. Fate might have thrown them together, but that didn't mean Hartley had had to look after him. The man was not his child or his brother, simply a fellow officer with a screw loose. He had been offensive, surly and possibly a coward too. He should have left him on the bridge in Greece.

Hartley turned over. No. He'd been right to take him. Like it or not, he had a duty to Royce. The man had needed help, and Hartley hadn't given him enough. He was his responsibility: Royce was a fellow officer and countryman. Liking or disliking a man had nothing to do with it. He might not like someone in this room, when he'd got to know them, but did that mean he wouldn't help him if his life was in peril? Certainly not. He had failed Royce. His inattention had all but killed the man. Perhaps he wouldn't be thinking like that in the morning, but now, in this room full of silent men, he felt guilty.

The mood at the *Appel* the next morning was subdued. It was a far cry from that of the previous morning. The tomfoolery, the sense of being back at school, was gone. Rensburg and his men were allowed to carry out the count efficiently and quietly, and within forty-five minutes they had all dispersed.

As he walked back to his room, Hartley found himself overcome by a sense of emptiness. There was nothing to do. He wasn't involved in any escapes. He didn't rate his chances of discovering a new way out – what could so many hundreds of men have overlooked during the past year and a half? Some of the Poles had been here longer than that, and they were the most inventive and desperate of them all. He faced boredom, unending cramped boredom. Perhaps he would read *Bleak House*, not that he found it particularly engaging.

'How are those tutus coming on?'

Hartley turned to find Edginton's smiling face behind him.

'I haven't started,' said Hartley, trying to hide his annoyance.

'Well, you'd better get on with it pronto, old chap, because we need them in a week.'

He'd had enough of this. He turned on his heel and walked into his room. He opened his cupboard, which was empty but for the sheet, the needle and thread, and pulled them out. He walked back to Edginton, who was standing in the doorway. 'Here. Do them your bloody self,' he said, and thrust them at Edginton, who was obliged to take them. 'I've got better things to do than make skirts all sodding day.'

'No need for that,' said Edginton.

Hartley's hands were clenching into fists. Calm down, he thought. Just lie down and forget it.

'You'll make a reputation for yourself if you behave like that,' said Edginton.

Hartley glowered at him. The man was insufferable. 'I'm not sure I care. Now, clear off!'

Edginton remained where he was. Hartley decided to ignore him. He lay down and picked up *Bleak House*. He tried to concentrate on the text, but he was too aware of Edginton staring at him. After he had reread the same paragraph four times, Edginton said, 'Thanks for nothing,' and left. Sod him, thought Hartley. He imagined a what-did-you-do-in-the-war-Daddy conversation with a putative son. If all he had to tell him was that he had been a dressmaker in an obscure German castle . . . well, it was hardly stirring stuff. He had to do something. He couldn't just lie here. And in a way, he owed it to Royce.

'You coming out to the park?'

Hartley looked up from his book. 'The park?'

'That's right,' said Huntington, who was jogging on the spot. 'Jerry lets us get a bit of exercise from time to time.'

'But I thought—'

'I know. Rensburg thinks it's better for us to let off steam by kicking a football around than to spend all our time cooped up in the *Schloss* trying to escape.'

'Well, of course I'm game,' said Hartley. 'When do we go?'

Huntington looked at his wrist. 'Force of habit – no watch. Taken by some bastard Jerry when I was captured in Belgium. About five minutes, I should think.'

Hartley stood up. 'Where is it?'

'You can see it from here.' Huntington pointed out of the window. 'Look through the trees and you can just about see a wired-off enclosure.'

Hartley followed the line of his finger and, sure enough, spotted a large cage about half the size of a football pitch. 'Doesn't Jerry think we might be able to escape from there?'

'Oh, yes. That's why the whole place is swarming with guards whenever we're in it. Even so, one of the French escaped from it a few weeks ago.'

'How?'

'Well, not the park exactly. He hid under that big house to the right when we were on the way down to it. He made it to Switzerland.'

'This was Dubois?'

'So you've already heard?'

'The colonel told me.'

'The Jerries suspect he got out from somewhere around there, so there's no chance to do anything now.'

Even though he had only been inside it for just over twenty-four hours, Hartley found it a relief to get out of the castle. It already represented to him a place of death, a place that sent people mad. And he missed Royce, even his complaining.

The route to the park took them through the courtyard of the Kommandantur. Hartley estimated that at least a hundred men had chosen to get some exercise that morning, and they were escorted by at least twenty-five guards so there was no chance of making a quick dash for it. Besides, thought Hartley, where would he go? He didn't have the faintest idea where the nearest station other than Colditz was, and he lacked documentation, clothing and money.

They passed through the Kommandantur on to a path that ran down to the park. If only Royce could have come to the park. It would have given him a sense of freedom, perhaps enough to keep him alive.

'That's it,' said Huntington, nudging Hartley and jerking a thumb in the direction of a large house. 'Dubois hid there. He waited for the guards to get round the bend, and *voilà*. He ducked into the house's basement. The next we heard was a few weeks later when the French got a postcard from Switzerland. They haven't stopped going on about it since.'

'There's quite a lot of competition between us and the French, then?'

'You bet! Although for the French, escaping seems to be an individual thing. For us it's a team effort.'

They walked down the path as it ran next to the house. Hartley looked for the entrance to Dubois's basement, but they were walking too quickly for him to identify it. They turned left and went into the enclosure, each man counted by two guards.

'Fancy some football?' said Huntington. 'I think a game of six-a-side versus the Dutch is on the cards.'

'Count me in,' said Hartley, 'although I should warn you, I'm really extremely good at football.'

Huntington laughed. 'I always thought you were crap. What did you make at school?'

'Only the house side.'

'Pathetic. Did you represent us at anything?'

'I was in the third eight.'

'*Golly.*'

Although Hartley's boast had been tongue-in-cheek, he acquitted himself better than he had expected, scoring one of the four English goals to the Dutch five. The exercise did him some good, and for the first time in weeks he forgot about the war. The Dutch were polite and pleasant, and he had particularly warmed to Captain Hans Mouwen, a slim, wiry man in his late twenties who spoke English so well he could have passed for a native.

'It was a good game,' said Mouwen, shaking Hartley's hand.

'We should have beaten you,' said Hartley. 'You were just lucky.'

'Nonsense! We were the far superior team.'

'I'm sure a rematch will prove you wrong.'

Mouwen laughed. 'We can bet on it if you like.'

'You're on,' said Hartley.

'What would you like to bet?'

'I don't have anything, but as I won't lose, you can bet what you like.'

Mouwen laughed again. 'Such confidence! All right. I bet you a jar of Red Cross jam.'

Hartley held out his hand, and Mouwen shook it.

'I'm looking forward to that jam already,' said Hartley.

'So am I, Captain.'

The two men walked out of the park together, exchanging life histories. Mouwen had been captured when the Germans invaded Holland in April 1940, and had marked his first year in the castle by getting caught as he tried to walk out of the castle disguised as a workman. 'That earned me two weeks in solitary,' he recalled.

'Sounds horrid,' said Hartley.

'It wasn't. I had peace and quiet, room to think and a good supply of books and cigarettes. I was really quite happy. I was glad to get out, but I had a chance to reflect.'

'And what did you conclude?'

'That I should try to escape again.'

'Good for you.' Hartley gazed up at the castle as they walked up the slope away from the park. 'So, those are your quarters, are they, next to ours?'

'That's right,' said Mouwen. 'And below us are the Poles. I'd say you get a better view than us. You can just about see the river from where you are.'

'Really?'

'Well, you'd have to strain your head as far as you can out of the window.'

The castle loomed over them. It really was an ugly thing, he thought, a jumble of vast, clumsy buildings plonked down next to each other. Its present purpose seemed fitting somehow, although Huntington had told him it had once been a lunatic asylum, for which it seemed totally unsuited. It had driven Royce to his death, and God knew how many others. Then Hartley's eye was drawn to an architectural feature that surprised him.

'What's that?' he said, pointing up to the Dutch quarters.

'What's what?' asked Mouwen.

'That,' said Hartley, indicating a long, thin built-out structure, attached to the outside wall of the Dutch quarters. It was about four feet wide and ran from the top floor to the ground.

'I'd not noticed it before,' said Mouwen. 'It looks like . . . Well, I don't know what it looks like because I'm not an expert on castles.'

'It looks like a shaft. I wonder what it was for?'

Mouwen was looking intently at the structure. 'I'm trying to work out where it is,' he said.

Mouwen counted the windows to either side of it as they walked.

'Did you get it?' asked Hartley.

'I think so,' said Mouwen. 'Who knows what it might be?' His face showed the trace of a smile. 'I think you may have spotted something quite exciting. Will you join me in the Dutch quarters for a little exploration?'

'Why not?' said Hartley.

The Dutch quarters were immaculate, as Hartley had thought they would be. Although he would have been the first to dismiss stereotypical national character-istics as a myth, he was beginning to find in Colditz that they existed.

He followed Mouwen along a dark corridor on the top floor. The ceilings were a little lower up here, the layout more warren-like and suitable for clandestine activities. Mouwen greeted each of his fellows with a broad grin, and introduced Hartley to one or two.

'OK,' said Mouwen. 'This is where our quarters end and yours begin. I estimate that the shaft is seven windows back into our quarters.'

The two men walked back slowly, sticking their heads into each room and counting the windows. Their presence caused a few bewildered Dutch faces to look up from reading or sketching. Window seven was in a major's room. 'What the hell are you doing?' he shouted.

'Sorry sir,' said Mouwen, and saluted smartly.

'So, it's the next room,' said Hartley.

'And do you want to know what it is?'

'Tell me.'

'The latrines.'

Hartley rolled his eyes.

Mouwen opened the door and they found a Dutch naval officer standing at a urinal.

'Morning, Hans,' said the officer.

'This is my new friend Hugh Hartley,' Mouwen told him. 'Hugh, this is Captain Chris Gordijn.'

'Hello there,' said Gordijn.

For a moment, the three men stood in silence while Gordijn buttoned his flies.

'Have you come in here for anything in particular,' asked Gordijn, 'or just to watch me?'

'We're looking for something.'

'What is it?' asked Gordijn.

Mouwen looked at Hartley, who shrugged.

'A shaft.'

'Where?'

'Just the other side of where you're, um, standing. Captain Hartley spotted a shaft that runs down the wall outside and I want to see if we can get to it.'

Gordijn grinned. 'Good luck to you. It'll be a dirty business trying to get through there.'

With that, he walked out, whistling.

'Why didn't he want to look?' Hartley asked.

'Chris thinks I'm full of crazy schemes. He's an escaper too, but more cautious.'

'Shall we get to work?'

They looked at the urinal with a degree of reluctance. It was little more than a wall built from heavy bricks, covered with creosote to chest height, and a small gully that took away the effluent. Despite the Dutch reputation for hygiene, the room stank of stale urine.

'Are you sure it's going to be there?' Hartley asked.

Mouwen nodded. 'I'm afraid so.'

Hartley walked up to the urinal and knocked on the wall just above the creosote. It was solid. Mouwen joined him, and they went over every inch.

'This is a pleasant way to spend a morning,' said Hartley. 'First losing to the Dutch at football, then rummaging around in their lavatories.'

'You should be honoured,' said Mouwen.

Hartley stood back. 'I don't think we're going to be able to get through it.'

'I wouldn't be so sure,' said Mouwen. 'We just need the right tools.'

'Do you have a sledgehammer? A pickaxe?'

'No, but we have table knives and forks.'

'Knives and forks?'

'That's right.'

Hartley exhaled. It would take ages, but ages was what they had. 'If we get through, we'll need to cover our traces,' he said. 'How are we going to do that?'

'Ask the Germans for more creosote.'

'They're hardly likely to give it to us.'

'Why not?' asked Mouwen. 'All the urinals in the castle are covered with creosote. We'll say ours is wearing thin, and that we need more. The Germans know we're obsessed with hygiene.'

'You sound confident.'

'Maybe, maybe not. It's our only hope. Anyway, what do you think we'll find on the other side?'

'I'm not sure,' Hartley said slowly. 'A shaft that goes all the way to the bottom, possibly to the ground. We tunnel out from there, under the path and into the slope with all the trees before the park.'

'It would be hard to dig a tunnel at the bottom of the shaft,' Mouwen mused. 'Any German walking past would hear us.'

'Perhaps,' said Hartley. 'But shall we try to get there first?'

'Of course, but first, Hugh, you must get permission from Wilds. Then we can start an Anglo-Dutch co-operation.'

'A bit like Shell Oil,' said Hartley.

'But more successful.'

If Hartley had had a glass, he would have raised it. As it was, the two men shook hands.

*

'You want to do *what*?' For once Wilds was animated.

'I'd like to help the Dutch start a tunnel from the lavatory in their quarters.'

'Yes, I heard you the first time, Hartley.' Wilds jabbed the stem of his pipe towards Hartley's chest. 'And how is this great escape of yours to be effected, eh?'

Hartley told him.

'What if the Germans don't give you any creosote?' Wilds asked. 'What if you can't get through the brickwork? What if this mysterious shaft of yours is blocked? What if you hit solid rock when you get to the bottom? How will you cover the noise of your tunnelling under one of the most trodden paths in the whole castle? If you do emerge into the park, how will you get out of it?'

Hartley kept his hands crossed behind his back. Deference, he was sure, would yield dividends. 'Reasonable questions, Sir.'

'Extremely reasonable, Hartley.'

Wilds started to chew his pipe again, which suggested to Hartley that his mind was made up. Damn him.

'However, sir, I would like to try. It would take my mind off Royce.'

Wilds stared at him from under his furrowed brow. 'Nasty business,' he said quietly. 'We hadn't lost a man until now. The Germans won't tell us anything about how it happened, or about funeral arrangements et cetera.'

Once again, that careful enunciation.

'The colonel is doing his best to ensure that your friend gets a decent send-off.'

'I'm very grateful to him,' said Hartley.

Wilds continued to stare at him. 'I suppose if I don't let you forage around in the Dutch lavatories, you're going to go mad, too. Is that what you're going to tell me?'

Hartley allowed a slight smile. 'Pretty much so, sir.'

Wilds chewed his pipe for a while longer. 'All right,' he said eventually. 'You can give it a go. But don't blame me when all you achieve is your room-mates' annoyance because you stink of Dutch urine.'

'Thank you, sir.'

The news of Hartley's involvement with the Dutch spread quickly through the English contingent.

'I gather you'll be spending the next few weeks covered with the Cloggies' piss,' said Huntington, as they sat down to a lunch of potato and turnip soup.

'How did you hear that?'

'Bush telegraph. Not many secrets in this place.'

Biddulph looked up from his bowl. 'Bit keen of you, isn't it? You've only been here a few minutes and you're off. Give us a chance, old boy – we've only just got to know you.'

Hartley laughed. 'It'll be a while yet. Anyway, Biddulph, haven't you got something up your sleeve?'

'Maybe,' he said.

'Johnnie's involved in the big canteen break,' said Huntington. 'He's just being modest. Isn't that right, Johnnie? He's one of our master tunnellers.'

Hartley's attention was now fully engaged. 'Can I ask you a question, Biddulph?'

'By all means.'

'What do you use to get through solid brick walls?'

'A sledgehammer.'

Hartley's heart leapt. 'You've got a sledgehammer? May I—'

His question was interrupted by peals of laughter.

'You can borrow my pile-driver any time you like!' Biddulph cackled.

'Or my car,' said Bettridge.

'And my aeroplane,' said Huntington.

Hartley held up his hands. 'All right, all right.' He smiled.

The laughter soon died down. Hartley knew he'd been absurdly naive, and that the laughter was not so much cruel as justified. 'So, what do you use?' he asked.

'These.' Biddulph waved a table knife.

'Is that all?' Hartley asked.

'Unless you've got a sledgehammer.'

*

It astonished even Mouwen that the Germans agreed to provide them with a tub of creosote. The senior Dutch officer had insisted, and the request had gone all the way up to the commandant, Colonel Steiner. He had been immensely suspicious, but as neither he nor his staff could work out how creosote could possibly be used in an escape, they allowed the Dutch a large tub. When it arrived two days later, Mouwen summoned Hartley to start work.

When Hartley arrived after morning *Appel* with a small knife, Mouwen looked at him witheringly. 'Is that all you have?'

'What did you expect? A sledgehammer?'

'No, but maybe something a little bigger. Like this.' He produced a chisel from inside his tunic. 'It's very blunt, but it's certainly better than that knife. Which brick shall we start on?'

Hartley looked at the urinal. 'Well, if we're going to want to squeeze through a gap, it makes sense to have one at about knee height.'

Mouwen laughed. 'Right in the middle of the urinal?'

'Right in the middle of the urinal,' said Hartley.

The sound of the door opening behind them caused both men to look round. A Dutch officer walked in. 'Sorry,' said Hartley, 'do you want to use . . . ?'

'No, he doesn't,' said Mouwen. 'This is Lieutenant Broek, one of our lookouts. He'll stay in the corridor, keeping an eye on the two men positioned at either end. They will listen for any warnings coming from the lookouts positioned at the bottom of the stairs. If the Germans suddenly make a raid, I estimate we'll have just under a minute to cover up our work with clay and the creosote.'

'Actually I do need to use it,' said Broek.

'Be our guest,' said Mouwen.

'But make sure you go at that end,' said Hartley. 'We don't want to have to be working through your, ah . . .'

'Sure,' said Broek.

'Isn't there somewhere else your fellow countrymen can do their business?' asked Hartley.

'We can always use your latrines, but we don't want word to get round that this one's out of action.'

'Fair point,' said Hartley. 'I suppose we'll just have to chip while people piss.'

They worked solidly for the next two hours but progress was frustratingly slow. Mouwen found that his chisel was little better than Hartley's knife at hacking away the mortar.

'Do you think we'll ever get through it?' Hartley asked.

'Maybe a week or two,' Mouwen replied.

Hartley examined his knife. He doubted it would last that long – he had to find something stronger. In the meantime, he continued to scrape away, each movement dislodging pathetic flecks of dust. So far, they had achieved a few scratches in the creosote, no more. If the Goons came, a small piece of clay would conceal their handiwork. Hartley could see that patience was a quality he needed to acquire. 'This is hard work,' he said.

'It is,' said Mouwen. 'Aha! A big bit!' It was no larger or thicker than a little finger-nail.

'Well done,' said Hartley. 'We'll be through in about a year.'

Playfully Mouwen made to strike Hartley with the chisel and the door burst open. It was Broek, and the look on his face left them in no doubt of what he was going to say. 'Germans!'

Hartley grabbed a handful of clay and smoothed it over the small dent they had made in the wall. Meanwhile, Mouwen was poised to spread creosote over it.

'Hurry!' said Mouwen.

'I bloody am!'

Hartley had never been much good at pottery at school, and his lack of sculptural prowess was much in evidence as he applied the clay. He smoothed it as best he could with a small piece of wood.

'That's enough!' said Mouwen.

Broek burst back into the room. 'They're coming up the stairs!'

How the hell had they known? Hartley wondered. Was there a traitor among them? Microphones in the walls?

Mouwen applied the creosote to the clay. Ideally the clay should have dried, and instead of masking it, the creosote was combining with it to form a reddish-black mess. It looked hopelessly unconvincing.

'For Pete's sake!' hissed Hartley.

Mouwen frantically slapped on some more. Seconds later it had started to mask the clay.

'That'll do,' said Hartley, and shoved his knife into his pocket.

Mouwen put the creosote on to the floor, and stuffed the clay down the front of his tunic. The urinal looked passable, except for the chippings of mortar that had accumulated at the bottom. They could hear footsteps outside. German jackbooted footsteps.

'*Raus!*'

'It's a snap search,' said Mouwen.

'Yes, but how are we going to get rid of all that?' asked Hartley, pointing to the mess.

'There's only one way,' said Mouwen, undoing his flies.

Hartley didn't have time to smile. Just as he was following Mouwen's lead, the door was flung open.

'Out!'

The two men faced a pugnacious NCO.

'Out!' he shrieked again.

'Can't a chap finish the job in hand?' Hartley asked.

Despite his tone, Hartley was so nervous he couldn't urinate. For heaven's sake, pee, he told himself. Mouwen was evidently suffering from the same problem.

'Hurry!' shouted the guard.

At last, Hartley's body did as told it. Soon, the evidence had been sluiced down the drain right under the German's nose. Hartley did up his flies, and walked past the guard, who eyed him with contempt. He and Mouwen did their best not to look relieved.

'Out!'

They stepped into the corridor, which the Germans had already filled with the contents of the Dutch officer's rooms. Clothes, books, crockery – even records – were all being thrown about haphazardly, many items breaking as they landed.

'This happens a lot,' Mouwen said, which hardly reassured Hartley.

'But what brought it on?'

'It's random. It might be your turn tomorrow, or next month.'

'Do they usually find anything?'

'Sometimes,' said Mouwen.

'But they're breaking everything!'

'Yes. But that's fair enough . . . It's amazing what hiding-places we've come up with after all this time.'

'You think . . . ?' Hartley's eyes went towards the lavatory door.

'We should be OK,' said Mouwen. 'Although I shall have to spend the rest of my day helping to clear up. After *Appel* tomorrow, yes?'

'I wish I could say I was looking forward to it but, yes, of course.'

The next morning's *Appel* went smoothly, barring occasional Dutch truculence, which the Germans took in their stride. They knew that any self-respecting prisoner did not like having the contents of his room smashed up, and even less the discovery of some of his carefully hoarded contraband. Keys, maps, Reichsmarks – all were found in the search, but to Hartley's relief, the barely scraped urinal was safe.

However, the morning's calm was about to be shattered by two pieces of news.

'Gentlemen!' Rensburg shouted. 'I have good news and bad news.' He paused to ensure that he had the attention of his audience, which he did. Hartley half expected him to quiz them on which piece of news they wanted first.

'First, the good news. I am happy to report that Captain Royce is alive.'

A murmur went through the courtyard.

'I say, old boy, that's great news,' said Huntington to Hartley.

'Quiet!' Rensburg shouted. 'He is presently convalescing in a civilian hospital. I am informed that his injuries, although serious, are not life-threatening. It is hoped that he should return to the castle within a month.'

At first, Hartley did not know how to feel. For the past few days, he had grown accustomed to thinking that Royce was dead and, because he had been so preoccupied with the wall, had dispatched him to the past with almost indecent haste. Now that he had heard Royce was alive, he felt a rush of guilt. 'Yes,' he said weakly to Huntington, 'it is good news. Thank God he's alive. Quite something.'

Huntington didn't reply. He, like the rest of the men in the courtyard, was waiting for Rensburg's bad news.

'And now for the bad news,' Rensburg announced, gesturing towards the arch that led out of the courtyard. The ringing smack of footsteps could be heard walking up the cobbled path.

Soon enough, the diminutive figure of a scruffy-haired, unshaven man shuffled in between two tall guards. His wrists were chained together, and his head was bowed.

'Keith,' said Huntington. 'Oh, shit. The poor bugger.'

It was James Keith, the Scotsman, who had been bundled out of the castle in a mattress. His return silenced the captives. Rensburg had certainly presented it well, thought Hartley, the bastard. He had made an example of him.

The prisoners watched Keith led in the direction of the solitary-confinement cells. Just as he reached the top, he turned and held up his hands to flash V-signs. Much to Rensburg's visible fury, a cheer went up, and a chorus of 'Good on you!' and 'Don't stay long!'. Nevertheless, as soon as Keith had disappeared, the mood became sombre.

'Bloody Rensburg,' said Huntington. 'I could kill him.'

Hartley didn't reply. There was no point. Everyone shared the sense of failure. Keith had been on the run for days, had most likely almost reached Switzerland before he was recaptured. And if they were depressed, it must be much worse for Keith. Hartley was reminded of his scraping. He had such a long way to go still.

And worse was to come. Two nights later, the canteen tunnel was rumbled. Hartley heard about it from others, among them Huntington. 'They bribed a guard,' said Huntington, 'but evidently he didn't play ball.'

'What happened?' Hartley asked.

They were sitting at their table, eating their meagre

lunch. Today it was turnips and potatoes, enlivened by two slices of nearly identifiable meat shared between the four of them.

'Well, Wilds was popping his head out of the tunnel when suddenly this goon says, 'Hande hoch!' They had been waiting for them. Wilds was hauled out while the others tried to scamper back to the entrance in the canteen—'

'– where the Germans were also waiting.' Bettridge had taken up the narrative. 'The guard had obviously spilled the beans weeks ago, and Rensburg had just let them carry on. Devious bastard.'

'So now all twelve, including our good friend Captain Biddulph, are languishing in solitary,' said Huntington, 'where they will stay, no doubt, for the next month. You can't image what a setback this is.'

'What happened to the guard?'

'If they've got any sense, they'll send him elsewhere,' said Bettridge. 'He'll be strung up if we get our hands on him.'

For a minute the table was silent.

'By the way,' said Huntington, 'how's your little Dutch escapade?'

Hartley bristled at Huntington's condescending tone, but he let it go. He was still a new boy, which wouldn't change until more arrived. 'Slowly,' he said. 'Still, I hope to be able to report some progress by the end of the week.'

'And then you'll be off, will you?'

Once more, Huntington's tone rankled. 'There's no need to be quite so cynical,' said Hartley.

'Touchy.'

'Yes, a little. At least I'm doing something though.'

He looked pointedly at Huntington, whose smugness dissolved. 'What's that supposed to mean?'

'That you spend all your time pontificating rather than getting on with something,' said Hartley. He regretted speaking out, but it was too late.

'Rubbish! I do a lot.'

Hartley folded his arms. 'Example?'

'A lot you don't know about,' said Huntington.

'That doesn't sound convincing.'

'It's not my mission in life to convince you, Hartley. God, you're just like you were at school. Still sanctimonious and holier-than-thou. Always so keen.'

Hartley couldn't deny it. 'Maybe I am,' he said, 'but you're changing the subject. Why don't you tell me just one thing you're doing?'

Huntington raised his eyes skyward. 'Because, as I've already told you, it's not for you to know.'

'I see,' said Hartley. 'Top secret, eh? Hush-hush? I'm impressed. I don't see you in solitary. At least Bettridge is honest about what he does and doesn't do.'

'Are you accusing me of lying?'

'No,' said Hartley, although he was. 'I just think you're a great talker but not much else.'

'Sod you.'

Hartley smiled. 'Say what you like,' he said. 'You may have been here longer than me, but that doesn't give you some sort of seniority. We aren't at school, you know.'

'You could have fooled me,' said Bettridge. 'Can you two just shut up?'

Huntington and Hartley stared at each other. Bettridge had a point.

'Sorry,' said Hartley. 'Anyway, I'm going.'

'Back to Britain?' said Huntington, determined to save face in front of the others with a joke.

'Yes,' said Hartley. 'You can stay here.'

Mouwen's prediction had been nearly correct: it took a fortnight to break through the wall, by which time the two men had become a standing joke among the Dutch. Hartley and Mouwen had worked in the lavatory for so long that they could guess now who was coming towards the door.

As the hole grew larger, so did the problem of disguising it. Hartley's solution was to cut pieces of wood to fit it, then cover them with clay and creosote. The Dutch were invited not to urinate against it.

'Who's going first?' said Mouwen, on the morning they broke through.

'I will,' said Hartley, 'so long as you give me some matches.'

While Mouwen went to find some, Hartley peered through the hole in an attempt to discern what lay beyond. It was impossible to see much, as his body blocked the light. He prayed that whatever it was had an exit, or they would have scraped in vain.

'Here we are,' said Mouwen.

Hartley took from him a book of matches emblazoned with 'Kissy Club'.

'Are they yours?' asked Hartley, with a wry smile.

'Oh, yes.'

'What's the Kissy Club?'

'Somewhere you and I should visit after the war.'

'May I remind you that I am a happily married man, Hans?'

'There's nothing to stop you looking.'

Hartley weighed up the suggestion. 'Well, if we get out of this, I'll accept your invitation.'

'Where shall you take me in return?' asked Mouwen.

'Have you ever been to the Travellers Club?'

'Do they have girls there?'

Hartley paused. 'Er, not really.'

Mouwen laughed.

'They do a good roast beef, though,' said Hartley.

'Don't talk to me about roast beef!'

Hartley stuck his arms, head and shoulders through the narrow gap. Then, after a few abortive fumbles with the matches, he got one alight.

'What can you see?' asked Mouwen, impatiently.

Hartley was in an antechamber, about the size of a large lavatory cubicle. A draught blew out the match.

'It's a small room,' said Hartley, lighting another, 'and there's a draught, which suggests there's a hole somewhere.'

The second match revealed that indeed there was: at one end of the chamber, about two feet wide, in the floor. Hartley stifled a whoop of joy. Instead, he extinguished the match and struggled back to Mouwens.

'There's a hole,' he said, grinning. 'Big enough to get a man through.'

Mouwen brought his hands to his chest and clenched them. 'That is good news – very good news. The Kissy Club beckons.'

Hartley laughed. 'Do you have a stone or something I can chuck down to find out how far it goes?'

The two men looked around the room. The floor was immaculate. Hartley cursed Dutch cleanliness.

'How about this?' said Mouwen, reaching into his pocket. 'It's my lucky stone. It's got a hole through it.'

'You won't want to lose it.'

'I'm not going to. I'll get it back when we reach the bottom.'

Hartley took the stone, slid through the gap and threw it into the hole. He strained his ears, but heard nothing until eventually a clack echoed in the shaft.

The stone had hit the ground dozens of feet below.

'I heard it,' said Mouwen.

Hartley crawled out. 'We're in business,' he said.

'What do you think the shaft was used for?' Mouwen asked.

'It's a lavatory,' said Hartley. 'I've seen one in a castle in Scotland. They built these rooms with holes overhanging the castle's walls. The gardener would collect the waste for use on the flowerbeds.'

'Then let's hope the gardener here did his job properly,' said Mouwen.

It took another week to make a rope-ladder and in this Mouwen and Hartley were assisted by a couple of other Dutch officers. They acquired the materials – sheets, blankets, broom handles and other assorted pieces of wood – through a mixture of appeals to the war effort and empty promises of chocolate and cigarettes.

'It had better hold,' said Hartley, as he and Mouwen attached the ladder to a washstand opposite the urinal.

'Of course it will.'

Hartley had won the toss to go down first, but now he could not see it as a victory. He was plagued with images of falling seventy feet to his death. He tugged at the ladder, which seemed satisfactorily strong.

'Is the torch working?' asked Mouwen.

Hartley switched it on. 'Looks good to me.'

The torch was on loan from a Frenchman called Jean-Marc Sauboua, who had swiped it from a visiting electrician. Sauboua was renowned as the best thief in the castle, so good, in fact, that many wondered what his job had been before he joined the army. He swore he had been a winemaker in Bordeaux, but nobody quite believed him. Hartley stuffed the torch into his trouser pocket and prayed it wouldn't fall out. Sauboua had said he would kill him if he lost or broke it, and Hartley believed him.

Hartley wriggled into the antechamber and took the rope-ladder, which Mouwen handed to him. 'Good luck, Hugh.'

'Thank you,' he replied. 'I'll bring back your stone.'

'Don't worry about it.'

After attaching it to a washstand, Hartley threw the coiled ladder down the hole, hoping he would hear the end hit the ground. They had made it longer than they had thought necessary, and their diligence paid off: the sound of the last rung striking the floor echoed up to him. Could it have been heard outside? Surely not – the walls were far too thick. Even so, Hartley knew he had to keep quiet.

He had an aversion to heights, and it was just as well that the shaft was dark: otherwise he knew he would have felt an overwhelming urge to climb back through the hole into the Dutch lavatory and return to his room.

171

He lay on his front on the floor and edged his feet into the hole, imagining his legs dangling over the invisible drop. Just get on with it, he thought. He took hold of the top rung and pushed himself into the hole where his feet connected with a rung.

'All right, Hugh?'

'Fine thanks.' He took a step down into the darkness, and found another rung. The ladder creaked alarmingly, but felt strong.

Hartley took another step down and swayed. The ladder groaned under his weight, which was not considerable but quite enough for this ramshackle object, composed of twigs and threads.

He descended gingerly, the swaying more pronounced now. Soon he was brushing against the walls of the shaft with each step. After thirty, he estimated that he was halfway down. Above, he could see the faintest chink of light from the hole, but it was no more than a smudge in the gloom. His breathing echoed in the shaft, more rapid than he had realised, and he did his best to control it.

When Hartley put his weight on the next rung, it splintered and snapped. He hung on tightly, foot thrashing for purchase, which it eventually found.

'Christ!'

It didn't matter, he told himself. It was just a bad rung, and he would remember it on the way back up. The rest of the going was easier, and a couple of minutes later, he reached the bottom. He turned on the torch, blinked and looked around.

The shaft measured no more than five feet by five. It was built from massive stones, but they did not concern him. He was more interested in the floor, which was solid rock. How the hell were they going to get through that? He shone the torch into the corners, trying desperately to find a patch of earth, but there was none. However, he spotted Mouwen's lucky stone and put it into his pocket.

He shone the torch at the wall that faced the park. Just a few inches of stone separated him from freedom, but it might as well have been a hundred miles. There was no way they could hack through the wall undetected, so tunnelling was the only option. But the floor was solid. It had been hard enough to get through the lavatory wall, so how could they get through this? And even if they could chip away at it, wouldn't they be heard by the guards patrolling outside?

Hartley had never felt more depressed.

'Why the long face? Escape not going well?'

Hartley ignored Huntington and lay down on his bed. He picked up *Bleak House* and turned to page forty-nine, which was as far as he'd got.

'What happened?' asked Huntington.

Hartley peered at Dickens's words. 'Why is it of any interest to you?' he asked.

Huntington looked flummoxed. 'You're right,' he said. 'It isn't.'

Hartley sighed and put the book down. The atmosphere between them had been rotten for days, and it hardly made life pleasant for those who had to share their room. The argument had come out of nowhere, fuelled by frustration and claustrophobia. It was the little things that got to you, thought Hartley. Huntington could have smelt like an old kipper, but he wouldn't have minded. It was his constant sarcasm that Hartley found objectionable.

'All right,' said Hartley. 'I apologise for flying off the handle. I suppose I'm too sensitive to criticism.'

Huntington didn't reply.

'Come on, Huntington,' said Bettridge, who was working on his accountancy textbooks, 'apologise to him now, and then we'll be able to live in some sort of peace.'

Huntington's shoulders sagged. 'All right, all right,' he said, his tone tinged with irritation. 'I'm sorry.' He walked over to Hartley and they shook hands.

Royce returned just after *Appel* the next morning. There was no ceremony, as there was with the return of a captured prisoner. He was just deposited in the courtyard as the prisoners were returning to their quarters.

'I say,' said Huntington, 'there's Royce.'

Royce was standing with a kitbag under his right arm, the left in a sling. Hartley ran towards him. 'Royce! How the devil are you?'

Royce smiled, which Hartley had thought he would never see. 'Not bad,' he replied. 'And you?'

'Keeping my pecker up. It's good to see you looking so well. I thought you'd killed yourself.'

'Well, that was kind of the intention.'

The words were delivered with a hint of ironic humour. The haunted look was gone from Royce's eyes, replaced instead with something approaching a twinkle.

'Whatever happened to you in hospital has certainly cheered you up,' Hartley observed.

The two men started to walk across the courtyard, feeling the gaze of their fellow prisoners on them.

'I saw sense,' said Royce. 'I realised I had a choice. Either I continued to crack up or I didn't.'

'And how do you feel about being back in here?'

Royce glanced round the courtyard and up at the walls. 'Oh, not so bad. God knows what came over me when I had that funny turn.'

'It was quite something. But we all want to know how you got out of the sickbay.'

Royce chuckled. 'I thought you'd be intrigued.'

'Well?'

'I pinched the key off the doctor. He left his tunic on the back of a chair when he was examining a patient. It was just a case of waiting for his back to be turned.'

'You sly dog!'

When they reached the room, Hartley gestured Royce towards the spare bed.

'Luxurious,' said Royce. 'I wish I was back in hospital.'

'I bet it was pretty comfortable. Were you well looked after?'

Royce nodded. 'Very much so. I couldn't have asked for better.'

'I'm impressed. I don't suppose we're giving sick Jerries the finest treatment back home.'

'Well, they've certainly done me a good turn. Apart from this,' he said, pointing to his broken arm, 'I'm pretty much fixed. My back's a bit sore, but otherwise they've made a whole new me.'

Hartley wanted to ask if the Germans had included a new brain, but decided not to chance it. 'So, what did you do?'

'When?'

'When you got out of the sickbay.'

Royce sat on his bed. 'I really can't remember. I'm pretty sure I tried climbing a gutter pipe, and I seem to remember falling – or, rather, jumping off – but other than that, not much. The next thing I recall is waking up in hospital. Which was where I met Rosa.'

'Rosa?'

Royce looked a little awkward. 'A nurse I've rather taken to.'

'What do you mean, "taken to"?'

'Well ... taken to. I'm not in love with her, though.'

'You do know it's, um, a pretty serious business to fraternise with the enemy?'

Royce waved it away. 'It's hardly that,' he said. 'I've only kissed her. Nothing else.'

'Not for lack of trying, I suppose.'

Royce indicated his broken arm. 'Not a lot I can do with this.'

Hartley pondered it briefly. Sex was at the forefront of most men's minds, and which of the single ones among them would say no to a kiss with a nurse, even if she was German? It wasn't the women they were fighting. In fact, kissing German women was a good way to get back at their men. 'Well, I don't suppose you'll see her again,' said Hartley.

'Aha! That's where you're wrong. I'll be in and out of that hospital for weeks – X-rays, the cast being taken off.'

'Good for you,' said Hartley. 'She appears to have done you a world of good.'

'She has. I can now face this place with a light heart.'

A brief silence ensued, which Royce broke. 'So, anyway, how are you? Been hatching any exciting escape plans?'

Chapter Five

MOUWEN AND HARTLEY stood at the bottom of the shaft, their expressions grim. The rope-ladder hung to one side. The top was secured inside the antechamber, and the hole in the wall had been sealed. They would be let out in two hours.

'Maybe,' said Mouwen, 'there is earth under the rock.'

Hartley could only admire his optimism. 'Well,' he replied, 'there's only one way to find out.' He held up an improvised chisel and mallet. The former was made from the sharpened handle of a table knife, while the blade was embedded in a piece of wood. The mallet was a real one from Sauboua's collection. He had lent it to Hartley in return for an exorbitant amount of chocolate.

Mouwen held up the chisel he had used to get through the wall. 'If we get out of here,' he said, 'this will be my most prized possession. Even if I become a very rich man, and my house is on fire, it will be the first thing I save.'

'And if we don't get out of here?'

'We will, Hugh.'

They bent down to examine the surface of the rock by the light of a small oil lamp. It smelt, but it was better than using Sauboua's torch, which required costly batteries that were singularly difficult to come by.

'We need to find some cracks,' said Hartley, 'where the rock'll be weaker.'

'How about that?' asked Mouwen, pointing to a long thin one.

'It looks like the obvious choice.'

Hartley placed the head of his chisel into the middle of the crack, and brought down the mallet hard. The noise reverberated up the shaft. The two men listened for any commotion outside. Nothing.

'That was bloody loud,' Mouwen whispered.

'What else can we do?'

'Try again.'

Hartley raised his mallet and brought it down. The sound seemed even louder. 'This is ridiculous,' he said.

'Just keep going. I'll start over here.'

'All right,' said Hartley. 'If we don't try, we'll never escape.'

Mouwen bashed away eagerly, working fast. Hartley brought down his mallet again, and soon both men were hammering as hard as they could.

After a few minutes, they paused.

'How much progress have we made?' Hartley asked.

Mouwen scanned the crack. They had made a few marks in the stone, but little more.

'Do you think this is possible?'

'If it takes a year, it'll be worth it,' Mouwen replied.

Hartley didn't fancy spending a year down there. If it really took a year, and they escaped only to be recaptured, he would probably go as mad as Royce had been. He raised his chisel and hit it with the mallet as hard as he could from sheer frustration. To his surprise, a piece of stone the size of his fist was dislodged. He hit it again, and the lump popped out.

'Well done!' Mouwen whispered. 'At this rate we'll be out of here in a week!'

After two hours, they had made far better progress than Hartley could have hoped for. They had cut about six inches deep into the crack, and had widened it by about three inches. To someone who hadn't seen it before they'd begun, it would have seemed unimpressive, but Mouwen and Hartley were much encouraged.

'We need some others to help us,' said Hartley.

'I agree. But shall we keep it an Anglo-Dutch affair?'

'Yes. Do you have anyone in mind?'

'Gordijn would be good.'

'All right. And Huntington. Do you know him?'

'He's tall, isn't he?'

'True, but he's flexible with it. He's like a beanpole.'

'A beanpole?'

'I can see you're not a gardener. I'll explain later. Come on, let's get out of here.'

Mouwen started to climb the rope-ladder. He went up quickly, and Hartley marvelled at his athleticism. Within a couple of minutes, he had reached the top and signalled his arrival with a couple of tugs on the ladder. Hartley extinguished the oil-lamp, hung it on a belt loop, then headed up after him. Two-thirds of the way to the top he was beginning to relax when he felt three jerks on the ladder. The warning signal. It meant that Goons were near, and activity had to cease. He looked up and, could just see Mouwen peering through the hole. 'Don't move!' he hissed.

Hartley froze. It was hardly a convenient place to stop, fifty feet above the ground on a dodgy rope-ladder.

Suddenly he could hear loud noises from above, mainly German shouts, coupled with bangs and crashes. It sounded like another search, but that was unlikely. The last one had happened so recently.

He wanted to climb up to the antechamber, but knew he couldn't risk bashing into the wall on the way. He tried to relax. They were perfectly safe in here. There was no way any Goon was going to find them. The urinal wall looked immaculate – Gordijn would have seen to that. All they had to do was to wait it out.

The noises were louder now, the sound of rooms being overturned coming from the wall right next to him. If he hadn't been feeling so vulnerable, he would have laughed at the thought of the Germans being so close yet unable to detect him. They'd be gone in a quarter of an hour, and then he and Mouwen could emerge from their dark world.

At first, Hartley ignored the creaking. He was used to the rope-ladder's noises, and this creak was no different from usual. Then, suddenly, he lurched down violently. The rung he was holding had become vertical and he kicked helplessly in the darkness for a support that wasn't there. One of the ropes had snapped. He felt his hand slipping down, and reached up with the other to grab the remaining rope.

'Help!' he whispered hoarsely, as loud as he dared, to Mouwen.

This was it, he knew. He was about to fall fifty feet to his death at the bottom of this shaft. The single rope would never hold. He wanted to yell but he knew he couldn't. Raw panic surged through him, and he froze. Don't give in to it, he told himself. You're still alive – you can get out of this. But how?

'I'll pull you up,' said Mouwen. 'Just hold on.'

He could hear the fear in the other man's voice.

'Gently, for Christ's sake,' Hartley blurted out.

He knew his chances were poor. The 'rope', fashioned from its combination of old bed-linen and other scraps, was hardly the stuff for mountaineering. He was going to die – and for what? He thought of Sarah, of how awful this would be for her. The telegram would arrive at the flat, and what she had always feared would be a reality, spelt out in capital letters on cheap paper.

Hartley felt a tug on the rope, which creaked terrifyingly. All he could do was to hold on, trusting God and Mouwen.

In the darkness, it was difficult to work out if he was rising, but he was pretty sure he was. He could hear Mouwen straining – and, through the wall, the noise of the search, the shouts, thuds and crashes.

'I've got you Hugh,' Mouwen was saying, 'Don't worry, I've got you.'

He just wanted to survive. He couldn't care less about the tunnel or the shaft. The rope was holding, but he knew it would break. Please, God, let it hold out just long enough for him to get to the top. He looked up – he was no more than ten feet from it.

Mouwen tugged again, this time so hard that Hartley swore the rope would break. But it held.

'Nearly there,' said Mouwen.

Another tug brought him within reach of the hole. 'Give me your hand.'

Hartley paused. Did he dare let go?

'Give me your hand, Hugh. I can reach you.'

'Are you sure you can hold me?'

'Yes! Come on, damnit!'

Hartley took a deep breath and stretched out his arm as far as he could. His hand grabbed at air.

'Here, Hugh!'

Hartley made out the movement of Mouwen's fingers. His hand brushed them, but he couldn't get a grip. He pulled himself up a fraction with his left arm, biceps straining, and grabbed Mouwen's wrist. He was going to live.

Mouwen hauled him through the hole, using the rope and his hand, and Hartley fell into the antechamber on his chest. He was too exhausted and too relieved to speak.

'Are you all right, Hugh?' Mouwen asked.

He nodded.

Mouwen let out a hysterical laugh. 'I think we need a new rope-ladder,' he said.

It took Hartley the best part of twenty-four hours to recover from his ordeal. It occurred to him that he should give up the whole mad scheme, do a Bettridge – learn something practical for after the war. He had nearly killed himself, and for what? Not much. What difference was one man going to make to the war effort? All that stuff about trying to escape to tie up German resources was nonsense. It wasn't as if they were diverting entire divisions from Greece and North Africa to chase after a few naughty *Englanders* in the Reich. All he would achieve would be to break his neck – or get shot.

However, by the following afternoon, Mouwen had strengthened Hartley's resolve. Mouwen told him that such things happened all the time in Colditz, then showed him the repaired rope-ladder.

'Look,' he said, pulling at various sections, 'it's stronger than if it were made of steel.'

Hartley touched it gingerly. 'You said that about the last one.'

'I know,' said Mouwen, 'but this one I'm sure about.'

'You'd better be,' said Hartley.

'So, you want to continue?'

Hartley paused. He couldn't let Mouwen down – or, indeed, himself. He had to keep going. Sarah would understand.

With the blessing of the recently released Wilds and the Dutch escape officer, the team working on the tunnel was increased to eight. With Hartley and Huntington, the English contingent supplied Ings-Chambers and Irby, which meant that, apart from *Appels*, work could continue round the clock. Progress was slow, but after three weeks of hacking and four feet of rock, the tunnellers struck their equivalent of gold: soft earth. Ings-Chambers discovered it: he emerged from the shaft bearing not only his trademark grin, but a handful of soil. Work could move on more rapidly now, and as there was only fifteen feet of tunnel to dig, which would take them under the path and out among the trees, Hartley and Mouwen estimated that it would take only two more weeks. The soil, said Mouwen, could easily be stored in the attic above the Dutch quarters.

One morning Hartley went to report to Wilds. As usual, he was the model of donnish inactivity, lying on his bed reading a book, still chewing his unlit pipe. Hartley noticed that he had gained a little weight in solitary – no doubt due to lack of exercise, rather than a superior diet.

'You look excited, Hartley,' he said.

'I am, sir,' Hartley replied.

'Oh, yes?'

'We've reached earth, sir.'

Wilds stopped chewing his pipe, which Hartley knew now signified that he was surprised. 'Have you, indeed?'

'Yes, sir. Captain Mouwen and I estimate that the tunnel will be ready in as little as two weeks.'

'Two weeks, eh?'

'Yes, sir.'

'Interesting.'

For Christ's sake, Hartley thought, why couldn't he

show a little enthusiasm? Maybe he was jealous. After all, his attempt had hardly been a great success, and it must gall him that this new boy might strike lucky at his first attempt. 'May I make a request, sir?'

'By all means.'

'I was wondering, sir, whether those who are intending to escape may be provided with some equipment. I was thinking clothes, sir, money and passes.'

More pipe-chewing, this time quite vigorous. Hartley didn't know if that was a good or bad sign. The latter, probably. Bastard.

'Of course,' Wilds replied.

Hartley didn't trust his ears.

'Well?' said Wilds.

'Sorry, sir. Thank you. I'm, um, very grateful.'

'One thing, though. We don't have an inexhaustible supply of passes. Or money. We lost a lot of kit when we were captured last month.'

'I understand, sir.'

'So we've only got enough for two of you. I assume that'll be you and Huntington.'

'That's right, sir.'

'We're in the process of making more, though. You'd better talk to Atkin-Berry about that, see how he's getting on.'

Atkin-Berry was the self-appointed chief British forger. An art teacher before the war, he was a master at producing convincing documents.

'Yes, sir.'

'Keep me in touch.'

'Of course, sir.'

Wilds resumed his reading. Hartley saluted him and turned to leave.

'One thing, Hartley.'

'Sir?'

'Your friend Royce.'

'Sir?'

'How is he?'

'He seems very well. Ever since he returned, he's had a new lease on life. The whole business of falling off the gutter made him see things properly.'

'I hear he's got some sort of nurse.'

'That's right – Rosa, at the hospital where he has his check-ups. He says he's quite taken with her.'

'Have you seen any pictures of her?'

'No, sir.'

'So you've just got his word that she exists?'

'I suppose so. Why do you ask, sir?'

Wilds removed the pipe from his mouth, a sign that he wanted to make himself absolutely clear.

'Well, I have to tell you, Hartley – and I know he's your friend – that some of us are . . . How do I put this? A little *unsure* about Royce.'

'Unsure, sir?'

'We think he may be a bad apple.'

'That's quite an accusation, sir.' Hartley felt the

colour drain from his cheeks. Royce? A traitor? Hartley recalled how he had felt when he first met him, but surely Royce had proved he had not been disloyal but going through a breakdown. As far as Hartley was concerned, his behaviour had resulted from something wilting in his brain.

'It *is* quite an accusation, Hartley.' Wilds was scrutinising him.

'Do you have any proof, sir, or is there anything to suggest why you might think that of Royce?'

'No proof, Hartley, just hints. *Indications*. You understand?'

'I do, sir. Any examples?'

Hartley was aware that he had sounded a little aggressive. He reminded himself to watch his tone: there was no point in making an enemy of Wilds.

'Example one. Ever since Royce has returned, there has been a marked increase in searches by the Germans that have borne fruit. What is more, they seem to know exactly where to look. Example two—'

'But, sir,' Hartley interrupted, 'there are any number of ways—'

'Let me finish!' Wilds had raised his voice for the first time in Hartley's memory. He had better shut up and listen, he thought.

'Example two,' enunciated Wilds, using the stem of his pipe to point to his forefinger, 'his so-called suicide attempt. His pilfering of the key sounds unlikely. That doctor has always been scrupulous in guarding the key to the sickbay. How do I know? Because we've tried to steal it on numerous occasions. Then, when he gets out of the sickbay, he manages to climb a gutter. Plausible, but unlikely. Why climb a gutter if you're trying to kill yourself? Why not jump out of a window? And the other problem is that if he *did* fall from the gutter, he wasn't killed. His injuries seem superficial for a man who fell from a great height on to hard ground.'

Wilds allowed Hartley to digest his words. What he had said made disturbing sense.

'Example three. He's been asking a lot of questions, a *lot* of questions. He seems to want to know who's doing what. At the very least he's being nosy, at the worst – well, as I say, he's a bad apple. I think all these trips to hospital are a way for the Germans to debrief him without arousing our suspicions. So they think.'

Hartley blew out a mouthful of air. 'This is quite something, sir.'

'Indeed it is.'

'May I ask what you're proposing to do?'

'We're going to question him,' said Wilds, 'and we want you to be there.'

Hartley swallowed. 'When, sir?'

'Tonight, Hartley, after the *Appel*. In the colonel's room. All right?'

'Yes, sir.'

191

Wilds returned to his book and clamped his yellow teeth round his pipe. Hartley's elation had been savagely dashed.

Hartley stood next to Royce at the *Appel*. He could tell that Royce sensed something was awry as he kept asking if everything was all right. Hartley wanted to tell him, but he knew he couldn't; if Royce was a traitor, he would flee to Rensburg.

'What do you fancy doing after this?' Royce asked.

'How about a game of rummy?' Hartley thought that if he suggested something, Royce might be less suspicious.

'All right,' said Royce. 'Play you for cigs?'

'Fine,' said Hartley, 'although you'd better have plenty to lose.'

Royce laughed. 'Always so cocksure, Hartley. Anyway, if I lose, I can always get some from Rosa.'

'Aha! So how is your *Fräulein* then? Any further . . . developments?'

'There has been some progress.' Royce smirked.

'I'm intrigued,' said Hartley. 'Tell me more.'

'Certainly not!' said Royce. 'This is between myself and her.'

Hartley couldn't tell whether Royce was being untruthful, insincere, or merely making light of the situation.

'So, has she given you a photograph yet?'

A brief flicker of something across Royce's face. Suspicion? Surprise? 'A photograph?'

'Yes, a snapshot. You know.'

Royce coughed. 'Well, we haven't quite got to *that* stage.'

'Sounds like you've already passed it.'

'This is preposterous!' Royce's reaction was both predictable and credible. 'I deny it all!'

The colonel had assembled what amounted to a court-martial, albeit an informal one, that included himself, Wilds and another major. Royce was made to stand in front of them, while Hartley sat to one side as the only 'witness'. Wilds, naturally, was chewing his pipe.

'Well, of course you do,' said Wilds, menacingly. Hartley felt antipathy towards him, but also respect and a little fear. 'It's only natural that you should deny treachery,' Wilds continued. 'After all, no man who is a traitor ever believes himself to be so. In his own mind he believes he is loyal to a cause that he has put above the good of his fellow countrymen. In your case, it would appear that you have decided to inform on our efforts. I am keen to explore the reason.'

Royce was clearly too flummoxed to say anything. He brought his one good arm up into the air, then dropped it.

'Is it for love, Captain Royce,' asked Wilds, 'of this – this supposed "Rosa" that you have decided to betray us?'

'What do you mean "supposed"?' barked Royce.

'Well, she seems very convenient, doesn't she? A nice excuse to see your friend Rensburg once in a while.'

'She's real, damnit!'

'All right,' said Wilds. 'Calm down. We're just *probing*, Royce, just having a rummage.'

That was disingenuous, thought Hartley.

'You know,' said Wilds, 'that fraternising with the enemy is a serious offence?'

Royce's shoulders dropped a little. Hartley could tell he felt on safe ground now. 'Well, I wasn't aware that it was against any laws, major.'

Wilds looked at the colonel, who shrugged his shoulders.

'I couldn't give a damn whether it's against any laws or not,' Kerr-Smiley replied. 'All I do know is that seeing a German woman is a security risk. After all, this Hun nurse could be primed to get information out of you.'

'That's nonsense, sir!'

'True love, eh?' said Wilds.

Royce seemed to be doing his best to keep cool. He took a deep breath. 'I wouldn't put it quite like that, *sir*.'

Hartley noted that Wilds didn't flinch at Royce's tone.

'You see, Royce, we've got a problem. Things have started to go wrong since you turned up. Escapes have been thwarted, equipment found by the Germans too easily.'

'That's unfair!' Royce protested. 'It's just circumstantial and you know it.'

'Circumstantial evidence is by no means inadmissible,' said Wilds.

'You're just looking for a scapegoat for all your – your failures.'

Royce was brave, perhaps foolish, to use that word, thought Hartley. Kerr-Smiley was bristling, but Wilds, true to form, remained calm.

'Well, I don't deny they were failures,' he said. 'This is a *Sonderlager*, after all. No one said it would be easy.'

'I don't see why I have to stand here and take this.'

'You will stay where you are!' the colonel shouted.

'Why the hell should I?'

That was unwise, thought Hartley. 'Royce,' he said quietly.

Royce turned to him, his face red with anger. 'What?'

'Just stay here,' said Hartley, soothingly. 'I don't think it'll help if you walk away.'

'But—'

195

'Please, Malcolm.'

Royce glowered at him. He turned back to his accusers. 'This is so unfair. You're accusing me of the most despicable crime, worse than murder, and expecting me to take it on the chin. How would any of you react if you were accused of treachery?'

The men didn't reply. Their expressions indicated that they believed the question to be facile and a little naive.

Wilds spoke first. 'You're doing a very good imitation of an innocent man, Royce. Angry. Hurt. Offensive. Indignant. Well done! No doubt you've been well trained by your handlers.'

'Oh, this is hopeless,' said Royce. 'Hopeless! There's nothing I can say to convince you of my innocence. You will simply twist everything I say to suggest that I'm guilty in some way. Well, all right, then, yes, I'm guilty. Send me under Traitor's Gate, or whatever it is, and string me up. There's no point in protesting, is there? I'm as bad as Lord Haw-Haw, aren't I?'

Hartley believed Royce was innocent. Tentatively he raised his hand.

'What is it, Hartley?' asked the colonel.

'I don't believe Royce is guilty, sir.'

'Oh? And why not?'

'Because despite how it looks, what's his motive? I've known him for little longer than any of you, and I just don't believe he has the makings of a traitor.

What would be the point? A German nurse? I doubt it! He may be a flirt, think himself a lady's man, but I hardly think he's so spineless that he'd sell us all down the river for a taste of German skirt, if you'll pardon the expression, sir. I know we're all desperate, but not that desperate.'

Hartley partially regretted his candour, but he felt that Royce deserved a few words in his defence. What they were accusing him of was monstrous.

'You're very trusting, Hartley,' said Wilds.

'Not especially. I just think there's an absence of proof. And there's not much you can do about it, either. Keeping an eye on him won't be any good because he's got to leave the camp for his check-ups. Getting him transferred won't work either, because his reputation will spread.'

The members of the 'court martial' looked at each other.

'He's got a point, hasn't he?' the colonel murmured. Wilds nodded.

'May I make a suggestion?' Hartley asked.

'I'm all ears,' said the colonel.

Hartley held up his hand to Royce, indicating that he should not interrupt. 'How about a period of quarantine?'

'Quarantine?' yelled Royce.

'Please, Malcolm,' said Hartley, 'this is the only way.'

'But then everybody will know I'm under—'

'I rather suspect they do already,' said Hartley. 'But this is the only way in which you'll be able to prove your innocence.'

Hartley looked at the colonel, not just because he was the senior figure but also because he was more likely than Wilds to be sympathetic to the idea. The colonel looked at Wilds, who in turn squinted at Hartley over his pipe.

'Tell me more,' said the colonel.

'Well, we put Royce into our own form of solitary confinement. For the most part, he stays in his room, and nobody is to talk to him about any escape plans. It should be explained to fellow officers that this action is only being taken as a precaution, and to remind them of that most basic principle of British justice that a man is innocent until proven guilty.'

'But in their eyes I'll be as good as guilty.'

'Not necessarily,' said Hartley. 'If escapes keep getting rumbled, kit gets discovered in searches, we'll know we're suffering from bad luck rather than treachery.'

'It won't let him completely off the hook,' said the colonel.

'Well, it's a start, isn't it? Come on, colonel, you could just as easily accuse me of being the traitor. After all, Royce and I arrived at the same time.' This was high-risk stuff, thought Hartley, but he had little choice if he wanted to see justice done. The tribunal did not stir, its members clearly considering what he had said. 'I mean,' said Hartley, 'it's not as though you were going to hang him.'

The room fell ominously silent. Royce wiped his face with his hand, as if he was trying to rub out the sight in front of him. Hartley wanted to do the same, but he kept his composure.

'That is the penalty for treason. You do know that, don't you, Hartley?' asked Wilds.

'Of course I do,' Hartley replied coldly, 'which is why Royce should be given every chance to prove his innocence.'

'Jesus Christ,' mumbled Royce. '*Jesus Christ.*'

'I think your idea is a good one, Hartley,' said Kerr-Smiley, 'so here's what we'll do. Quarantine it is, for a month, administered by Major O'Neill here. We shall then hold another of these informal meetings, in which we shall decide what to do with you. Got that, Royce?'

'Yes, sir.'

'All right, dismissed, both of you.'

Hartley and Royce saluted, walked out of the room and made their way down the corridor to their room, where Royce smashed his fist on to the table. 'They actually want to hang me!'

He was close to tears.

'I know,' said Hartley, 'but, look, it's not going to happen.'

'How can you be so sure?'

'Well, you're innocent aren't you?'

'Of course I bloody am!'

'Well, then.'

'But that doesn't make the slightest difference! They've got it in for me, plain and simple, and there's sweet Fanny Adams I can do about it.'

There was nothing Hartley could say. Royce was right – there was something about his face that didn't fit, which made him perfect scapegoat material. 'Look,' said Hartley, 'I'll make sure nothing happens, all right?'

'It's kind of you to say so, but I don't—'

'I promise they won't hang you. It'll be over my dead body if they do.'

Royce laughed, but not very convincingly.

As Hartley and Mouwen had predicted – and, indeed had prayed – the tunnel-building went smoothly. No rock troubled them: most was above, which meant that the tunnel's roof was supported naturally and there was no need to requisition bed boards to prop up unstable ground.

One of Hartley's major concerns lay in trying to establish where they should end the tunnel. It was intended to come out in the trees on the slope next to the path, but the last thing he wanted to do was poke his makeshift spade out of the ground in full view of a passing sentry. He solved the problem by ordering that the digging would take place at night.

Two and a half weeks after they had broken through the rock, he was breathing fresh air. It smelt delicious – it did not reek of sweat and mud, but carried the scent of freedom.

He replaced the earth as best as he could, then crawled backwards along the tunnel, and turned in the little space they had made at the bottom of the drop through the rock.

'We've done it!' he whispered.

'Excellent!'

It was Huntington's voice – Hartley wished it had been Mouwen's. He crawled out of the tunnel and the two men shook hands, the gesture stiffly formal.

Hartley wiped his brow.

'When shall we go?' Huntington asked.

'Soon, I hope. I'd like a wet night so that the Goons are keeping their heads down. All the kit's in place, so we've just got to wait for the weather. And I've got to make a pushwood.'

'What's that?'

'An invention dreamed up by Wilds, that pipe-smoker *extraordinaire*. It's a piece of wood that slots into the end of the tunnel. The top's disguised to look like the missing ground. He used one on the canteen tunnel.'

'Is it really necessary?'

'It is if we want others to use the tunnel after us.'

After consultation with Wilds, it was agreed that the first break would be made on the first wet night. Two pairs of prisoners were to go – Hartley and Mouwen, Huntington and Gordijn. Hartley and Mouwen were to be disguised as labourers, and would make their way by rail to the town of Singen, two or three miles north of Ramsen, a Swiss village that lay at the head of a small salient into German territory. Huntington and Gordijn, who spoke passable French, would dress as French workmen and travel north to the coast, then stow aboard a boat bound for neutral Sweden. It was well known that the Germans bought steel from the Swedes, and Huntington staked much confidence in his theory that countless boats plied Baltic waters.

Hartley could barely contain his excitement.

'You look like the cat who got the cream,' Royce said over lunch one day. Huntington and Bettridge were also in the room and shot a wary glance at Hartley. So far, Royce's quarantine had gone well, at least from his position. A search by the Goons of the British quarters had revealed a cupboard with a false back full of contraband, which suggested that such discoveries were more the result of luck than inside information.

'I'm sorry Malcolm,' Hartley replied. 'You know how it is.'

'Of course.' But there was wistfulness in Royce's words. Both men knew that without Hartley Royce was as good as abandoned.

'You'll have a drink for me when you get back, will you?'

'Of course,' Hartley said, with a smile. 'Where would you like me to have it?'

'At your club, of course.'

'The Travellers?'

'Well, it would seem appropriate.'

'No problem. There's just the small matter of getting there, of course!'

Rain started to fall at seven o'clock the following evening. Hartley was sitting in the courtyard, enjoying a cigarette and trying to read *Bleak House*. His progress with the book had been slower than hacking through the rock, and almost as painful. When the first fat raindrop fell into the middle of page 143, he knew he would never read any further because the book couldn't feature in an escape kit.

He looked up and saw a mass of grey-black cloud. When the multilingual groan went round the courtyard, Hartley smacked the book shut, and stood up. He made his way to the foot of the staircase, and went up with a grin. Perhaps this would be the last time he walked down the dim corridor, the last time he would knock at Wilds's door.

'Come!'

Hartley was mildly surprised to find that Wilds was not lying on his bed but gazing out of the window.

'It's raining, sir,' said Hartley.

'So I'd noticed,' Wilds replied, without turning. 'What are you going to do about it?'

'I'd like to escape, sir.'

Silence.

'You have my permission.'

'Thank you, sir. I'm very grateful.'

'Good luck, Hartley. I can't deny I'll be jealous if you make it. But if you escape, in a way we all escape.'

'Thank you, sir.'

'You'd better get a move on.'

Hartley saluted.

He spent the hour until the *Appel* rounding up his fellow escapers and preparing himself. His labourer's clothes were suitably shabby, as were his dog-eared identity card and travel permit. It still seemed unreal, all this dressing-up and crawling through tunnels, still felt like a *Boy's Own* adventure. At the *Appel*, he and Huntington did their best to act normally. Because of the pelting rain, the count took place quickly.

'Our last *Appel*,' Huntington whispered.

'This time in a week it'll be beer in Zürich,' Hartley murmured back.

'Or Sweden,' said Huntington.

Hartley didn't feel very confident, but as long as they were cautious and sensible, their chance of success was marginally greater than slim. Then he reminded himself that he was trying to get half-way across Germany with a handful of Reichsmarks and over one of the most heavily defended borders in the world. They would more than likely slip up, be caught and brought back to this castle, or even shot as spies. The Germans had threatened that, but so far it hadn't happened. That was not to say it never would, and part of Hartley had no wish to put himself in such danger. But the alternative – countless years in here – was almost worse than death. He couldn't let that happen to him.

The four men stood silently in the lavatory with a fifth, a Dutchman who would reseal the hole. It was eleven o'clock, and it was still pouring with rain. No doubt the sentries were keeping their heads well down, despite orders to the contrary.

'This is it,' said Hartley. 'Good luck, everybody.'

Mouwen and Gordijn were smiling in the dim light. Huntington failed to respond.

'Huntington?'

He was silent.

'Huntington? Are you all right?'

He looked up, and Hartley saw that he had lost his nerve. 'I . . .' He faltered.

'Yes?'

'I'm – I'm not sure I can come.'

'*What?* Why the hell not? Come on, man, we're all nervous. You can't stay here now – we've got to go.'

'I can't.'

'What do you mean you can't?'

'I'm sorry, Hartley, I don't think I'm up to it.'

'Of course you are! You'll be fine as soon as we get out of the tunnel. We'll be free! No more sitting around here, waiting for the war to end. Come on, man! This is your chance!'

Huntington looked at the floor.

Hartley recognised the symptoms: this was a soldier who didn't want to go into battle. He had been warned of how a decent man could snap at the crucial moment. And it had happened now, to someone who had tunnelled as hard as the rest of them. 'Huntington,' he said. 'This is your last chance. Are you coming or not?'

Huntington said nothing.

'Yes or no?'

Huntington shook his head.

'Jesus Christ! You'll ruin everything! For fuck's sake, Huntington, just get moving!'

But Huntington was rooted to the spot.

Hartley looked at Mouwen and Gordijn. 'Stay here,' he said.

'Where are you going?' Mouwen asked.

'To find an understudy.'

'But how are you going to get this past Wilds?'

'I'm not,' said Hartley.

'But what will he say when he finds out?'

'Who gives a damn? We won't be here to find out.'

'There are more deserving cases than me. Look at Biddulph – he's forever trying to get out of here.'

'True, but Biddulph isn't expecting to be strung up by his fellow officers at a moment's notice. Come on, Malcolm, this is a way to save your neck.'

The two men were standing in the corridor outside their room. Hartley had more or less dragged Royce out of bed, much to the surprise of the room's other occupants.

'But I don't have a pass, clothes—'

'You can use Huntington's – he's only a little taller than you. Come on, what do you say?'

The men's eyes met.

'Of course I'll bloody do it.'

'Let's go then.'

'Now?'

'Yes, damnit.'

Royce turned back towards the room. He had the

look of a man who had just shut his front door and was wondering whether he had left the fire unguarded.

'Come on! There's nothing to take with you.'

'A letter. From Rosa.'

'And what if we're searched and they find it? "My Dear Malcolm" isn't going to look too good, is it?' Hartley glared at him. 'Follow me,' he said, and with it turned on his heel and began to walk away. He heard Royce tuck in behind him.

Huntington's jaw dropped when he saw Royce. 'You're taking *him*?'

'You've no right to an opinion,' said Hartley. 'Come on, swap clothes. Give him your papers, your money – everything you've bloody well got.'

'If I'd known you were going to take—'

'Shut up!'

He turned to Mouwen. 'A change of plan, Hans,' he said. 'Why don't you go with Gordijn and I'll go with Royce?'

Mouwen shrugged his shoulders. 'It's best that Royce goes with someone he knows,' he said.

The two men swapped clothes, Huntington taking his time. If he had any regrets, he had the good sense not to voice them. If he had, Hartley would have probably floored him.

'Let's get moving,' said Hartley. He looked at Huntington. 'Goodbye,' he said, voice expressionless.

Huntington nodded. 'Good luck,' he said.

'Thank you.'

Huntington left the room, head bowed. Hartley hoped never to see him again – yet another reason to make a successful escape.

'Where are we going?' asked Royce, mystified. 'Down the lavatory?'

Hartley grinned.

As Hartley made his way down the rope-ladder, he couldn't quite believe that he was on his way out of the castle. In a few minutes, they would emerge into the open air and start their long trip back to freedom – or a shorter one back to captivity. The men made their way down silently, and Hartley was impressed that Royce negotiated the ladder without hesitation. At the bottom of the shaft, the four men stood cramped together, the yellow glow of the oil-lamp illuminating their faces like a Rembrandt painting.

'See you in London,' said Mouwen, and gestured Hartley towards the tunnel. 'After you, Hugh. We'll follow you in five minutes.'

'Are you sure?'

'You were the one who discovered the shaft.'

Hartley eased himself down the hole, then began to crawl along the short tunnel. He could hear Royce behind him, breathing heavily. When he reached the end, he paused. This was it. There was no going back.

He lifted the pushwood, expecting the barrel of a rifle to be shoved into his face.

Instead, to his delight, heavy rain hit his face. He hauled himself out of the hole and dragged himself over a combination of mud and tree roots, a layer of natural grime now supplementing what had been artificially applied to his clothes. Even though he was under the cover of the trees, he felt vulnerable: his back was exposed to the aim of an observant sentry. One almighty thump in the middle of the spine, and that would be that.

He crouched, looking back towards the hole. The castle loomed above him. A moment later, Royce's head emerged, and then he wriggled out. Hartley replaced the pushwood, brushed a few twigs and some mud over it, then made his way down the slope, avoiding more treacherous roots. One stumble, one trip, and a guard would be on to them. Royce was seemingly making one hell of a noise, but Hartley knew that he was too – he hoped the rain was drowning it.

When they reached the bottom of the slope, they paused in front of the exercise park. Hartley pointed to the left. He and Royce would be running across open ground, but a few sheds would provide useful cover. He glanced at Royce, who gave him a thumb's-up.

Hartley stood up and sprinted to the first shed,

and waited for Royce to join him. At any moment, he expected a shot to ring out from the castle walls and a bullet to smash into the back of Royce's head. But none came, and Royce reached the side of the shed, panting.

They had been out of the tunnel for a minute, perhaps less, but to Hartley it felt like an age. There was so much to take in – shapes in the darkness, the lie of the land, whether they would find the railway station – that his brain was flooded with information. He had to keep things simple, try not to worry about anything except achieving the next small stage of their journey.

'Let's go!' he whispered.

Together they ran up a hill towards the park's wall. Hartley had studied it, as had most of the prisoners, and although it was some eight feet high, scaling it would not present much of a challenge. The wall was old, and many of its stones were missing or loose so there were plenty of foot- and hand-holds, of which Hartley was now taking advantage. He heaved himself up, hands occasionally slipping on the wet surfaces. Within a few seconds he was at the top, and stretched a hand down to help Royce up. It was easier than the last wall they had climbed together. In fact, thought Hartley, it was all a little too easy. It crossed his mind that they might be walking into a trap, that they were being lured to a place where they would be shot as spies, their deaths used by the Germans as some sort of deterrent to others.

It couldn't be a trap. Not even Rensburg would be so cunning as to let a couple of prisoners run around the park in the middle of the night – too much of a risk for him to allow them that much freedom. He dismissed his fears and let himself gently down the wall – there was no point in twisting an ankle for the sake of speed.

When he landed, he felt an almighty surge of elation. Now they had truly left the castle. It might not be for long, but for the time being they were free. And even if they were recaptured, he could always say he had escaped from the castle at Colditz. That might mean something one day, he thought, as Royce landed next to him.

'Where next?' Royce whispered.

Hartley pointed to a path that led up the hill away from the castle. 'That way,' he said.

'What happens up there?' asked Royce.

'Leisnig,' said Hartley. 'It's six miles away, and that's where we're going to catch our train home.'

Despite the rain, they made good going. Using the silk map and the compass they had been given, they successfully navigated the network of tracks and roads that crisscrossed the gently undulating countryside. The occasional set of headlights and a dog barking were the only hazards they encountered, both of which they avoided by lying in fields or giving farmhouses an even wider berth. The only unavoidable hazard was mud, of which there was plenty. Although they were dressed as workmen, Hartley knew that if they were absurdly filthy they would look like what they were – prisoners on the run.

They arrived in Leisnig as dawn was breaking at four in the morning. Instead of trying to slip into the town, Hartley thought it best to walk down the main street as real workers would. Unsurprisingly at that hour, it was empty, and there was none of the curtain-twitching he had anticipated.

'Which way is the station?' asked Royce.

'Speak in German, you fool! From now on, we only speak German. We even think in German, if that's possible.'

'Sorry,' said Royce.

'And I don't know where the station is.'

They walked in silence for a while, until Royce said, 'I'll miss my nurse.'

'Come off it!'

'She's a good woman.'

'There'll be plenty of good women waiting for you back home.'

'I don't know.'

Common sense found the station for them, and soon they were standing at the ticket office in a queue of workmen, who spoke Polish among themselves. Thank God for that, thought Hartley. They wouldn't need to make awkward conversation about Germany.

At the ticket window, Hartley asked for two seats to Ulm, a city near the Swiss border. To his surprise he felt calm, as if adopting the persona of a German workman was second nature to him. He felt at home with the play-acting. In a way, it was even fun. Reassuringly, the clerk showed no more interest in his request than he had in any other, and informed him that he would need to change at Leipzig, then Regensburg.

They waited on the platform for forty minutes, where they ate a little bread and smoked a cigarette. There were at least a hundred labourers with them, and Hartley was gratified to notice that their own clothes did not look out of place. The muddiness of their boots was perhaps a little distinctive, but not remarkably so. To the casual observer, they were just another couple of scruffy workmen.

The train was small, and Hartley and Royce had to stand in the aisle of their third-class carriage. There were already plenty of other workers on the train, many of whom Hartley fancied were Czechs and Yugoslavs. Their faces looked drawn, sallow, empty, their bodies overworked and underfed. There was no banter, not even a game of cards. And these were the paid workers, thought Hartley, not the slaves that the

Germans had made of the Jews and Communists unlucky to have been caught in the tide of Hitler's so-called master race. These workers were the lucky ones, Hartley reflected, because they had something approaching freedom.

Some two hours later the train pulled into Leipzig. The station was vast, and the platform bustled with workers, soldiers and skinny young women. Like the rest of the inmates at Colditz, Hartley had heard about the invasion of Russia, although he had no inkling as to how it was going. He was tempted to buy a newspaper, but he knew it would be full of lies and, besides, a workman reading a newspaper would be an unusual sight.

They had two hours to wait until their train to Regensburg.

'What shall we do?' asked Royce.

'Stay here,' Hartley replied. 'It's busy, and nobody's going to notice a couple of workers sitting around waiting for a train.'

The two men sat down on a bench and watched the crowd. The lack of sleep was beginning to catch up with Hartley, and he felt woozy. But now was the not the time to drop off – he could do that on the train.

'There's a cafe over there,' he said. 'I'm going to get some coffee.'

'Good idea,' said Royce.

They walked across the station, pausing for a group of Luftwaffe personnel to march past. Hartley studied their faces. They were even younger than he was, and each man wore a look of joyful determination. They were hungry and fit for battle, he thought, ready to destroy the hated Soviets. How many would last the war? At the rate it was going, probably all of them. The idea depressed him, and he dispelled it.

The cafe was thick with steam and cigarette smoke. Nobody looked up at them as they walked in, although an elderly man in a suit glanced disdainfully at their muddy boots. There were only two seats left, and Hartley and Royce took them. They found themselves opposite a pair of young soldiers. Hartley's heart pounded. He prayed that Royce kept cool. So far he had been fine, but there was no guarantee that he would remain so.

'Two coffees, please,' Hartley said to the waitress, a surly middle-aged matron.

'Anything else?'

'Any biscuits?' asked Royce.

The waitress paused.

Oh, shit, thought Hartley. Of course they don't have any bloody biscuits. Don't you know there's a war on?

'What sort would you like?' the waitress asked.

'Some *Lebekuchen*, please, Fräulein,' said Royce, grinning at her.

Hartley tried not to look too relieved.

*

The train to Regensburg was busy but not full. They found seats in a compartment, and settled in next to a Luftwaffe officer in his thirties, two middle-aged men in suits and a pretty young woman. As they sat down, Hartley could feel the officer staring at them. He nodded politely at him.

'Are you Jews?'

'Good God, no!' said Hartley, momentarily taken aback.

'Good,' said the officer. 'If you were, I would have thrown you out.'

'Quite right,' said Hartley. 'I wouldn't want to share a compartment with scum.'

The officer smiled. 'Imagine the smell!'

Hartley pinched his nose theatrically. The rest of the carriage was watching, making a show of amusement. To do otherwise would have suggested some sympathy for the Jews, and it was their duty to laugh, especially with an officer of the glorious Wehrmacht. Hartley noticed that the man was wearing a chestful of medals. 'You have a fine collection,' he said, pointing at the officer's tunic.

'Thank you.' His voice was tinged with false modesty.

'You must have seen a lot of action.'

'I have indeed. Spain, Holland, Belgium, France, England, and now Russia.'

'England, eh? How was that?'

The officer's face darkened. 'A disaster,' he replied. 'We lost a lot of men over there. But we will be back, my friend, as soon as we have polished off the Russkis.'

Hartley raised an imaginary glass. 'Here's to being in England!' he said.

The officer did likewise. 'I'll drink to that! Perhaps one day you will go there as well.'

Hartley smiled. 'I'd like that very much.'

'Papers!'

Hartley and Royce stirred in their seats. It was around midday, and they had been asleep for the past few hours. Bleary-eyed, Hartley stared at the policeman standing in the doorway to the compartment. He had a long, thin face and narrow eyes, the face of an inquisitor. This was a moment of truth, Hartley thought. In a few minutes, they might be in handcuffs and on their way back to the castle. Hartley prayed that Atkin-Berry and his team had done a good enough job.

The two men fumbled in their pockets for their identity cards and passed them to the policeman. Royce's hand was trembling, which was understandable but annoying. The policeman studied them carefully. 'Where are you going?' he asked.

'To Ulm,' Hartley replied.

'Why?'

'We are electricians,' said Hartley. 'We've been ordered to go to one of the big companies there to work in their factory.'

'Which company?'

'Krupps,' said Hartley.

'I didn't think Krupps was in Ulm.'

'Not yet,' said Hartley, without pause. 'It's a new factory.'

The policeman nodded, his expression uncertain. 'A new factory, eh?'

'That's right.'

'You must be very good electricians if they brought you all the way from Leisnig.'

'We'll go anywhere for work,' said Hartley.

The policeman held out the passes. Hartley and Royce stretched out their hands to take them, but the policeman did not let go, his attention drawn to something on one of them. He pulled it back and looked closely at it.

'Why haven't you signed it?' he asked, holding up Royce's pass.

'Haven't I?' said Royce.

'No.'

Hartley closed his eyes. They were done for because Huntington hadn't signed his papers. Why the hell not? Had he known he wouldn't actually go?

'I'm sorry,' said Royce. 'I can sign it now if you like.'

The policeman was regarding him as if he were some sort of dolt. 'It's not supposed to . . .' the policeman began. 'Oh, get on with it, then.'

He gave both men their passes, then reached inside his tunic for a pen, which he handed to Royce, who scribbled.

The policeman inspected the other passengers' passes, then left the compartment.

'Paperwork, eh?' said the Luftwaffe officer jovially.

'I know,' said Hartley. 'My friend here has always been useless with it.'

Royce attempted a smile, but it was clear to Hartley that he was still frightened.

'I thought all you electricians were supposed to be neat.'

'Not me,' said Royce.

'Heaven help Krupps!'

The two men arrived in Ulm at three o'clock the following morning. They had spent much of their time asleep, or gazing out of the window at the German countryside. The other occupants of their carriage had ignored them and, thankfully, none had tried to engage them in conversation. Their one problem had been a lack of food. There had been little on offer at Regensburg station, but they had bought some more biscuits and eaten them with the scraps of bread they had brought with them. Both were carrying bars of Red Cross chocolate, but Hartley told Royce they should save them for an emergency, and eat them only when they were alone. He could imagine the faces of a carriageful of Germans watching them scoff something that had been unavailable to most of them since the start of the war.

While they travelled, Hartley reflected on what life was like back at the castle. He imagined the *Appels* without them, and how angry Wilds would be when he found out that Royce had left without his permission. Hartley smiled to himself – hopefully the man's pipe would have fallen out of his mouth and smashed on the cobbles.

Although they were many miles and many hours away, he could still feel the pull of Colditz. There had been camaraderie and laughter, a sense of stability and safety. He never wanted to see the place again, but a small part of him missed it.

At the Ulm ticket office, Hartley asked for two tickets to Singen. The woman behind the desk peered at him suspiciously.

'Singen?'

'That's right,' said Hartley.

'But it's on the Swiss border.'

'Yes, I know. What of it?'

'You need to talk to the railway police if you want to go to the frontier zone. Why are you going to Singen anyway?'

Hartley was tempted to tell her it was none of her business, but he kept his opinion to himself. 'My friend and I could do with some mountain air. Is that a crime, Fräulein?'

'That's for a policeman to decide.'

'Are there any policemen around?'

'Wait here. I'll have a look.'

Hartley watched her disappear through a door at the back of the ticket office. Now what? Wait here for a policeman and chance it, hoping he would believe their story? Or run away and try to catch a train further down the line? He turned to Royce. 'What do you think?' he asked.

'Our papers have been good for all the checks so far. If he says we can't go, we'll just smile along with him and try another way of getting there.'

'Agreed,' said Hartley. 'Anyway, it would look too suspicious if we ran away.'

Eventually the woman returned with a short, rotund man dressed in the dark blue uniform of a railway policeman. 'You want to go to Singen?' he said.

'That's right.'

'Why?'

'Because we'd like a little mountain air,' said Hartley.

'Why?'

'We'll be working in a factory for the next few months, and some air will do us some good.'

222

The policeman looked quizzically at them. Evidently he was not a man who cared for air.

'Papers?'

Hartley and Royce handed them to him.

'So, you're from Saxony, eh?'

'That's right.'

'Plenty of air round there.'

'Yes,' said Hartley, 'we miss it.'

'Then why didn't you stay?'

'Because there's no work.'

Did all the Reich's citizens have to put up with such questioning? Hartley wondered. They probably did.

'But why Singen?'

'A friend of mine went there and said it was pretty.'

'Did he now?'

'Yes.'

'And how long will you be there?'

'Two days.'

'Where will you stay?'

'We don't know. I'm sure there'll be a guesthouse or two.'

'There might be, there might not . . . Singen is in the frontier zone.'

'Yes.'

'Well, you'd better be careful,' said the policeman, handing back their passes. 'If you step into the wrong place, you'll be shot.'

'Thanks for the advice,' said Hartley.

The policeman walked off, yawning.

'Single or return?' the ticket woman asked.

'Return.'

Just forty hours after leaving the castle, Hartley and Royce were looking at the Swiss border. It was a fabulous afternoon, and the town of Singen, with its whitewashed cottages set against green pasture, was postcard pretty. Under different circumstances, it would indeed have been a pleasant place to visit. Nevertheless, suspicious faces watched them as they alighted from the train: the town was small enough for two strangers to be noticed.

'We should hide,' said Hartley.

The two men walked out of the town, passing a group of farmhands coming towards them. They, too, stared at Hartley and Royce, evidently wondering what they were doing, walking along the road purposefully. Any of these people might report them, thought Hartley, and that would be that. But it was not going to happen. He would not let it.

They found a small wood, and lay among some thick foliage. The sun barely penetrated the branches, and Hartley found himself overtaken by drowsiness. 'Royce,' he said, 'I must sleep. Can you keep watch for two hours? Then we'll swap.'

'Certainly,' said Royce. There was something odd in his tone.

'What's the matter?' Hartley asked.

'Nothing.'

'Really?'

'Yes.'

'All right,' said Hartley, and lay back. No doubt Royce was nervous. Well, so was he. In his heart, he had never expected to get so close, yet here they were, just a mile from the Swiss border. It would be the longest mile of their journey, he knew, because no amount of bluff would get them past any sentry. It was a case of finding cover, and being as stealthy as wild animals. It would not be easy but the price of failure was no longer a return trip to Colditz but a bullet in the back.

In the darkness, Hartley could make out the frontier post straddling the road a couple of hundred yards to their left. To their right, some three hundred yards away, there was a sentry post, which was barely visible. For the past two hours, a guard had paced between the two. On the other side of his beat lay at least a hundred yards of open ground before the border – a field the two men would have to get across when the guard had gone, if he ever went. Freedom was tantalisingly close.

They waited another two hours, and still the guard

paced. The night was clear and mild, and Hartley wished it had been raining. The moon washed the countryside in a silvery sheen, a backdrop against which they would be easily spotted. In a perfect world, they would have waited for a wet night, but that was impossible. They had one chance, and this was it.

Their break came half an hour later. The guard had stopped his patrol – perhaps he was about to be relieved – and disappeared into a small hut at the frontier post. For the past minute he had not emerged.

Hartley turned to Royce. 'This is it.'

'Are you sure?'

'No. But it's the least worst moment. Come on.'

The two men stood up, and ran as they had never run before. The ground was pockmarked with burrows and hoofprints, making it dangerously uneven. Hartley's tiredness had disappeared, replaced with adrenaline. They were going to make it, he thought. They were going to bloody make it! He could hear Royce behind him, feet thudding over the hard ground. It occurred to him that perhaps they should crawl, but he dismissed the notion. When no one was around it was best to run – get the hell over the border fast.

He was breathing hard now, feeling tired. He was running more slowly, legs stiffening. They passed the guard's beat, and were now into the open field. There was just two hundred yards to Switzerland, two hundred yards to freedom. The air scorched in and out of Hartley's burning lungs.

'*Halt!*'

If his heart had not been pumping so hard, it would have stopped.

'*Halt!*'

A whistle somewhere behind him. Dogs barking. Oh, Christ, no, please, let this not be true! Keep running!

A shot echoed round the mountains, then another. He kept running.

'Hugh!'

He carried on running.

'*Hugh!*'

He turned his head. Royce was clutching his left shoulder. 'I think I've been hit!' he shouted.

He couldn't leave him. He ran back to Royce and, without a word, hauled him over his shoulders.

'Let me down, Hugh! You go over – go on!'

'I can't leave you!'

A bullet whizzed past his ear with a high-pitched whine, followed by the sound of another shot.

'Put me down! Save yourself!'

'No!'

'I insist!' Royce was struggling to get down. Hartley let him fall as gently as he could. Royce gazed back up at him. 'I'll be all right, Hugh. You go – just go!'

Hartley opened his mouth, but no words came out.

The border was too close, too seductive. He gave in to it.

Chapter Six

April 1973

THE TAXI SMELT heavily of stale tobacco, and the small metal ashtrays were overflowing with cigarette ends. No matter, thought Hartley, as he removed a packet of Silk Cut from his mackintosh. He lit one, the first of the day, and unfolded *The Times*. Strikes, and more bloody strikes. He half folded, half crumpled the paper, and tossed it on to the seat. He took a long drag on the cigarette, coughed and blew out the smoke through the window. The wet streets were as grey and filthy as the inside of the cab. There was rubbish everywhere, and many pedestrians looked as though they spent the night in it.

Hartley took another drag on the cigarette, and pushed it out of the window. He didn't like his smoking, and neither did Sarah, but he needed it. One day, he would give up, perhaps next week when they went fishing in Scotland. He would be unbearable for a few days, but Sarah would tolerate it, as she always did. Indeed, there was much to tolerate – late nights home, countless trips abroad, phone calls in the middle of the night, broken-off dinner parties – all of which she took in good part. It wasn't so much for herself that she had minded, but for their two boys. He had missed too many football matches, one too many prize-givings. They were grown-up now, and although they were friendly, they were not close to him. Maybe things would get better when they had families of their own. Perhaps then they would understand.

Had it been worthwhile, though? Only he knew the answer to that, and he couldn't even tell Sarah, because she would want to know why. Some of them did tell their wives – they denied it, of course – but Hartley didn't want to burden Sarah with the weight of his secrets. It had been worth it because knowing what your enemy was planning to do was the most important information of all. And he had found out a lot, and stopped them doing some of it. But he couldn't stop it all, and that was why the game was so frustrating: you could never quite win, and it would never end.

It was expensive too, and Hartley had lost many men. His superiors told him that that was natural, that it was a by-product of doing what he did, but he could never get used to it. And now that he was one of the superiors, he had to tell young men that losing agents was all part of it. It didn't mean they shouldn't care, but they couldn't take it personally. Deep down, though, Hartley did take it personally – and badly. He masked his feelings, often wondering whether he was too decent for all this. He was not one of the grubby ones, but he had been corrupted by it, because throwing shit around meant that a lot stuck to your hands. It was unavoidable, and the only place you could wipe it off was all over yourself, because no one else could help you get clean, not even your wife, and you certainly didn't want her covered with it.

'Just here, please,' said Hartley to the driver.

'Righto.' The cabbie pulled up beside a newsagent.

Hartley got out, taking the newspaper with him. The rain was just heavy enough for him to rue his lack of an umbrella, but the macintosh would keep him dry.

'How much do I owe you?'

'Call it one fifty, guv.'

Hartley took a handful of change out of his pocket. He was still not entirely used to the new money, especially as he had been away when it was introduced. He found three fifty pence coins and passed them over with a few coppers. The cabbie raised a finger to an imaginary cap and drove off.

Hartley started down the street, dodging rubbish. Like everyone else that day, he kept his head down.

He was walking along a London thoroughfare with more than its fair share of concrete office blocks, ugly anonymous buildings that had sprung up like geometrical fungus over the past few years.

He changed his route into work every morning, and when he took a taxi, he always had it drop him a few yards from the office. He was sure that half the cabbies guessed where he was going, and some even winked at him. There weren't too many men like him around these parts, which made people like him stick out somewhat. So much for tradecraft. If they had been in the middle of St James's it would have been so much easier, and far more convenient, but this was where the gods had told them they should be, and there were to be no arguments about it. We've all got to tighten our belts, even you people. You should count yourselves lucky that you're not *really* having to slum it. These are tough times.

Hartley opened the revolving doors and stepped into a muted brown lobby. There was a battered brown corduroy sofa next to a large brass floor-mounted ashtray. He had never seen anybody sit in that sofa, or read the copy of *The Times* that was put there dutifully every morning. It was not the type of place where visitors sat around.

'Good morning, sir.' Terry's friendly, nicotine-stained face grinned at him from behind a large desk.

He had been here for as long as Hartley could

remember. The poor bugger only had one arm – D-Day – and his CO had wangled him the job immediately after the war. 'Morning, Terry.'

Hartley produced his pass from his inside jacket pocket. There was nothing on it to reveal what he did, and all anyone could glean from it was that Hugh Hartley was a civil servant.

Terry examined the pass carefully. He always checked everyone's thoroughly and conscientiously. Hartley had once lost his and Terry had refused to let him in. The Head Man had had to come down and vouch for him.

'How are you this morning, Colonel?'

'Not bad, Terry. And you?'

'Very chipper, sir. I'm off on holiday next week. Taking the missus down to the coast.'

'Lovely.'

'You going anywhere, sir?'

'Scotland. Spot of fishing.'

'Bring us back a salmon, would you?'

Hartley grinned, genuinely. 'Who do you think I am, Terry? Midas?'

'Nah. Poseidon.'

'No flies on you this morning.'

Hartley walked to the lift door. He would have used the stairs, but a sign indicated that they were 'Out of Order'. Hartley wondered how that could be, but the lift arrived with a weak ping that distracted him. The doors opened and a man of similar age to Hartley, wearing, like Hartley, a pinstripe suit, stepped out. 'Morning, Hugh.'

'Clive.'

'You're in early.'

'You're off early.'

That was the extent of the conversation between the two men. Clive Ramsay despised Hartley as the man who had stolen his job. There was some truth in the allegation: Hartley had lobbied the Head Man hard for it, saying that Ramsay ran a loose ship – too many agents were being lost or, worse, turned. Ramsay had denied it, citing the operational difficulties and caveats they always cited, but the Head Man had sided with Hartley. What made Ramsay more livid was that since Hartley had taken over the material had vastly improved, and the network, although smaller, was far more productive. Hartley knew he had been lucky, but that was half the game.

The lift took him to the top floor. Hartley noticed yet again that only one of its two bulbs was working. It had been like that for a few weeks now. Had the country even run out of lightbulbs? They'd be using candles soon. The doors opened on to a small vestibule, with threadbare brown carpet that matched the sofa downstairs. A large unhealthy-looking pot plant drooped in one corner, and a commissionaire sat behind a desk.

'Morning, Colonel.'

'Morning, Frank.'

There was less banter to be had with Frank, and Hartley merely showed him his pass. The man stood up to unlock a large wooden door.

'Thanks.'

Hartley stepped into a long, empty corridor. Like the lift, it was only partially lit, although some attempt had been made to cheer it up with crookedly hung prints of London scenes. Hartley didn't notice them as he went to his office. He never had. They were as anonymous as the building: their presence would only be remarked upon if they were removed.

Hartley's door was marked with the jumble of letters and numbers that designated his department. He turned the handle and stepped into a reasonably spacious, bright room, its walls covered with shelves, which bowed under the weight of box files and books.

'Good morning, Colonel.'

Primrose, his secretary, was near to retirement, and Hartley would miss her when she had gone. 'Good morning, Miss Beal.'

Hartley removed his macintosh and hung it next to Primrose's thick woollen overcoat, which she wore every day, even during the summer. Then he walked to his desk, briefly acknowledging the grey view, the best that London could offer that morning. No landmarks, not even St Paul's, just a messy assortment of office blocks and the occasional spire.

'I see Picasso has died,' said Primrose.

'Who?'

'Picasso – you know, the painter.'

'Oh, yes,' said Hartley.

His brevity had nothing to do with rudeness: it was just that he had nothing to say about Picasso. In fact, he had little to say about art in general, an English characteristic of which he was almost proud. Sarah despaired when he fell asleep at concerts, or looked at his watch when they visited a gallery.

'I rather liked his stuff,' said Primrose.

'Can't say I know it.' Hartley sat at his desk and heaved a wire tray stacked with paper towards him. There was a lot to go through. He reached into his pocket and took out his packet of Silk Cut. He glanced at the wall clock as he lit the cigarette. Three minutes past eight. He would have finished this lot by lunchtime.

He exhaled a long jet of smoke. Today he was feeling every one of his fifty-five years.

An hour later there was a knock on the door.

'Come in.'

A man in his forties entered the room.

'Morning, Holland.'

'Good morning, sir.'

Holland was Hartley's deputy. At six foot four, he had been too tall for this line of work – far too noticeable – but he was a good operator. He knew East Germany almost as well as Hartley did, and he had a brilliant memory.

'I'm sorry about that mountain, sir,' said Holland, pointing to Hartley's desk.

'Not at all, Holland. Paperwork, the privilege of seniority.'

'Surely you mean the curse, sir?'

'I rather think you're right. Anything interesting come in last night? Weren't we meant to hear from Crowbar?'

'We did, sir, but it's pretty feeble stuff. The Russians are planning another FTX next month. He's got a round-up of the kit they're deploying, but it's pretty predictable stuff.'

'Let's have a look,' said Hartley.

Holland passed him a manilla file. Inside, a single piece of paper listed an assortment of Soviet military equipment for a field training exercise. Holland was right: it was pretty tedious stuff.

'Hardly sets the world alight.'

'Indeed, sir,' Holland replied. 'Crowbar's been a bit weak of late.'

Hartley wasn't surprised. Agents went through bad patches like everybody else, perhaps more often as they were subject to so many more forces. Crowbar was an East German colonel who supplied the West with information for the simple reason that he liked money. He was reliable, and pleasant – Hartley had even met him. He preferred the gold-diggers to the idealists, because you knew where you stood with them. There was no need to appeal to fine sentiments and high morals: it was simply a case of getting out a wedge of dollars. Easy, if expensive, but often worth it. It was Crowbar who had told them about a new tank last year, and even supplied them with the specifications, which had earned the service a gold star from the army.

'Anything else?' asked Hartley, passing the folder back to Holland.

'Not much,' said Holland, 'although there was this. Curious little item from Sparrow in Leipzig.'

Hartley took another manilla folder from Holland and opened it.

HAVE HEARD REPORTS FROM A DOCTOR FRIEND THAT
AN UNNAMED ENGLISHMAN IS IN A LUNATIC ASYLUM
FIFTY KMS SE OF LEIPZIG STOP AWAITING INSTRUCTION
STOP SPARROW

Hartley read the cable again. With exaggerated calm, he lit a cigarette.

'Sir, you've gone pale. Are you all right?'

'I feel as if someone's just walked over my grave.

Or, rather, as if I'd just walked over someone else's.'

Holland knitted his eyebrows. 'I don't follow you, sir.'

'I'll explain at lunch,' said Hartley. With almost reverential care, he closed the manilla folder and placed it in the top right-hand drawer of his desk, which was reserved for his own operations.

'It's about time I put you up for this place,' said Hartley, 'but you probably think it a bit dusty.'

Holland put down his glass of claret and looked around the dining-room of the Travellers Club. The sun had come out and illuminated even the darkest and most conspiratorial corners in which an assortment of old men, wearing three-piece suits and regimental or old-school ties, were having lunch. 'Well, there are a few cobwebs,' he said.

Hartley followed Holland's gaze. 'Him?' asked Hartley.

'Who is he?'

'Sir Bill Dawson.'

'Wasn't he our man in Latin America somewhere?'

'The very same. Argentina.'

'So where did he pick up his K?'

'It was his father's. He's one of the Lloyd George barts. I'll introduce you after lunch.'

Despite the chitchat Hartley was unable to stop thinking about Sparrow's cable. His face must have revealed his distraction, because Holland asked him politely if something was on his mind.

'That cable troubles me.'

'May I ask why?'

Hartley cut into a piece of overcooked beef. The knife was a little blunt, so the meat slid around his plate. Eventually he succeeded, and supplemented it with green beans and a piece of roast potato.

'Of course.'

Hartley chewed, aware that Holland was waiting for him to finish, but he wanted time to get his thoughts together, to know where to begin. He would need Holland's help, and it was only fair that the man should know the full story. He emptied his mouth, put down his cutlery and took a mouthful of wine (slightly too cold).

'This goes back to the war,' he began, 'to my days in Colditz.'

He could see that he had gained Holland's attention. Everyone knew about Colditz: there had been numerous books and films about it. Hartley had been offered countless deals by publishers to write his story, but he had always refused. Perhaps a retirement project, he said, but for now it was best that he remain an anonymous civil servant.

'I escaped with a chap called Malcolm Royce. I'd met him in Greece and taken him under my wing. He had a screw loose, or rather a few screws loose, and tried to kill himself. Well, to cut it short, many of the senior officers had it in their heads that he was a stool pigeon, mainly based on the "evidence" that the Germans were rumbling escapes after Royce had arrived. Well, I thought it unfair, so when I went out, I took Royce with me. It was the only way I could save his neck.'

'Do you think he would have been hanged?'

'Oh, yes. It was disgraceful. Real kangaroo stuff. If I hadn't got him out, he'd have been swinging from the rafters.'

'So what happened?'

'Well, we got out, and our trip went pretty smoothly until we reached the Swiss border. We were at a little place called Singen – you probably know it from all that business with General Steiner.'

'I remember it well,' said Holland. 'Pretty little place.'

'Well, not for me. We made our break across the border late at night, and that was where they shot him. He took a bullet in the shoulder and insisted that I go on. I did so reluctantly, eventually made it back to Britain and joined MI9.'

'From where you joined the Service.'

'That's right.' Another swig of claret. 'Shall we get another bottle? This one's running dangerously low.'

'You're the boss, sir,' said Holland.

Hartley caught a waiter's eye. 'Peter,' he said,

'another of these, please. And could you tell Vincent that the greens were so soft I thought they were made of paper.'

The waiter smiled. Colonel Hartley always complained that the greens were overcooked, and every time he reported it back to the chef, Vincent replied that Colonel Hartley must be an Italian: did he want his bloody greens raw?

'I will, sir.'

'So, what happened to Royce?'

'I don't know.' Hartley tried to say it casually, as though what had happened was of no great consequence.

'You don't know?'

'That's right,' said Hartley, draining his glass. 'I've no idea.'

'Are you sure he didn't die?'

'Don't know. There are no records of his death and, believe you me, I checked. In 'forty-seven I even interviewed the German officer – a Hauptmann Wangenheim, I recall – who was responsible for that part of the border, and he told me Royce went to a military hospital. That's where the trail goes cold.'

'He just disappeared?'

'So it would seem. The hospital records at Ulm show that he was admitted a day after he was shot. After that, nothing.'

'How extraordinary.'

'Isn't it? Well, you can imagine what my fellow captives said later, can't you? "He must have been a traitor, old boy, stands to reason, doesn't it? Went to ground with his Jerry friends, et cetera et cetera." '

Wilds had been one of Hartley's chief tormentors after the war, but Hartley had refused to accept that Royce was a traitor, saying that it was despicable to slander a man who might be dead.

'What makes you so sure he wasn't a traitor?'

'A gut feeling. Now, I know I've told you dozens of times not to trust your guts, but in this instance. I've broken my own rule. I don't deny that Royce could have been a traitor, but why? What was in it for him? He wasn't a Fascist, because if he was he would have been banged up before the war.'

'Money?'

'Unlikely. I've yet to hear of a British officer being corrupted like that. That leaves us to *chercher la femme*, who in this instance was a nurse called Rosa at the Leipzig military hospital. Royce had fallen for her when he was being treated for his injuries after he'd tried to kill himself.'

'Did you find her?'

Hartley nodded. 'I did indeed, but with some difficulty. You can't imagine what a mess Germany was in during the years after the war. Finding people was absurdly difficult. The hospital records showed that there were at least eight Rosas working there, and

it took me two months to find all of them – on top of
my ordinary duties. Sod's Law, she was the last one
on my list. Anyway, she denied having seen him, and
even thought my enquiry was a bit odd. She said she
and Royce had never been an item. Yes, she had liked
him, but things had turned sour after he had forced
himself on her.'

'In a serious way?'

'Oh, no. Nothing like that. Schoolboy lunge, she
said.'

'So, a bit one-sided, then?'

'Precisely.'

'Did you believe her?'

'No. I had her watched for a couple of weeks. It
turned out she had a new boyfriend, a Russian soldier.
We saw them kissing.'

'So that ended that?'

'Quite. If Royce was alive he'd have been a little
upset.'

Peter arrived with the wine, which he poured.

'At last,' exclaimed Hartley. He tasted it and
nodded that it was fine.

'Did you try to recruit her?' asked Holland.

'I did think of it, but in the end I decided she was
too flighty, too low-grade and too pregnant. Besides,
we had bigger fish.'

'And you gave up?'

'I had to. I had plenty on my plate, and I was

making myself pretty unpopular in pursuing a private investigation.'

'What do you think happened?'

'Well, either he died, which is not unlikely as the wound could have turned septic, or he escaped from the hospital and was killed somewhere else. That's the most likely explanation. Who knows? He could have fallen off a cliff, or drowned crossing a river, something like that.'

Holland seemed vexed. 'But what about the cable from Sparrow?'

Hartley didn't speak for several seconds. Instead, he swilled the wine around in his glass, studying its colour. 'I have a feeling that our mysterious Englishman is none other than Royce.'

'How can you be sure?'

'I'm not sure at all.'

'But what makes you think he might be?'

'Because the only lunatic asylum fifty kilometres south-east of Leipzig is Colditz.'

'Really?'

'That's what it's become.'

'But there's nothing to say that the man in there is Royce.'

'You're quite right, of course, but it appeals to my romantic instincts to think that he might be. Maybe Royce's mental condition worsened after he was shot and recaptured – God knows, mine would have –

and he ended up incarcerated in some German asylum. And now, after thirty-odd years, he's locked up in the place he tried to escape from during the war. It would be a cruel irony.'

'You've no proof that it's him, sir, just a hunch.'

'I don't deny it. Which is why I'm going to get Sparrow to do some digging for me.'

Holland coughed. 'Are you going to ask the Head Man?'

'No,' Hartley replied. 'It's none of his business. Sparrow's one of mine, so I can do what I like with her. I'd like you to keep quiet, if that's not too much to ask.'

'Of course not, sir,' said Holland, stiffly, his manner suggesting that it was indeed an enormous thing to ask.

'Come on man,' said Hartley. 'I'm only going to get her to ask a few questions.'

'But what if it is Royce?'

Hartley drank some more wine. This bottle was a little warmer, and the flavour was better.

A silence.

'How's Rachel?' Hartley asked. 'All well I trust? Ned behaving?'

'How are things in your section?'

'A little quiet, if truth be told, sir.'

The Head Man had his back to him. He was staring

out of the window at the same patch of anonymous skyline that Hartley endured from his office.

'Nothing from the Praesidium?'

'Not yet, sir, although Aerial normally delivers the goods.'

'I don't like it, Hugh. Since you took over, things have been rather busy with your boys. Have you spoken to Mike?'

Mike Baker was the station head in Berlin. He was a good man, a real operator, fast track to the top.

'I'm calling him this afternoon, just after five.'

'Well, shake him up, would you?'

This was unlike the Head Man. He sounded irritable, short-tempered. Hartley didn't speak.

'It's all a little bit too quiet, these days,' said the Head Man, turning to face Hartley. 'We need some oomph. It's as though we're getting bogged down with the rest of the country.'

'I agree, sir. But we've known quiet patches in the past.'

'And I didn't like them then.'

'Well, sir, I shall certainly shake things up.'

The Head Man was probably right. These two-bottle lunches were becoming a little more frequent, a sure sign of sclerosis. Since he had come back to London, Hartley had found it all too easy to slip into the role of St James's grandee. He felt he deserved it after years in the field, busting his guts in the middle of cold East German nights to meet some low-level source with astonishingly trivial information. He was by no means lazy, it was just that he delegated well, and the networks were running themselves quite nicely. Nevertheless, things were getting a bit stale. Perhaps this was an opportunity for a trip to Germany.

'I could go out there, sir,' said Hartley.

The Head Man shook his head.

'No, Hartley. I'm not having that. I don't like letting my big fish swim around on their own. No jaunts. Leave the shaking up on the ground to Mike. OK?'

'Of course. It was just a passing thought.'

Hartley spent the rest of the afternoon on his paperwork. At five o'clock, he picked up the phone and asked to be connected to Berlin. It was a couple of minutes before the line came up, and when it did it was atrociously crackly, with a distracting delay.

'Mike!' Hartley shouted

'Hello, sir. How are you?'

'Fine. I'll get straight to the point. The Head Man thinks things are too quiet at the moment, wants a little more oomph. His word. I'll cable you exactly what he wants.'

'More "oomph", eh? Well, we're doing our best, sir.'

'I know that, but I thought I should pass on the request.'

'I understand, sir.'

'One thing, Mike, before I go.'

'Sir?'

'That cable you sent me from Sparrow. Anything else with it?'

'No, sir, that was all.'

'Well, get her to find out more, could you? I'd like to know everything about this chap.'

There was a pause.

'Don't worry, Mike. I'll reveal all soon.'

'All right, sir. I don't know how long it'll take.'

'No matter. Whatever she can find would be a help.'

The taxi home smelt no better than that morning's. Hartley did his bit to make it worse with at least two Silk Cut between the office and his home in Kensington. He didn't take in the passing city because he was lost in thought, his mind transported back thirty years. At this distance, Colditz didn't seem real. Now he felt almost as though his time there had been a film he had watched rather than something he had experienced.

A lot had changed, a lot had happened. The children, the countless postings abroad, the scrapes he had had - some far worse than being shot at crossing the Swiss border. He had never told Sarah of the risks he had taken, not only because they were secret but also because he felt guilty about them. He had lived for adventure, a taste he had acquired in Colditz. That was its legacy to him – or, perhaps it was a curse. Ever since the escape he had craved excitement, and he had found it. He couldn't bear the idea that at twenty-three his adventures were over, but joining the Service had provided him with plenty more. Eventually he had lost that taste, or thought he had, but today it had quivered into life again.

But it wasn't just about adventure. It was friendship. If poor old Royce was stuck there, he knew he had to help him. Hartley had buried his guilt over abandoning Royce: he could have carried him, he knew it. The border hadn't been much further on – they would have made it together and the Swiss would have patched him up. Now he couldn't let the man rot after what they had gone through together. He owed it to him to do his best, to come good, help the man finally escape.

'You seem preoccupied, darling. Is anything the matter?'

Hartley looked at her over his seven o'clock whisky and soda. They were sitting in the drawing room, Sarah flicking through a copy of *Country Life*. 'Just work, darling, that's all.'

'Anything you can talk about?'

'Not really.'

Sarah knew better than to ask any more. She was the perfect wife for a man like him, not that she had known how he would turn out. She had thought she was marrying a soldier, not a man who lived in the shadows.

'Christopher rang today,' she said.

'How is he?'

'As well as can be expected, with his finals coming up.'

'Working all hours, is he?'

'Sounds like it. I told him not to tire himself out, but you know what he's like.'

'Well, we've all been there.'

'I haven't, darling.'

It was the source of some annoyance to Sarah that she had been badly educated. She had a first-class brain, and had wanted to go up to Oxford, but her parents had not allowed it.

'There's nothing to stop you doing a degree now.'

Sarah scoffed. 'How would you manage without me? You'd be hopeless.'

'You don't have to go away. You could sign up for Harold Wilson's Open University – about the only good thing he did.'

'And what would I study?'

'German?'

'I'm sick of all things German.'

'How about English literature? I'd like to do that if I started all over again.'

Sarah put down the magazine. 'Maybe . . . and maybe not. I don't fancy slaving away on some degree, not now that I've got you back.' She stood up and walked over to him, bent down and kissed him. 'Anyway, now I'm going to see about supper. Are you hungry?'

'Not really. I had lunch at the club.'

'Let me guess. Roast beef and a bottle of claret.'

'Hole in one.'

'Just the one bottle, was it?'

'Er, yes, I think so.'

Sarah smiled. 'You're the worst liar in the world. Do you know something?'

'What?'

'You'd make a terrible spy.' She whisked out of the room. 'Tomato soup is all you're getting,' she called back.

A week later Sparrow sent her reply. Holland brought it in with all the other overnight traffic. The uneasy smile on his face told Hartley all he needed to know.

'It looks like you've got some news for me.'

'I have, sir,' said Holland.

Hartley opened the file and took out the cable.

NAME OF PATIENT IS ROYCE STOP FIFTY-FOUR YEARS
STOP ADMITTED 03/03/73 STOP CONDITION SUSPECTED
MANIC DEPRESSION AND PARANOIA STOP

So there were names for it now, thought Hartley. He didn't care for all these new-fangled psychiatric terms, but there it was. God knew how Royce was being treated in Colditz. The place had driven him mad all those years ago so it was unlikely to be doing him a world of good now. He would be better off here, in a British hospital.

Hartley looked at the cable again. Something troubled him. Why was Royce being treated under his British name? And how had Sparrow come across the information so easily?

'Are you thinking what I'm thinking?' he asked Holland.

'That it's a trap?'

'It's like offering ice-cream to a three-year-old – they want me to wolf it down.'

'It certainly looks that way, sir.'

'But there's the element of double bluff. If they were wanting to woo me, you'd have thought they'd have made it a little harder.'

'Maybe they wouldn't have got your attention otherwise,' said Holland. 'After all, news that an Englishman is stuck in a loony-bin behind the Curtain is no great shakes. We know of several ex-servicemen who defected to the East after the war.'

'Some of them are on our books.'

'What are you going to do, sir?'

Hartley drummed his fingers on the table. 'First, I shall think about it. And then I shall think a bit more.'

'Can we move on to other matters now, sir?'

'Of course.'

Hartley's mind was already made up. He would go, even if it was a trap, and even if the Head Man wouldn't allow it. He couldn't let Royce down. He wouldn't be able to live with himself.

'I don't believe this, Hugh.'

'I'm sorry, darling, but you know how it is.'

'You said work was quiet at the moment. "Soporific", even.'

'Well, I'm afraid it's no longer that. You know I'd much rather be in Scotland with you.'

'I'm beginning to find that hard to believe. When you came back to London, you said there wouldn't be any more trips. "It's just a desk job," you said. "They're either easing me into retirement or preparing me for the big one." Do you remember?'

'I do.'

'You also said that the closest you'd get to Germany was drinking their wine.'

Hartley nodded. There was no point in

interrupting Sarah when she was in the middle of one of her verbal assaults. He had been the victim of them on numerous occasions but this was a particularly bad one. And it was justified: she had been looking forward to this holiday for months.

'How long are you going to be away?'

Hartley didn't know, but he had to give her an answer. 'A week, maybe ten days. We could go up to Scotland as soon as I get back.'

'But it's all booked, Hugh! You know it's a popular time of year. The Mackinnons have other people staying after us.'

'We'll find somewhere else.'

'Where?'

'Glenelg?'

'With whom?'

'We could stay at the pub.'

'It's not quite the same, is it?'

'It'll be fine.'

'You always say that when you know perfectly well that it won't. And I can't stand staying in pubs.'

'All right. I'll find somewhere nice, I promise.'

'How? You're going to bloody Germany. Will you book it from there?'

Hartley didn't reply.

'So, as usual, it'll be me who'll have to run around trying to find somewhere.'

She was right.

'I'm sorry,' he said. 'There's really nothing I can do. You know I wouldn't go if it wasn't important.'

'Future of the free world again, is it?'

'Something like that.'

'If you don't go we'll all be speaking Russian by next week, I suppose.'

Hartley smiled. '*Da*.'

'Ha-bloody-ha. Well, it'd better be important, because at the moment, given the choice between the whole country speaking Russian and us going on holiday, I know which I'd prefer. Christ, Hugh! Have you seen the papers? Half the bloody country wants us to be ruled from Moscow as it is.'

'I'm aware of that.'

'So where does that leave you, eh? Who are you fighting for?'

'Please, Sarah, let's not get into that.'

Sarah put her hands on her hips. 'You *never* want to get into it.'

'Look,' said Hartley, 'this really will be the last time, I promise.'

'I find that very hard to believe, not least because I've heard it many times before.'

'I know – but you must believe me when I say I really wouldn't go if I could help it.'

'Why doesn't your deputy go? Isn't that what deputies are for?'

'He's not experienced enough. They need an old hand.'

Sarah threw her arms into the air in a gesture of hopelessness. She sat on the sofa and picked up the copy of *Country Life* she had read the week before. 'Hadn't you better go and pack?' she asked.

Hartley left the room, tail wedged firmly between his legs. He felt awful. At one point he had almost surrendered to her. If Royce was so far round the bend, there was little anyone could do for him. The whole idea was reckless, foolhardy. It was a trip from which he might never come back – he could spend the rest of his days locked up in some prison in Berlin, never to see Sarah again, never to see the boys get married, give him grandchildren. But he owed Royce. He had abandoned him, and now he was going back for him. It was as simple as that.

Hartley went into his study at the top of the house, a retreat from family bustle. The room held nothing particularly sensitive – all such papers were kept at work – but there was the odd memento: East German currency, Soviet magazines, photographs, even a dried flower given to him by a German girl, Ingrid Hoffmann, one of his best agents. She had been shot in 1957, a loss from which Hartley had never quite recovered. He had loved her – not in a way that would have threatened Sarah, more as a daughter or younger sister.

Hartley stood in front of the bookcase and took out a hardback copy of *Bleak House*. He still hadn't read it, and neither was he about to. He opened it, and took out the West German passport that was tucked between its pages. It was in the name of Manfred Schmidt, an industrialist from Hamburg, who had been born on the same day as Hartley, and who bore a more than striking resemblance to him.

'Hello, Manfred,' said Hartley. 'It's time we had another trip together.'

He sat at his bureau and opened a drawer, scrabbled around and brought out two more West German passports, which were blank.

Holland was apoplectic, as Hartley had known he would be. The two men were strolling through Regent's Park, Holland carrying his habitual tightly bound umbrella, which Hartley had never seen him open.

'Sir, I really would advise you to think again. It could be a trap.'

'I shall be careful, Holland. I know what I'm doing. You must think this is the whim of an old man, but I assure you it runs deeper than that.'

'But what are you going to say to the Head Man?'

'That I'm going fishing in Scotland.'

Holland was speechless.

'There's really no reason why he needs to know

what I'm up to. This is a private matter and, besides, I'll be going there on my leave.'

'And your wife?'

'Thinks I'm going on a job. It's quite simple, Holland.'

'You do realise you're asking a lot of me, sir?'

'I thought there was no point in lying to you, Holland. You'd have worked it out for yourself, anyway. If anything goes wrong, I'll leave a letter that explains to the Head Man what I was up to, and that you were in the dark. All right?'

'I suppose so.'

'Good.'

'One thing, sir.'

'Yes.'

'How do you plan to get him out?'

'Via Berlin. Our normal route for this sort of thing.'

'Yes. But what about the hospital – I mean the castle?'

'In case you'd forgotten, Holland, I know that place like the back of my hand. There are plenty of ways out of it.'

Holland didn't reply.

'Anyway, Holland, there are a few things I'd like you to do.'

Hartley reached inside his pocket and brought out the blank passports. 'Can you get David's lot to sort these out? One needs to be in the name of Carl

Bergmann, born on the fifth of July 1917 in Stuttgart. He's an electrical engineer and his address is Nachsommerweg forty-seven, Stuttgart. Married. Two children. The other needs to be in the name of Maria Klein, address Hohenheimer fifty-eight, also Stuttgart. Born on the eighth of May 1946. They both need entry stamps into the DDR dated for next week.'

'I assume one's for Royce. Who's the other for?'

'You'll see.'

Holland sighed. 'What are you going to do about photos?'

'I shall take one of the office Polaroid cameras.'

'All right, I'll do it. Is there anything else?'

Hartley grinned. 'It's very good of you to ask.'

'Call it misplaced loyalty.'

'Cheeky! I need two invitations to the Leipzig Trade Fair from our friends at Kombinat in Dresden. They'll need to be made out to myself as Schmidt and one for Herr Bergmann, both of us working for Hübers in Bonn.'

'I assume you don't want this to go via Mike.'

'Good God, no! Mike would have a fit if he knew I was paying a visit.'

The two men walked in silence. It was a pleasant afternoon, thought Hartley, bright, crisp.

'What about a drink?' said Hartley. 'You can wish me *bon voyage*.'

'I'd rather you weren't going on any *voyage* at all, sir.'

'At least you're honest, Holland. It's an admirable quality, although perhaps not useful in our profession.' Hartley's smile was a little forced. He had lied to Sarah, dragged Holland into the shit and was about to risk his neck – all for Royce. They would understand if he told them, but he couldn't.

'I will come back, you know,' he said, 'no doubt about it.'

He said it less for Holland's benefit than his own.

Chapter Seven

THEY ALWAYS LOOKED the bloody same, these people. Perhaps it was the peaked caps, or that their faces seemed to have been moulded in some sort of laboratory, but every East German border guard in Hartley's experience had been identical – cold eyes, thin lips, squashed noses, pugnaciously round faces. Like a bloody cartoon, thought Hartley. The specimen who had thrust himself through the open window of Hartley's Mercedes was no different.

'Papers.'

Hartley handed over his passport and his accreditation for the Leipzig Trade Fair. He had hired the Mercedes because he wanted to appear the model of West German capitalism, the type of figure despised in the East but whose money they didn't object to. Hartley wouldn't be the only businessman driving east over the next few days. Indeed, a few cars back he could see a large BMW – and was that a Jaguar?

The guard flicked through the papers, face impassive. Hartley wasn't worried, confident that the Schmidt alias was a good one. It was brand new, and he had a whole life set up for him in Hamburg. The Stasi could ring a woman who would swear she was his wife, ring a company who would say, yes, Herr Schmidt was indeed their chief electrical engineer. They could even get one of their agents to discover from his war records that he held a second-class Iron Cross won during the invasion of France. Nevertheless, the Service had to be careful: perfect records, especially in heavily bombed Germany, were always suspect, so there were engineered gaps in Schmidt's paper trail.

The guard walked off with his papers to a large cabin. This was no Checkpoint Charlie, thought Hartley. It was far more basic. He lit a cigarette – a Peter Stuyvesant – and stared blankly out of the window. Ahead of him lay the road to the south-east, blocked at the moment by a large barrier. He looked to left and right, at a network of fences, watchtowers and concrete tank traps. If the border with Switzerland had been like this in '41, he would never have stood a chance.

He threw the cigarette out of the window and reached for his briefcase on the back seat. He opened it, and brought out a copy of *Bleak House* in German – *Kahles Haus*. His progress with the German version was almost as slow as it had been with the English one. The briefcase also contained some engineering magazines, which Hartley had rendered suitably dog-eared, a selection of papers displaying data on various pieces of machinery and some business cards, in the name of Manfred Schmidt and others, whose owners could all testify that they had met Herr Schmidt – had it been in Munich or Düsseldorf? All these trade conventions were the same! Hartley glanced at his watch. It was half past two. On a good day he'd be away by four.

Four o'clock passed, as did five. Hartley was not worried, although plenty of cars behind him had been let through, including a succession of BMWs, Mercedes and even the Jaguar. There was another like him, a tall blond man in his late thirties, whom Hartley fancied was CIA but couldn't quite tell. He needed to exchange a few words with him to make sure, but not now. The men in the cabin would be watching for that – hoping for it, even. More than anything he wanted a cup of coffee, but there wasn't a cafe for ten kilometres. Besides, the diuretic effect meant he would have to ask to use a lavatory, which the guards often took pleasure in denying. The cigarettes would see him through.

He could imagine the phone calls. The checkpoint would ring the Stasi in Berlin, who would search through their voluminous card indexes. They did not have a computer yet, to the best of Hartley's knowledge. He was not a fan of such machines: the bloody things kept breaking down, losing information or giving out hogwash. The Stasi in Berlin might be cabling London, Washington and Moscow, and there would be a long wait for replies. Eventually, someone in Berlin would make an assessment, which would be telephoned to the checkpoint. Let him in and watch him. Let him in and detain him for further questioning. Don't let him in, but watch him. Whatever happened, as far as the Stasi was concerned, Manfred Schmidt would be an enemy of the state. He would have a file all to himself, and the card would soon fill with marks, observations, scraps. Chilling.

At half past five, the guard was in earshot, and Hartley wound down the window. Complaining would be in character for a West German businessman. Only the guilty would sit there without kicking up a fuss. 'Hey!' he shouted.

The guard ignored him.

'Hey! You!'

The guard turned his head.

'When are you going to let me through?'

No reply.

'I'm trying to do business with your country. This is no way to treat me.' Still no reply. Hartley knew that the very notion of 'business' meant nothing to him. 'The least you could do is to tell me how much longer.'

The guard remained rigid. Hartley shut the window angrily. He had not overdone the histrionics: bad acting was a sin, worse than doing nothing. It was so easy to spot, and a quick way to get yourself incarcerated. Since Colditz, Hartley had found it easy to act, perhaps disturbingly so. He often wondered whether there was something missing in him, some core part of his character that should have rebelled against changing who he was. In his experience, bad actors were usually strong characters, well defined. Did that make him weak? Was this just a way of proving something to himself? He liked to think he was doing his duty, but a small voice said it wasn't that. It was the longing for drama, action, danger that had dogged him since Colditz.

Hartley lit another cigarette, the sixth or seventh since he had arrived. The atmosphere in the car was becoming a little unpalatable, but there was nothing else to do. *Kahles Haus* had not held his attention, and the magazines were so stupendously boring he could not bear to read them a second time. Eventually the cabin door opened and a major stepped out. He walked slowly towards the car, making a note of its numberplate on a pad. He tapped on Hartley's window. 'Herr Schmidt?' His voice was friendly – too friendly?

Hartley rolled down the window. 'Yes?'

'I'm sorry to have kept you. It's a busy time for us, with the trade fair. Please accept our apologies.'

This was unusual. 'It's been nearly four hours!'

'I know,' said the major. 'And I'm afraid it'll be a little longer. We need to search your car.' He beckoned to two guards.

'Fine,' said Hartley. 'How long will it take? Another four hours?'

'No, no, Herr Schmidt. Five, perhaps ten minutes. It is just a formality. Surely you have been to East Germany before?'

This was a trap: Hartley's passport indicated that he had not. 'No, I haven't.'

The major's smile faded. 'Anyway, if you will get out of the car, please?'

Hartley opened the door and stepped out. It felt good to stretch his legs. The search did not concern him: the passports and the camera were embedded in the side panels of the front offside door. They would have to dismantle the car to find them, and Hartley knew that the East Germans could not do that to every vehicle that passed through.

The guards were thorough, good at their jobs. Hubcaps came off, mirrors were held under the chassis, even the radio was removed and replaced. They did not damage the car – like the best sort of interrogation, Hartley thought. Leave no marks.

'I hear the trade fair is quite an event,' said the major.

Small-talk, thought Hartley. Be careful. 'So I understand.' he said. 'I gather it's been going for centuries.'

'I wouldn't know about that. All I know is that it's very good for the Democratic Republic. It shows that we are a world leader.'

The poor deluded man, thought Hartley. There was no way he could reply honestly. 'Which is why I'm going,' he said. 'Your electronics are very advanced.'

'Is that so?'

'Oh, yes.'

The search appeared to be complete. The major reached into his tunic and took out Hartley's papers. 'Your passport and accreditation, Herr Schmidt. I hope you have a successful trip.'

'I'm sure I will,' said Hartley, as he took the documents.

He walked back to the car and started the engine. It coughed into noisy life, and soon he was away, passing through featureless countryside. The road quality was appalling – he always forgot this when he was at home. Constant inspection of his rear-view mirror hold him he wasn't being followed, at least not visibly, so he took the opportunity to pull into a small parking space.

It didn't take him long to find it, because they had planted it in the third place he suspected. The first was the boot, the second was under the bonnet, and the third was not so much inside the aerial but the aerial itself. They had done a good job in trying to make it look dirty, but there was no doubt that it was new and slightly thicker than the original one. As well as receiving radio signals, it broadcast a signal that meant he could always be located. Hartley smiled. No wonder they had made him wait so long: it must have taken them hours to find the right fit. There weren't too many Mercedes in the German Democratic Republic. Hartley got back into the car and drove off. Let them track him. He was going nowhere suspicious – at least, not in this car.

Hartley approached the outskirts of Leipzig just after eight o'clock. This was his fourth visit to the city since '41, and he had a fondness for the place that some would have found strange. It was your typical Sovbloc craphole, he thought, all concrete and grey, soulless and without hope. The occasional nineteenth-century building was still visible, doing its best to remind its inhabitants that the city hadn't always had such a dehumanising presence. There was even the odd church, and in the centre of the city, a fairly convincing re-creation of the central market area, which had been obliterated by the RAF and the

USAF. Hartley had made two great coups here – the escape from Colditz, and recruiting the Bulgarian General Obretonov.

The Inntourist hotel was located just north of the Tröndlinring, the ring road round the city centre. A typically charmless block, it reminded Hartley a little of the office, an irony that was not lost on him. He parked in its underground car park, where he noticed a plethora of other Western cars along with the odd Zil. He would be among plenty of fellow Westerners here. How many were being watched? All of them? It was possible. The Stasi was massive, these days, capable of anything. No doubt some would find themselves the targets of honeytraps and blackmail: tempted by attractive young women (and men), they would receive a set of black and white pornographic prints in which they played the leading role. It was a nasty business, but they used it in the Service too. There was no point in being moral about these things: to fight a dirty enemy, you had to get as dirty as he was, if not more so. It was how he had recruited Müllheim – they had used a boy they had found in Soho, given him a thousand pounds, and a month later he was dead, having spent it on drugs. The Head Man liked to say that Müllheim had probably saved many lives with his information, so they had made a 'profit'. Maybe, but Hartley still felt uneasy.

Hartley knew his room would be bugged so he

didn't bother to check it. He would say and do nothing
in it that would be of interest to the Stasi, so let the
buggers listen. The wiring was predictably atrocious,
and those bulbs that worked gave out only a feeble
light. The small bathroom was sordid: the basin was
cracked, if nearly clean, while the lavatory was seatless
with only a few sheets of rough paper beside it. Thank
God he had brought his own, and a plug for the bath.

After a quick wash, Hartley left the hotel and
headed for the city centre. He dodged the creaky light
blue trams on the Tröndlinring, and walked up the
Hainstrasse, an almost attractive street. He carried a
map, which he didn't need, and consulted it
frequently. Whoever was following him – and
someone must be – would surmise that he had never
been there before, which would fit with what he had
said at the border.

He reached the Markt – the central square – and
decided to sit down at the first café he came to. The
evening was relatively mild, and he deserved a drink
before supper. Besides, he wanted a look at whoever
was following him, partly out of curiosity but also to
see whether he had retained the ability to spot a tail.

'What would you like?' The waitress's face was
rather sour.

'A beer, please, Fräulein.'

'Is that all?'

'Yes.'

Hartley watched the passers-by. For the most part they looked happy – students arm in arm, a few middle-aged men laughing, the odd married couple – far from the stereotypical image of the East. It was the buildings that were grim, not the people – or, at least, not ninety per cent of them anyway. The service estimated the other ten per cent were Stasi informers, which meant that whenever two average families got together for lunch, at least one member of the party was an informer. It might even be one of the children, especially a teenager, perhaps forced into working for the Stasi because he had been discovered with the wrong sort of magazine, or a radio tuned to the West. He would have been informed on by someone in his housing block, and he in turn would inform on others, thereby continuing the Stasi's perfect hold on the country's own people.

The beer arrived and tasted better than he had expected, although he would have preferred a West German lager. He sat back and continued his search for his tail. After a few minutes, a female student walked past. Hartley noticed that she was wearing a pair of jeans and carrying a large handbag over her right shoulder. She was keeping it as still as possible. Smile, he thought, you're on camera. His impish side wanted to raise a glass to the concealed lens, but the fact that he had detected his surveillance would mark him out as a spy. So that was number one, he thought. There would be at least three more.

He spotted numbers two and three almost immediately. A young couple – their arms were linked but their faces were expressionless. Hartley made eye-contact with the man, then looked away slowly, as if he had merely been observing his surroundings.

Five minutes later he finished his beer, a little frustrated. There should be another tail. He looked around him. The man with the beard next to him or the fellow with the large moustache (perhaps not: face too distinctive)? Maybe the two young women who had sat down a few minutes after him (again, perhaps not, one of the girls was noticeably pretty). Hartley left some change on the table and stood up. The waitress came across and picked up the money.

'Fräulein, is there anywhere nice to eat on the square?'

'You'll be wanting Auerbach's,' she said, and pointed to the other side of the square.

'It's in a cellar over there. You can't miss it.'

'There?' asked Hartley, pointing.

'Yes. You can just see the sign.'

'Thank you, Fräulein,' said Hartley. He had known she would say Auerbach's, but he had to give the impression that he was a newcomer. He had been going there anyway because he had a reservation – or, rather, an appointment.

*

The entrance to Auerbach's was under an ornate arch. Hartley had been there twice before, and it was the best place to eat behind the Iron Curtain. It was always busy, stuffed with Party men and their mistresses by night, Party men and their families by day. He walked down a large staircase, his ears already detecting the sounds of merriment. He opened one of two large doors and walked into a vast cellar, its lighting subdued, its volume anything but.

'Good evening, sir.'

This waitress was rather more charming than the one who had served him the beer.

'Do you have any spare tables?' Hartley asked. 'I'm on my own.'

The waitress consulted a large sheet of paper on a lectern. 'You're in luck. We're very busy with the fair at the moment.'

Hartley started to take off his coat. He had known there would be a spare table because it was for him. The waitress took his coat and hung it on a large rack. Hartley noticed numerous peaked caps, indicating a vast variety of uniforms.

'This way, please.'

She led him past table after table of bigwigs stuffing themselves. The food looked hearty, and reminded Hartley that he had not eaten properly all day. Occasionally someone glanced at him, but here he was just another businessman from the West – there were plenty like him at this time of year. Auerbach's was the only place they came to – it was the only place they would want to go to.

'Here you are.'

Hartley sat at his table and the waitress walked away. A single candle flickered gently in front of him, reminding him of his solitude. Normally Sarah would have been on the other side of it, not a room full of ugly East Germans. He should have been in Scotland with her, having dinner with the Mackinnons, perhaps enjoying some salmon they had caught that day. Still, he would make it up to her. He had promised, and he would deliver.

He looked down the extensive menu and decided on the veal shank. By East German standards it cost a fortune – perhaps two weeks' wages for the average worker – but judging by the tables around him, it was going down well. That's what he hated so much about this country: the hypocrisy. It was not a workers' state in which every man could have his shank of veal. He'd be lucky if he had beef five or six times a year, let alone veal. Instead, he would eat a sausage of dubious origin that his wife had bought after queuing for a few hours. It was a pathetic way to run a country, thought Hartley, and he found it hateful, despicable. It was the type of regime he had fought against, yet here it had been imposed by people who had been their allies. What had they fought for?

The veal was good, the Saxon wine less so – too flimsy – but it was the best on offer. He noticed a lot of vodka being knocked back, and over the course of his meal, the surrounding tables grew drunker and noisier. The table that intrigued him was almost immediately opposite: two West German businessmen (clearly so – the suits, the shoes) were having the time of their lives with two attractive young women. Stasi girls, thought Hartley. He would have liked to warn the two men of what they were getting into but of course, he couldn't. He lit a cigarette. Anyway, they weren't children. If they wanted to cheat on their wives, then it was their own funeral. He had never cheated on Sarah, and never would.

'Have you finished?'

Hartley looked up at the waitress.

'Yes. It was very good.'

'Pudding?'

'No, thank you.'

'That's a shame. I've a friend who would love to share some with you.'

Here we go, thought Hartley. The obvious approach to the seemingly smashed West German businessman. Well, let them try.

'And who is your friend?' asked Hartley, raising an eyebrow.

'She's lonely.'

'Well, I'm a little lonely too.'

The waitress grinned. 'So, can she join you?'

'Of course. Tell her she'll be more than welcome.'

The waitress returned about a minute later with a strikingly tall brunette – in her late twenties, thought Hartley. She was obviously another Stasi girl, because women like her were never lonely. Her make-up was crude but effective – bright red lipstick, too much mascara, blue eye-shadow.

'May I join you, Herr . . .'

'Schmidt, Manfred Schmidt,' said Hartley, standing up.

He gestured to the girl that she should take the chair next to him, rather than opposite.

'What would you like to drink?'

'A glass of champagne.'

Hartley was impressed. 'I didn't think there was any in the German Democratic Republic.'

'You just have to know the right people.'

'And do you know the right people?'

'That's what I'm trying to find out,' she said coquettishly.

Hartley caught the eye of the waitress and ordered a bottle of champagne.

'French or German?' she asked.

'German champagne? I don't think so. It had better be French.'

'Certainly.'

'So,' said the girl, 'what brings you to Leipzig?'

Hartley leant forward conspiratorially. 'You do,' he said.

'Me?'

'Of course, my little Sparrow.'

The girl grinned. 'It's good to meet you at last,' she said, 'although I think you'd better call me Heidi this evening.'

Hartley knew perfectly well that her name was Christa Gussveld. She had been born in Leipzig on 3 June 1946, had studied medicine at the local university but never graduated. The Stasi had seen to that because she had bloody-mindedly asked if she could go on holiday to West Germany. 'If we are so free,' she asked, 'why can I not go where I please?' They had marked her card and after that, she found that, no matter how hard she studied, no matter how well she thought she had done in her exams, she always failed. One day, she was ushered into the Stasi headquarters at the Round Corner, and was introduced to a perfectly pleasant major, who told her in a perfectly pleasant way that she was required to become friendly with a visiting British business-man, and that if she got friendly enough, she would earn her degree. And if she did not? She would never get a job, which, as Fräulein Gussveld knew, was breaking the law, and if she broke the law she would go to prison, and if she went to prison her family would be disgraced, her widowed mother would lose her job as a cleaner, and her little brother would have no hope of going to university. Christa had had no choice, and the following week she had found herself in the arms of a British businessman called Mark Lello, who was not a businessman at all but a member of the Service. For the past five years Christa, now armed with her medical degree, had been a double agent – Heidi to the Stasi, Sparrow to the Service.

'So, Heidi, how have you been?'

'Very well, thank you, Herr Schmidt. It's a pleasure to meet a man I never knew existed until earlier this week.'

Hartley shrugged. 'Well, there's no point in you—'

'Don't worry, I know how it works. Does Mark know you're here?'

Hartley shook his head. 'No,' he said. 'I am here on my own.'

Christa frowned. 'Really?'

'Keep smiling, Heidi,' said Hartley. 'Whoever's watching us will want to think you're doing a good job.'

A rictus grin spread over her face.

'With your eyes as well, Heidi,' said Hartley. 'Smile like you mean it.'

Christa let out a genuine laugh.

'Good,' said Hartley. 'No, I'm afraid Mark doesn't know because this is a private matter.'

'You're taking a great risk,' said Christa. 'The man at the asylum must be very important to you.'

Hartley tried not to look uneasy. 'He's very important. There's not much more I can say.'

'Well,' she said, touching his nose with her forefinger, 'I'm always happy to help.'

'Thank God my wife's not here,' said Hartley.

'They all say that,' said Christa, and they laughed.

'Do you really want some pudding, or is that the normal chat-up line in these parts?'

'Of course I do!' said Christa. 'You don't think I eat here every night, do you?'

They maintained the charade for the next hour, making fake small-talk and working their way through the champagne. Hartley enjoyed himself, and forgot for a dangerously long time that he was on a job. When he remembered, he cursed himself. He had been in plenty of situations like this with women, but none had been as attractive as Christa. He didn't need to pretend that he was attracted to her, and had to remind himself that her flirtation was for the benefit of their spectators. He found himself wondering whether she would have flirted with him anyway, but dismissed the thought as the musing of a dirty old man. She was more Christopher and Tom's age than his.

They left the restaurant arm in arm, Christa giving him an occasional peck on the cheek for good measure. Whoever was watching them would have no doubt that a West German businessman had fallen head first into the honeytrap.

'Let's walk a little,' said Hartley.

'Sure,' said Christa, 'but not for too long. It's not very warm.'

They walked across the Markt, which was almost empty. Hundreds of black windows surrounded them, reminding Hartley of the night at Colditz in which Royce had tried to kill himself. It was strange to know he was only a few miles away, languishing in some God-awful psychiatric ward, poor bugger.

'How did you find out about Royce?'

'My real job,' said Christa. 'One of the nurses at the hospital told me that a friend of hers is a nurse at Colditz. This nurse had to look after an Englishman, and thought it a little odd.'

'How did she know he was English?'

'Because he spoke English in his sleep, or when he was drugged.'

'How did you find out his name?'

'In the registry here in Leipzig. All psychiatric patients come under our jurisdiction at the general hospital.'

'So his file was listed under his English name?'

'No,' said Christa, 'a German name – Helmut

Knopf. But in the file, under aliases, it says "Malcolm Royce".'

It seemed extraordinary to Hartley that the English name was on the medical file. Could it be a genuine slip-up?

'What else did the file say?'

'Not much. He'd only just been admitted, transferred from Berlin.'

'Are you sure?'

'Absolutely.'

It was clearly a trap. He was a fool for coming here. Royce was probably dead, and had been for over three decades. Someone in the Stasi had found out about Hartley's wartime exploits and used them to tempt him over. Why didn't they pounce on him now? Because he had done nothing wrong. The Stasi wanted to maintain an outward show of playing under the rule of law, even if it had been created and moulded for their convenience. He should drive back to the West tomorrow, and forget about this business. He could be in London by tomorrow night, hand in his resignation to the Head Man, then fly with Sarah to Scotland. Balls to the Service, balls to all these childish games.

'What's the matter, Herr Schmidt?'

'Nothing,' said Hartley. 'I'm just turning things over. I assume there's no photograph on his file.'

'No,' said Christa. 'You think it's not the man you're looking for?'

'I can't be sure. There's only one way to find out.'

'How?'

'I've got to go there.'

'But they've got a whole team on you!'

'Then I'll have to give them the slip.'

'But how are you going to do that?'

Hartley's expression was rather more condescending than he had intended. 'It's my job,' he said. 'Getting away from people is what I do.'

Christa hugged his arm, drawing herself into him.

'And how are you going to get rid of me this evening?'

Did she mean it, or was it part of the charade? He didn't reply, because he didn't know what to say.

'They'll expect things to happen tonight,' she said.

'And if nothing does?'

'I'll get into trouble.'

'Christ! What have they got?'

'A camera in the broken ceiling fan. A bug in the headboard.'

'No surprises, then.'

Hartley knew that many middle-aged men would kill to be in his shoes – forced to have sex with a beautiful woman to keep his and her cover. But betray Sarah?

'What are they expecting from me?'

'They tell me you're an electrical engineer. They want to know all about your business, whom you work for, whether you work for the British and American military.'

'Well, I can certainly give you something.'

'Oh, yes?'

'I'll tell them we're working on a new missile for the French.'

Christa paused.

'Is it true?'

'Sort of.'

She stopped. 'You're married, aren't you?'

'Yes.'

'We don't have to . . . you know . . .'

'But what about you?'

'I can say that you were too drunk. We can just lie in bed together. That would be all right, wouldn't it?'

Hartley chewed his bottom lip. 'We'll have to kiss, though,' he said.

'Nobody is too drunk for that.'

Hartley nodded. 'All right.'

Hartley gripped Christa's arms and kissed her. When he broke off he said, 'Don't take this the wrong way, but I feel wretched.'

Christa giggled. 'It must be a terrible burden to kiss a woman like me.'

'Waltraut would kill me . . .'

Christa giggled louder. 'Waltraut? Your wife is called Waltraut?'

'I'm afraid so.' Hartley let out a small laugh. It was easier to pretend he was being unfaithful to a Prussian baggage called Waltraut. He could see her now, a buxom Nordic hammer-thrower, a panzer of a woman. Christa came forward and kissed him again. He could taste her lipstick, scented and cheap. Kisses with Sarah were affectionate, but not like these. He wanted to give in to his desires, to go with what his body wanted, but he had to stop himself. He was a drunken West German businessman.

He made a great play of falling back on to the bed. Although he was not a heavy man, the bed must have taken a lot of punishment over the years, because an almighty crack signalled its demise. He found the two sides folding in on him, and gazed up at Christa as though from a ravine.

Christa howled with laughter, as did Herr Schmidt. For once, he didn't need to act.

For appearances' sake, Hartley spent much of the next day at the trade fair, hours wandering the stands, fabricating enthusiasm for machinery and electronics. He joked with many an East German factory supervisor, took the telephone numbers of many firms, and was weighed down with product-information sheets, some of which were for hopelessly outdated articles. It was always good to remind oneself of how technologically backward the East was, Hartley thought. It gave one hope. Nevertheless, he knew well enough that the technology he saw here was not representative of what the Sovbloc countries were making secretly – the weaponry, the espionage devices. Many examples had crossed his desk and were vastly more sophisticated than what was available in the West.

He left the fair just before four, negotiating his Mercedes along the pot-holed roads. He would have thought, with the number of international visitors, that the East Germans would have made more effort with the routes they knew the foreigners would use. Perhaps they had forgotten, or perhaps they just didn't have the money and the materials. As he drove to the hotel, he monitored his rear-view mirror. Sure enough, there were three cars behind him, one of which was a light blue Trabant. It had followed him that morning, and it would be hard to shake off, but he didn't need to do so yet.

To no great surprise, he noticed that his room had been searched. His suitcase had been rifled, and although an attempt had been made to replace the contents exactly as he had left them, there were slight deviations. His clothes too had been searched, no doubt X-rayed. Thank God he had nothing to hide – at least, not in the room.

He took a bath; the water was nearly warm and smelt of chlorine – he might as well have gone to a

swimming-pool. Then he dried himself, and shaved.
He dressed in an East German's idea of casual clothes
– pleated cream trousers, a grey shirt and a synthetic
green jacket. He looked at himself in the cracked
mirror on the wardrobe door. It was an awful
combination, right down to the grey plastic slip-on
shoes. Why did Germans have such bad taste? The
finishing touch was a pair of blue-tinted sunglasses,
which he would never have dreamt of wearing under
normal circumstances, but now they helped to create
the right effect. He slipped his passport into his jacket,
along with his wallet, all his money, a penknife and a
packet of cigarettes. He looked round the room,
knowing he would never see it again. The
chambermaid was welcome to his clothes.

He stepped out and walked down the long brown
corridor to the staircase. There was nobody behind
him, but all of the hotel's exits were covered. Hartley
walked slowly down the five flights of stairs to the
underground car park, gathering his thoughts. What
he was about to do was risky, perhaps absurdly so,
but with any luck he would be back in West Germany
by daybreak. A lot could go wrong, but much might
go right. He had the fluttery feeling in his chest that
he had experienced on the night he had escaped from
Colditz. Well, now he was going back.

Hartley unlocked the car door and sat down. Eyes
darting between the mirrors, he removed a piece of

panelling from the car door and removed the passports. He also took out the Polaroid camera, which was bulky but would fit inside his jacket pocket. Then he started the car and drove out of the car park, heart beating hard and fast. He took a couple of deep breaths, then pulled into the line of traffic heading east.

Hartley drove slowly, but not too slowly. He smiled as he saw the same light blue Trabant slip into the sparse line of traffic two cars behind him. Good. He drove for a quarter of an hour, keeping within the speed limit and attempting no sudden manoeuvres. Block upon block of concrete passed him, relentless in its drab uniformity.

A few minutes later, he pulled to the side of the road next to a block of flats. He got out of the car and watched the blue Trabant pass him, then walked to the front of the car and opened the bonnet. They would think he had broken down. He removed the distributor cap and took out the rotor arm – no bigger than half a cigarette – and slipped it into his trouser pocket. He slammed the bonnet.

Then he lit a cigarette and looked about him. A few curious faces had appeared at windows, and passers-by stared at him with bewilderment. It was not often that a Mercedes broke down outside their block of flats. As far as Hartley could tell, he was not being followed, but it would not be long before the blue Trabant had turned round, radioing his position back to headquarters at the Round Corner. The passenger in the Trabant would doubtless get out to follow him on foot, and Hartley had to beat him or her to it.

He walked under the entrance arch to the block of flats where a faint odour of urine assaulted his nostrils. Some brave graffiti, 'Fuck Milch', complemented the seedy atmosphere. Milch was the head of the Stasi – whoever had daubed that obviously had a death wish. Hartley emerged into a small courtyard, and looked up to see more faces staring down at him – far too many. Over to his right another arch led to another courtyard. He had clearly entered a concrete maze, which suited him.

For the next ten minutes, Hartley walked round the housing estate. Sometimes he would emerge on to an aerial walkway, at others he was submerged in underpasses. He never seemed to get anywhere, as though he was stuck in an Escher painting. As far as he could tell, nobody was following him, but there was no way he was going to rest on an assumption. Even if he was stopped, he had the perfect alibi – his car had broken down, and he was looking for a telephone.

A few minutes later, Hartley came on to a main road with a tramline running down it. Ideal. He ran to the tram stop, and joined a group largely composed of teenagers. He received no more than a few cursory glances, although one asked him for a light, which he gave. The tram arrived a few minutes later, and Hartley boarded it. He took a seat at the back and watched out of the window to see if he was being followed. Still nothing. None of his fellow passengers appeared to be tails either, and Hartley took heart that he had been the last to arrive at the tram stop.

The vehicle screeched and rumbled down the road. As each yard passed, Hartley's confidence grew. So far, things were going according to plan. Around him, teenagers were laughing and flirting, although the rest of the passengers looked sour. What were they thinking? They were the same faces he had seen thirty years ago, thin and abused. They had merely exchanged one regime for another. In fact, under Hitler they had been better off, at least before the war had started. It felt troubling to think that he had spent his whole life fighting regimes like this, to free people, like the old woman over there, to see their cousins in the West. He had failed. These people were still captives, and his efforts had made no difference – escaping from Colditz, joining MI9, then the Service. And now he was playing chase again. But at least he was doing it for a tangible reason rather than an abstract notion.

The tram drew into the city centre at a quarter to seven. Hartley stepped off, looking briefly left and right. The streets were nearly empty, there being nothing to entice the average Leipziger. Hartley removed the sunglasses and put them into his top pocket, then walked purposefully down a side-street. He turned left, left again, and then once more, until he was back where he had started. No one was following him, either ahead or behind. He was as sure now as he possibly could be.

The hospital was miserable compared to one in the West. The walls were damp and peeling, although large, garish paintings showed heroic doctors tending old women and children in a sunbathed Communist paradise.

The entrance atrium was just busy enough for Hartley's purposes. While the crones at the enquiries and admissions desk dealt with a queue of people Hartley slipped past and made his way to the lift doors, one of which was open. He briefly consulted a metal plate that listed all the departments and pressed a button.

Nothing happened. The lift was clearly out of order. He stepped out and pressed the call button, hoping that no one would question him. For half an agonising minute he waited for 'Hey, you!' but none came. The next lift arrived and he stepped in, hoping it would do its job.

It seemed to take an inordinately long time to reach

the third floor – it was slower than climbing the stairs. He walked out of the lift, glancing about for any human presence. There was none. The corridor was silent, but for an electrical hum coming from the ceiling. Hartley noticed that the green lino was peeling, and that dirt lined the area where it had once met the wall. This hospital would make you feel worse, thought Hartley.

He consulted a large, hand-painted wooden sign, and found the department he was looking for – Paediatrics. He walked briskly in the direction the arrow told him, occasionally turning his head to inside wards and offices. A few nurses saw him go past, but barely registered him. Invisibility was the trick. The ideal agent was the one nobody noticed. Grey hair, medium build, a pair of glasses were the ideal attributes.

A sign hung down from the ceiling, informing Hartley that Paediatrics was to the left. He entered a depressing room, decorated in the same green as the lino. The ward was filled with at least twenty beds, each of which contained a child. They looked up at him, then slumped back, disappointed. Some were in a terrible way – pale, disturbingly thin. It was heartbreaking. One boy reminded him of when Christopher had had malaria, his face white and sweaty for days.

'Hello?'

The nurse had appeared as if from nowhere, catching Hartley temporarily off-guard.

'Hello.'

'Who are you looking for?'

'Dr Gussveld?'

'Dr Gussveld?'

'That's right.'

'And who are you?'

'Professor Manfred Schmidt. I was one of her tutors at the university.'

The nurse smiled. 'Are you a paediatrician?'

'Radiology. Unfortunately I lost Fräulein Gussveld to the children!'

'Well, that's no bad thing. Dr Gussveld is in the office over there.'

'Thank you,' said Hartley, his smile perhaps a little too insincere.

Hartley walked over to a door made largely of frosted glass and marked 'Duty Doctor'. He knocked.

'Come in.'

He turned the handle and walked into a small office. Christa looked up, her face showing her astonishment.

'Hello, Dr Gussveld.'

'Well,' she said, 'what a lovely surprise.'

'I was walking past and thought, why don't I see if my favourite pupil is around? And here she is!'

Christa gave him a fierce stare. 'It's . . . er . . . good to see you.'

'I was thinking it might be nice to have coffee in the canteen,' said Hartley, 'for old times' sake.'

His face told her she was in no position to refuse. She glanced at her watch. 'Well, I suppose I could spare you twenty minutes.'

'I'm flattered.'

Christa put down her pen and stood up. Hartley grabbed it and scribbled: 'I need a white coat.' He screwed it up and put it into his pocket. Christa nodded, walked to a cupboard and opened it. It contained medical apparel, including a somewhat dirty doctor's white coat. She passed it to him, and Hartley draped it over his forearm.

'It's so nice of you to pop in,' said Christa.

'I thought so,' said Hartley, as they stepped out of the room. 'I haven't seen you in far too long.'

Christa exchanged a few words with the nurse, who smiled knowingly at Hartley, no doubt thinking he had come to see the good Dr Gussveld for all the wrong reasons. They walked out of the ward, Hartley nodding at a little boy on the way.

'What is wrong with him?' asked Hartley, as they went down the corridor.

'He's got leukaemia.'

'Can you do anything for him?'

'No. Could you?'

'I wouldn't know. I don't think so.'

They walked in silence to the lift. Once they were

in it, Christa turned on him. 'What the hell is this all about? Why the white coat? What are you doing here?'

'I need your help.'

'Oh, really?'

'Yes.'

'You could have warned me.'

'I had no choice, and no time. I want you to come to Colditz with me.'

The lift door opened to reveal a policeman's uniform. Hartley's heart leapt, but then he noticed the flowers in the man's hands. He steered Christa towards the main door.

'I'm not coming,' she said,

'I'm afraid you are,' said Hartley.

They stepped outside and walked down a series of shallow concrete steps.

'This is madness!' she said.

'Be quiet,' he said. 'You'll be back here in a few hours.'

Hartley carried on walking and, despite her complaints, Christa kept pace with him. 'What are you going to do?' she asked.

'We'll drive to Colditz and pick up Herr Royce.'

'And what if I say no?'

'You can't, can you? I'm your superior, Christa, remember that.'

'Are you threatening me?'

'Certainly not.'

It was a lie, and they knew it. He hated what he was doing, but he had done worse. Spying wasn't a gentlemanly business. It was for nasty little men, and Hartley was having to be just that.

'Where's your car?' she asked.

'I don't have one any more.'

'What happened to it?'

'It broke down.'

'But I don't have one either, so how are we going to get to Colditz? There won't be any trains at this time.'

Hartley smiled. 'There is nothing in this world quite so easy to steal as a good old East German Trabant.'

Hartley found his victim down a side-street. He sidled up alongside it, and wrenched at the driver's door. Although it was locked, it gave way easily. He got in, and sat down, then unlocked the passenger door for Christa.

'How are you going to start it?'

Hartley removed a penknife from his pocket and inserted it in the ignition.

'Shouldn't you have a key?'

'I don't need one,' said Hartley, and twisted the penknife sharply to the right. The two-stroke, two-cylinder engine coughed noisily, then went silent. Hartley twisted the penknife again, and the engine let out a couple more coughs. Then he turned the

penknife and held it until the coughing transformed.
He grinned. 'Bingo?' he said.

'Bingo?'

'Don't worry,' said Hartley, crunching the car into
what he assumed was first gear, 'I'll explain everything
one day.'

'Everything?'

'Well, not quite.'

Hartley guided the noisy little car out of the parking
space, the view in his mirror obscured by a cloud of
light brown smoke. Like mustard gas, he thought.

'Have you been to Colditz before?' Christa asked.

'Just once. And I've always wanted to go back.'

Chapter Eight

HARTLEY TOOK THE Dresden road out of the city, heading south-east. Colditz was a good fifty kilometres away, and he estimated that the journey would take over an hour, which meant they would arrive in Colditz at around nine o'clock. The Trabant was worse than he had remembered from previous experiences: at the slightest incline it felt as if it needed pedal power. For the first ten minutes, Christa kept looking back, but Hartley reassured her that they had not been followed.

When they left the city, Hartley fished around in his jacket pocket, then pulled out a packet of cigarettes and a lighter. He passed them to Christa. 'Do you want one?' he asked.

'No, thanks. I'm a doctor, remember?'

'Could you light me one?'

'You've got to be joking!'

Hartley took a cigarette out of the packet and lit it. Smoke filled the car and Christa opened the window.

'Sorry,' said Hartley, 'I'm a hopeless addict.'

She coughed.

He hadn't expected Christa to be quite so appalled by his smoking, but he needed the cigarette – he really was a hopeless addict, and he was nervous.

The road worsened as they drove, and Hartley swerved violently to avoid pot-holes that would have destroyed the Trabant. The fuel was running low, but he estimated they had just enough to reach their destination. As the flat countryside crawled past, he recalled the train journey he had made with Royce so many years ago. It had seemed so innocent, like a great game of goodies and baddies – at least until Royce was shot. He wondered what had happened to the Luftwaffe officer with whom they had shared their carriage on the train. It was most likely that he had died, his Me-109 blown to pieces on the eastern front. If he was alive, what then? Would he be keeping his anti-Jewish feelings to himself, telling his generation that he for one had nothing against the Jews, that it was all the work of the diehard Nazis, and besides, they only knew about the transports and the camps after the war? No one knew about them, thought Hartley, no one saw the trains, no one saw the ghettoes being razed, no one heard of Jews disappearing, no one saw a thing. Of course they didn't. The same thing was happening here and now, even in the village a few miles over there to the right, the same process of complicity and denial. What would happen if the regime collapsed? What then? Would it be the same as after the war?

Hartley lit another cigarette. There was no way to tell what would happen, no way to guess. Besides, the idea of the regime collapsing was too fantastical. All he and the service had done was to weakly scratch the surface, dressing up the occasional intelligence coup as a major blow in the cold war against the Warsaw Pact countries. It was almost pathetic what they had achieved, feeble. Did that make his life a farce, something to be mocked? All that promise as a young man, and now what? What did he have to show? Very little. He should have done something decent with his time, rather than pissing it up a rope playing spies. Because it was just another game, no more of a game than what he and Royce had done. That young man was a better man than he.

'We should turn off here,' said Christa.

Hartley looked at the road sign: Grimma, Grossbothen and Colditz. It still existed. It wasn't just locked in the past, or dreamt up by film-makers, it was there, painted in black on a white sign. He turned right. Colditz was drawing him back, insisting that he should be inside its walls.

The road through the countryside was empty, and even Christa appeared to relax. At one point, they drove under a railway bridge, which Hartley knew carried the line that he and Royce had taken from Leisnig to Leipzig.

'What are we going to do when we get there?' Christa asked.

'We're going to drive up to the castle and ask to see Royce.'

'And what if they won't let us in?'

'Then we'll find another way,' said Hartley.

'How?'

'There are plenty of entrances into the castle.'

'How do you know?'

It hadn't occurred to Hartley that Christa had no idea he had been imprisoned in it. Should he tell her? Why not? It would do no harm.

'I was a prisoner here,' he said, 'during the war.'

'The castle was a prisoner-of-war camp?'

'Yes. Didn't you know?'

'I thought it had always been a mental hospital.'

'It's famous in Britain as a POW camp. It was special – for naughty boys.'

'And that was what you were?'

Hartley laughed a little. 'Yes. Some would say I still am.'

There was just enough light to see it. The Trabant crested a small hill, and there, perched a couple of miles across the valley, was the castle. Hartley pulled in to the side of the road, the wheels of the Trabant sinking into the soft verge.

'What are you doing?' asked Christa.

'I won't be a minute.'

Hartley stepped out of the car. The *Schloss* was still just as sludge-brown grey as Hartley remembered it, but it seemed smaller. Perhaps it was the distance. It wasn't small, but it lacked its earlier menace. As he sank back into the car, he felt almost disappointed. He found first gear and drove off, the wheels spinning on the mud.

The town was as Hartley remembered it. It was still small, although a few new concrete blocks suggested that an attempt had been made at expansion. As they drove over the river, the castle reclaimed some of its wartime majesty – Hartley recalled walking across the same bridge with Royce all those years ago. There was the weir, looking just as it had then, like the one at school.

Hartley turned right after the bridge, aware of the castle on his left. His old friend was behind one of those windows. Hartley fancied that, of all the people in the world, only he would be able to rescue Royce. And it was right to try. But he still worried that he was walking into a trap. It had been too easy so far – but, then, sometimes it was. The Stasi was not omnipresent, despite its efforts. He had slipped through its tentacles now as he had on several occasions.

Above the noise of the engine, Hartley could hear a bell chiming. Once again, his heart leapt – it was the bell he had heard when he was imprisoned and the feelings he had experienced then flooded over him: claustrophobia, frustration, hopelessness, camaraderie . . . The bell came from a church in the town, and every quarter of an hour its peal had drifted up to the castle's walls.

'Are you all right?' Christa asked.

'What?'

'Are you all right? You seem distracted.'

She was right. It was time to snap back into his role, to stop wallowing self-indulgently in the past.

'Sorry,' he said, 'I'm trying to find the right road up to the castle.'

It took Hartley a few minutes to navigate the maze of cobbled streets to the entrance, but eventually he found the right one, and after a steep hairpin, he and Christa were outside the grey walls.

'Hello again,' Hartley said, under his breath.

They stepped out of the car and Hartley took in the jumble of the town's rooftops. Just the same, he thought. It was the one advantage of Communism: it preserved things in aspic.

Hartley half expected to see a couple of sentries standing outside the first gateway, but there was nobody, and they walked through the arch and over the bridge unhindered. The coat-of-arms was as he remembered it.

After the second gate, Hartley paused at a door on his right marked 'Reception'. 'We'd better do this by the book,' he said, and opened the door.

He went into a small office, where a fat woman sat wearing horn-rimmed glasses and a matron's uniform two sizes too tight for her. A thick fug of Trabant-like smoke emanated from a cigarette that dangled from her lower lip. What a sight, thought Hartley. Nevertheless, she was the gatekeeper, and she had to be charmed.

'Good evening, Fräulein.'

The woman nodded. 'Yes?' she asked suspiciously.

'My name is Dr Manfred Schmidt from Leipzig Hospital, and this is my assistant Dr Gussveld. We are here to see one of the patients.'

'Inmates, you mean.'

'I prefer to call them patients.' A real doctor would have exercised such authority, Hartley knew. Just act the part, and everything will fall into place.

'As you wish,' said the matron. 'Inmates, patients, it's all the same to me.'

Clearly the patients at Colditz Psychiatric Hospital were the recipients of the best and most sympathetic treatment, thought Hartley.

'Which one do you want?'

'Helmut Knopf,' said Hartley.

The woman spun a book on her desk through 180 degrees with a practised flourish. 'Sign here,' she said, pointing a fat yellow finger at the open page.

Hartley took a pen and scribbled. He passed it to Christa, who paused slightly. He wanted to tell her that it would be all right, that she would be out of the country in twenty-four hours, that it didn't matter if she left a trail. Christa signed, her handwriting as illegible as Hartley's.

'He's on the third floor, ward six.'

'Thank you, Fräulein.'

She grunted.

Hartley and Christa left the office and walked into the courtyard that had once belonged to the Kommandantur. A couple of nurses were walking towards them, chatting noisily.

'Do you know where the ward is?' Christa asked.

'No, but I'm sure we can work it out.'

Hartley walked in the direction the nurses had come from, towards the arch under the old Kommandantur building. He felt uneasy: he was walking through an area that had been forbidden to him thirty years ago. He looked up at the windows, expecting to see faces in the half-light, but there were none. The building was so quiet it might have been empty.

A spiral staircase presented itself to them. 'This is it,' said Hartley, and bounded up the steps two at a time. After they had climbed a floor and a half, he heard footsteps coming down the stairs, and paused. Once again, his imagination told him it would be a guard, but it was a young doctor, who wished them a good evening. To Hartley's relief, strange faces were obviously commonplace in Colditz. That had not been the case during the war.

At the third floor, Hartley's pulse was racing. This was it. He was about to set eyes on a man he had last seen a long time ago. He would have changed – perhaps he would be unrecognisable. He looked down a long corridor. A succession of thin strip-lights cast a sickly light over the green linoleum. The last vestiges of daylight crept in through the windows, but not enough to make the corridor look anything but unwelcoming.

He and Christa walked briskly down it. Somewhere a door slammed, and footsteps rushed into the distance. The wards were to their left, and Hartley glanced inside the first. The room was not large, and held only six beds, all of which were unoccupied. The second was the same, as were wards three and four.

'Do you think we're in the right place?' asked Christa.

'I'm not sure,' said Hartley.

Something was wrong. The whole place was too quiet, too empty. This was not a hospital. Hartley wanted to run back along the corridor, down the stairs and through the courtyard, then drive away in the Trabant. But he had to keep going. He couldn't turn back, not when he was so close. Ward five was empty.

He approached ward six slowly. He wanted a gun in his hand. He paused before the open door and listened. He heard nothing but the crackling of a loose electrical connection. He strained his ears and caught a low sound: someone breathing heavily, or perhaps sobbing. Royce?

Hartley edged forward and craned his head past the door frame. He looked into the room, which was dimly lit by a single bulb. All the beds were empty, except one. An old face, topped with a few wisps of grey hair, lay on a grey pillow. It was Royce. Hartley stepped into the ward, eyes focused on his old friend. He was skeletally thin, his eyes dark pools in a cadaverous face.

'Royce!'

Not a flicker passed over Royce's grey features. He breathed heavily, and his eyes were red, from tears or tiredness.

'Royce! Can you hear me?' Hartley shook him gently. He was so thin and so delicate. He lifted Royce's left arm and turned it over. Needle marks, and a new plaster. The man had been doped into a state of oblivion. He laid the arm gently on the bed, and bent so that his face was only inches from Royce's.

'Royce, it's Hartley,' he whispered. 'You must remember me. The Swiss border. You told me to leave you, and I did. Well, I've come back for you now, to take you home. Do you hear me?'

Hartley couldn't be sure what crossed Royce's face, but it might have been a smile. His mouth opened a little, like a crack forming on dry ground. A desiccated hiss issued through it that seemed to say, 'Hello, Hartley.' Then Royce grinned.

'You can hear me?'

A nod.

'I'm here to take you home.'

'Home?'

'That's right. Back to Britain.'

Hartley felt Christa move beside him. She was sniffing. 'What's the matter?' he asked.

A tear trickled down each of her cheeks, their progress almost symmetrical. 'He's my father,' she said.

At first, Hartley said nothing. It couldn't be true, he thought, as he watched her bend down and kiss Royce's forehead.

'Have you . . .' Hartley twisted off.

Christa turned her head. 'Yes, I have,' she said. 'I met him for the first time last month.' The tears were flowing now. 'I'm so sorry,' she said.

'Why?'

She closed her eyes. 'I've betrayed you.'

If Hartley's heart had been weaker, it would have stopped. 'Betrayed me?'

'Yes!'

She sounded almost hysterical.

'Look behind you!'

Hartley turned swiftly, and saw a man dressed in the uniform of a Stasi colonel standing in the door. He was smiling, his hands behind his back. Next to him two junior officers were pointing pistols into the room.

'Good evening, Colonel Hartley.'

For a moment Hartley said nothing, his brain whirling. Christa was Royce's daughter, a woman he had trusted, and she had been used to lure him to his capture.

'You stupid idiot,' he said calmly, as he gazed into the colonel's eyes.

They must have blackmailed her – help us snare Hartley and your father will be all right. Given the same choice, Hartley knew he would have put family before country and politics.

'I'm so sorry,' she sobbed.

'Don't apologise,' he replied. 'I understand.'

He had been a fool – he had been played along brilliantly. They had known he would come for Royce. It had been simply a matter of waiting for him. He might as well have handed himself in as soon as he had crossed the border. He thought of Sarah and the boys, how he had let them down by making this ridiculous journey. Had all that stuff about friendship just concealed a base desire for adventure and boyish thrills? He hoped not. He wished he had never escaped from this damn place, had never developed a taste for outwitting an enemy. He should have sat it out and studied law, ornithology, or how to paint landscapes.

'I am arresting you for the theft of a vehicle,' said the colonel.

'Isn't that a police matter?' asked Hartley, knowing that the charge was simply an excuse to detain him.

The colonel chuckled. 'Come, Colonel Hartley, there's no need to play the *naïf* with me.'

Hartley saw that he was going to get to know this man rather well. He would be questioned for weeks, perhaps months, on end, although he would not know how much time had passed. He had to regard himself as dead. If he didn't talk, they would torture him, and the Stasi were good at that. This colonel looked like an expert, his mean face and short body the classic hallmarks of a little man who liked to take revenge on a world inhabited by people larger than him. Hartley took a deep breath. He had to keep his mouth shut. Scores of lives depended on it, perhaps hundreds. If he talked, they wouldn't just arrest the members of Hartley's networks: they would round up their friends and families, question and torture them as well. Hartley wished he had a cyanide pill secreted in his collar. It would be a merciful release from what was to come.

'Are you ready, Colonel Hartley?'

Hartley said nothing.

They marched him down the stairs and across the courtyard. He wondered what would happen to Royce, whether they would kill him now and call it euthanasia. Probably. The Germans had done that before, and there was nothing different about this lot. They would probably kill Christa too.

The colonel led Hartley up the passage and out into the old prisoners' courtyard. It looked just the same, although a small tree had been planted in the middle, a beacon of green in a sea of grey.

The solitary-confinement cells. That was where he was going. So many others had been locked in here, but not Hartley. He had got out too soon for that. Oh, well, it was his turn at last. He thought of the Head Man, who would go spare when he found out what had happened. He would probably wrap up all the networks, get as many agents as possible out of the country. 'Abandon ship,' he would order. 'Swim for your lives.'

'In here,' said the colonel, and pointed to a cell.

Hartley walked in. It was empty – there was not even a bed or a chair.

'This is your new home,' said the colonel. 'I hope you like it.' He stood in the doorway, his hands on his hips. He looked proud of himself, and well he might: he had netted a big fish, the biggest of the lot, the man who ran British capitalist spies in the GDR.

'It's a warm night, isn't it?'

Hartley looked at him blankly. He was already trying to escape to a world within himself, to lock out what was around him.

'On a night like this there is generally no need for bedclothes . . .'

Hartley shut his eyes briefly. He knew what was coming.

'. . . so I think you should strip.'

Was there any point in refusing? No. Dumb compliance was required. He had done this in training many times, been forced to strip and, although it was hardly second nature, he could handle the indignity better than a civilian. The last time he had done it he had been with the Special Air Service two years ago, on an interrogation course in Wales. The star interrogator went by the name of Mr Rudler, and he had been particularly adept at castigating the nature of men's genitals. Rumour had it that Rudler's day job was as the deputy headmaster of a prep school, but it had never been proved.

Hartley removed his clothes swiftly. He wanted to show this two-bit colonel that he wasn't ashamed, that for him it was no great shakes. He knew what the man was doing – he was trying to break him. Well, it wasn't going to work. Hartley even removed his underpants before his shirt and socks, and made no attempt to hide himself.

'Very good Hartley,' said the colonel. 'I'd always thought Englishmen were little pricks, but now it seems I've been proved right.'

That old chestnut, thought Hartley. He stood naked, his hands by his sides. To have put them behind his back would have been asking for trouble.

'We now have to search you, Colonel.'

Hartley shrugged. This was also to be expected. It was uncomfortable, unpleasant, but it did not last long. It was also reasonable – after all, they did it at the Service whenever they interrogated someone.

'Bend over,' said the colonel.

Hartley turned round and bent forward. He heard a latex glove being put on, and within a few seconds a jabbing sensation up his backside. Hartley had to remind himself that this was probably more unpleasant for the searcher than the searched – after all, Hartley couldn't see it happening. The finger was removed, and Hartley stood up, glad that it was over. He watched the junior officer remove the glove, disgust on his face.

The colonel picked up Hartley's jacket and took out the contents slowly. When he came to the blank passports, he smiled. 'So, how were you going to take Mr Royce and Miss Gussveld out of the GDR?'

Hartley said nothing.

'I assume you had a plan.'

Of course, Hartley thought, but he was damned if he was going to tell this runt. He let the man's words wash over him.

'Very well,' said the colonel. 'No doubt you shall tell us soon.'

He fished around in the jacket like a child with a Christmas stocking. 'Now then! What is this?'

He produced the camera with a flourish. 'Polaroid,' he said. 'Ah, yes! I've heard of these! You were going to take a picture for the passport, yes?'

Hartley said nothing. He was at home, having dinner with Sarah, the boys and their girlfriends. What were their names? Deborah and Sue. He preferred Sue, not because she was more attractive but because she was livelier. Deborah was sweet in her own way, but Christopher could do better. At least, that was what Hartley thought. Sarah disagreed.

A flash interrupted him. The colonel was cackling away, the camera in his hands. He had just taken a picture.

'Now what do I do?'

The colonel pawed at it, not knowing how to extract the film, then passed it to one of the junior officers, who also struggled until, triumphantly, he removed the small black square. The colonel's face was wreathed in disappointment. 'There is nothing!'

Just you wait, thought Hartley.

'Sir,' said one of the officers, 'something is happening – look!'

The three men crowded excitedly round the print. Clearly Polaroid cameras were something of a novelty in the GDR. They laughed as the image became apparent. The colonel held it up to Hartley's face. 'Don't you look happy?'

Hartley studied it. His torso was pale against the darkness of the cell's walls, his profile visible. His expression was as blank and emotionless as he had hoped. Show no emotion, tell nothing. Your secrets are inside your head. They cannot unscrew it and get them out.

'I shall keep this is as a souvenir,' said the colonel, and put it inside his tunic.

Hartley wondered what other souvenirs the man kept. Underwear? Extracted fingernails? He was tempted to ask, but kept silent. He thought about dinner again, about reprimanding Christopher for not offering his mother a drink, thought about the boys' exams, thought about anything but being where he was.

The colonel examined the rest of Hartley's clothing. He broke open the cigarettes and tossed them on to the floor, but put the lighter into his pocket. Hartley would be allowed no privileges. Prisoners had to earn privileges. It was the same the world over.

'You know,' said the colonel, 'it's touching that you came back for your friend.'

Hartley flinched a little.

'It all worked out so much better than we could have hoped. But we knew how gallant you would be.'

Hartley didn't respond.

'Your friend is a very sick man, Colonel Hartley. He might not live long.'

That was clearly a threat.

'He needs better treatment,' the colonel continued. 'Maybe we can give it to him, but psychiatric care is very costly to the state.'

There was no psychiatric care in this God-forsaken hellhole that could help Royce, Hartley knew.

'You see, Colonel Hartley, I'd hate to see him stay here. I don't think it would be very good for him. I know how much you want to help him, so why don't you help us?'

Hartley stood still. He was not even tempted. He would not put Royce above the safety of his agents.

'Anyway,' said the colonel, 'why don't you sleep on it? We can talk again in the morning. Good night.'

The three men laughed as they left. The cell door slammed, and a key turned in the lock. If only he had learnt how to pick locks when he was here last, he thought ruefully. Mind you, he had nothing to use as a pick. He might as well try to sleep, which he knew would be impossible, not just because of his nakedness and the lack of furniture but because of his state of mind. At that moment, Hartley hated himself more than anybody else ever could. It was self-pity, but there it was. Sometimes it was allowed, and now was one of those times.

The door opened at exactly six o'clock the following morning. Hartley had slept after a fashion, albeit only for a few minutes at a time. The stone floor was cold and uncomfortable, and with a drop in the air temperature in the middle of the night, his teeth had literally chattered. The opening of the door was therefore almost welcome: it signalled the end of the night. Now all he had to do was to survive today. He knew they would keep him alive, but in what condition?

Hartley looked up at a pair of black leather jackboots, a pair of grey-blue breeches with red piping tucked into them, and above them a tunic festooned with medal ribbons. A small misshapen head was perched on top. It bore a pugilist's face, complete with broken noise and cauliflower ears. Hartley knew the face well: he had seen it in countless photographs, at medal-giving ceremonies and march-pasts. It never smiled. It belonged to General Gunther Milch, the head of the Stasi, and the man whom Hartley had spent the best part of his working life trying to outwit. And now he had failed. Milch had outwitted him.

Hartley sat up, and drew up his legs to hide himself. He did his best to look dignified, but knew it was impossible. Milch regarded him as a piece of excrescence.

Eventually, Milch cleared his throat. 'You are a professional, Colonel Hartley,' he said, his voice slightly hoarse and plebeian. Hartley recalled that Milch had been a Communist street-fighter in his youth, and had earned his spurs by killing a policeman in Munich in 1934. After that he had fled to Moscow, and the next anybody heard of him was when he appeared in Berlin in 1946. The Russians had been good to him, and Milch was certainly good to them. A real lickspittle, in fact.

Hartley had nothing to say to the man.

'You're well aware that my organisation always gets what it wants,' Milch went on. 'And that our methods can be somewhat testing for the interviewee. So what I suggest is this. You can have some clothes and some breakfast, and we shall meet in one hour for a talk. Do you agree to this?'

Hartley had little choice. He might as well accept, not least because he needed food. He had not eaten since lunch yesterday and felt weak. He nodded.

'Good,' said Milch. There was no triumph in his

voice. Hartley knew that Milch knew that he was buying time. Milch turned on his heel and strutted imperiously from the room.

Hartley accepted Milch's offer of a cigarette. He needed to feed his habit, and there was no point in punishing himself with nicotine-withdrawal symptoms. It was after breakfast – black bread, water – and he was sitting opposite Milch in what Hartley had known as the castle's theatre. They were alone in the middle of the large room, and behind Milch, Hartley could see the camp stage. He recalled the conversations he'd had with Edginton about the tutus. They belonged to someone else's lifetime. The Hartley who sat opposite Milch was not the same man who had been here thirty years ago.

'First of all, Colonel Hartley, I don't want you to think that you can harm me. I have only to shout and twenty men will be in here, ready to blow you to pieces. Do you understand?'

Hartley nodded. He had already worked that out for himself.

'Second, I don't want you to waste my fucking time!'

Hartley was taken aback by the sudden explosion, but he nodded again.

'All right,' said Milch. 'Let's begin.'

Hartley folded his arms. There was nothing on the

table in front of Milch, not even a pencil and paper. Their conversation would be recorded, then replayed and analysed ad nauseam. Hartley had spent countless cigarette-filled nights replaying confessions, trying to establish the truths buried among the half-truths and lies.

'When were you recruited to the Service?'

The easy question first. The question that seemed innocuous, that he would be tempted to answer . . . that would get him into the answering-questions frame of mind. Milch obviously knew all about Hartley, just as Hartley knew all about Milch. It would be pointless to tell him nothing because that was a quick route to torture.

'I'm surprised you don't know,' said Hartley.

'Humour me.'

'If you insist.'

Milch flashed him a look that indicated he most certainly did insist.

'May 1945.'

'And who recruited you?'

'Robert Sloman.'

Sloman had been the Head Man back then, and he had died at least twenty years ago. There was nothing harmful in revealing that Sloman had recruited him and, besides, it was information that Milch would already know.

'This was straight from MI9. Am I correct?'

'Yes.'

'And why were you recruited?'

'Because I had experience of East Germany.'

Milch leant back.

'Your "great escape", yes?'

'If you want to put it like that.'

'Ironic that you are back here again.'

'Very.'

'And your friend Mr Royce. Back here as well. Quite a reunion.'

Hartley smiled weakly.

'And his lovely daughter, Dr Gussveld. That must have been quite a shock for you, eh?'

'It was a little.'

Milch harrumphed. 'A little!'

'What's going to happen to her?'

Milch studied his fingernails.

'She will continue with her duties.'

It was clear that he would not be more forthcoming.

'Let's get back to 1945.'

Hartley relaxed slightly. He did not mind talking about 1945, because 1945 was ancient history, Paleozoic. There were some elements of those years that he would not reveal, but for the most part 1945 to 1947 had been a succession of stumbles and bungles mixed with occasional success. They had thought they were so slick then, so professional, and it had taken them far too long to realise that the

Russians were well ahead in the game. They had men like Milch, trained in Moscow for well over a decade, ready to come in, take over, and start implementing the new order. The service then had been a collection of officers, dons and former policemen, motley and amateur. Hartley was probably a little less amateur than some, but compared to the machines that came from the East, he was a very primitive spy.

'What were your initial duties? Where were you posted?'

'Berlin,' said Hartley. 'I was there to find suitable agents to operate in the Russian sector.'

'And whom did you recruit?'

Hartley had recruited dozens of agents, many of whom had been useless, but a couple of goldmines. One was still alive, a Russian air force major who had now retired with the rank of general, and Hartley had no wish to imperil him. 'I recruited lots of agents.'

'Who?'

'You want to know all of them? They're dead now anyway.'

'Who?'

'All right. Let me see. The first was a Frau Renate Lippmann. She was a cleaner at Soxmis, your military mission. She supplied me with the contents of the bins. They were occasionally fruitful, but not often.'

'What did she find in the bins?'

'I can barely remember.'

Milch flashed him a slow look. Hartley knew it would serve him well to remember, or even to make something up. Anything to buy time – but for what? To escape? Hardly.

'What did she find?' asked Milch.

'She found details of postings, leave schedules, that sort of thing.'

'Be more precise.'

Well, thought Hartley, if Milch had all day, so did he. He could spin this out for hours, even days, and still come nowhere near to revealing anything that was remotely confidential. Just keep rambling, he told himself, bore Milch with your encyclopaedic knowledge of defunct networks, anything to delay the more searching questions.

The tactic worked. Milch lapped up Hartley's reminiscences, and Hartley had to stop himself getting carried away. It was too easy to show off, especially after years of keeping everything secret. He even wanted to tell Milch about the really big fish and some of the coups, just to watch the bastard's face. But he kept himself in check, concentrating only on low-grade stuff. Milch would have known this was small beer, but he was no doubt building up the level of questioning, ready to slip in something that was a little more searching, a little more delicate. It was like a game of chess in which Hartley was on the defensive, having to sacrifice a pawn from time to time to keep his king out of check.

At one o'clock, Milch told him it was time for lunch.

'I am pleased with you, Colonel,' he said. 'Of course, we have only just started, but I am glad you are making life easier for yourself.'

Hartley felt marginally guilty that he had opened up quite so easily, but he had said nothing that Milch probably did not know. Judging by his indifferent expression, that would appear to have been so. He had registered surprise – a raised eyebrow – only twice, and hardly in response to groundbreaking material.

Milch walked out of the room, leaving Hartley alone. Was this an opportunity or a trap? Hartley got up and walked over to the stage, remembering how old Gerald and that Dutchman had started their successful attempt from right underneath it. That had been after Hartley had escaped. Gerald had reminisced about it to him and published his memoirs. He examined the front of the stage, looking for a loose board, a trapdoor, anything. There was nothing. He turned to the door – no one was there. What harm would it do to get on the stage and look for an exit? None.

He stepped up and walked across it, temporarily grateful that his feet were bare. He tried to recall

GUY WALTERS

Gerald's memoirs, tried to think how Gerald had got beneath the stage. He padded around softly, peering into the gloom for a loose board. Nothing. There had to be something, or perhaps the Germans had discovered the route and sealed it up. It wasn't unlikely.

'Engaging in amateur dramatics, old boy?'

The words were spoken in English and Hartley spun round. There in front of him was one of the junior officers from last night, bearing a tray of food. 'Something like that,' he said.

'I used to creep the boards when I was at school,' said the officer, placing the tray down on the table. 'Here's your lunch. It looks pretty ghastly, I'm afraid.'

The man spoke extraordinarily good public-school English, and Hartley told him as much as he stepped down from the stage.

The officer smiled. He had a friendly face, thought Hartley, unlike many of the Stasi men he had come across. 'I like to practise,' he replied.

Hartley sat at the table and examined the food. It was gruel of some sort. A plastic cup of water stood next to it, which he drank in one gulp. 'Have you been to England?' he asked as if he was talking to someone sitting next to him on a plane.

The officer laughed. 'I don't think I'm in a position to tell you one way or the other, Colonel Hartley.'

The man's fluency was chilling. If the Stasi had

326

agents like him all over Britain, the country was probably infested with even more moles than they had thought. He ate the gruel, doing his best to ignore its slightly rancid taste. If this was what they fed the patients here, heaven help them. The man left the room, and once more Hartley was alone. He finished his lunch, then darted back to the stage, determined to find Gerald's exit.

Just as he was stepping on to it, the door opened again and Milch came in. 'What are you doing, Colonel Hartley?'

'I was in a play here once,' he said. 'I was taking a trip down what we British call Memory Lane.'

Milch nodded. Hartley hadn't expected a smile, but he got one.

'No doubt you are looking for the small trapdoor your associates cut into that stage thirty years ago. I think it was Gerald Heard who used it to get out, along with a Dutchman. They wore German uniforms, didn't they? And they marched straight out of the castle. Heard's memoirs make for a good read.'

Hartley stepped down, deflated. Why had he expected Milch to be so easily hoodwinked?

'You see, Colonel Hartley, we know all about this castle. I know that you were the first Englishman to escape, which must be a badge of honour. Did you get a medal for it?'

'The Military Cross.'

Milch nodded. 'Well done! And tell me, how did you and Royce get out?'

'You don't know? Hasn't Royce already told you?'

'Royce cannot remember much.'

'I see. Well, we got out hidden in mattresses. Some French workmen were removing all the old ones, and we decided that two of us should be sewn into them. Royce and I were chosen, and that was it. We were bundled into a lorry and twenty minutes later found ourselves half suffocating under a pile of mattresses in a warehouse in the town.'

'Ingenious,' Milch commented, 'although you look a little big to be stuffed into a mattress.'

'I was much thinner back then,' said Hartley.

'What happened next?'

'We waited until it got dark, left the warehouse, and made our way across country to Rochlitz, where we caught the train to Chemnitz.'

'You make it sound simple.'

'The best plans usually are.'

'A bit like this one, then,' said Milch.

Touché. Hartley walked back to the chair, doing his best not to look excited that the East Germans had clearly not discovered his tunnel. During the war the Nazis had certainly never discovered it, although they suspected that the park was a weak spot and posted guards around it twenty-four hours a day, thereby rendering the tunnel obsolete. There was a chance that it was still open, although Hartley knew that was too much to hope for. Besides, the rope-ladder would have rotted in the damp years ago, and it would be impossible to get down.

'We shall now move on to 1953,' said Milch.

'Fire away,' said Hartley.

The questions continued for the next three hours. Hartley was beginning to feel pleased with himself because he had fed Milch dross. He had given him nothing that was of any relevance, but he knew that this was all part of the lulling process. By the time the questioning got to 1965, he began to feel uncomfortable. He did his best not to show it, but Milch would have detected the pauses before his answers, pauses that grew longer with every minute.

'Now tell me about General Stöller,' said Milch, matter-of-factly.

'General Stöller?'

'That's right, General Helmut Stöller.'

'What about him? All I know about him is that he wears a lot of medals and drinks a lot of beer.'

'You have had him under surveillance, then?'

'We tried once when he was in Bulgaria.'

'Why?'

'We like to keep an eye on as many of your senior officers as possible.'

Hartley was on dangerous ground here. Stöller

was one of his top agents. He felt deeply anxious that
the man had already been exposed. He might have
been a double agent for years, feeding the Service
rubbish. But Hartley doubted it. If that was so, Milch
would not have mentioned him: he would want to
keep Stöller out of the conversation. The most likely
explanation was that the Stasi suspected him, which
was a death sentence in the German Democratic
Republic.

'Who spied on him in Bulgaria?'

'Bulgaria is not my department.'

'No, but Stöller certainly is.'

'Well, he would be.'

'What do you mean?'

'He would be if he was an agent.'

'I see. And you're telling me he's not an agent?'

'That's correct.'

'In that case, why don't you just tell me who your
agents really are, rather than wasting my time? What
could be simpler? Do that, and you and Mr Royce will
be safe. I'll even put you on a plane back to England.'

Hartley believed him, he really did. They had done
it at the Service a few times. Once a spy had been
thoroughly interrogated, perhaps over two or three
years, they sent him back in exchange for one of their
own. The homecoming for any captured spy was a dark
under-the-stairs affair – an RAF plane from Berlin to
Northolt, then a van to Courtfield House where the

spy was interrogated on what he had told the enemy. And he had usually told them everything, which meant a lot of 'There, there, old boy' and 'You did well to hold out for so long', but all the time he would be regarded with contempt for handing over whatever part of the Crown Jewels he had had on him, then pensioned off and told to go and live somewhere quiet – Devon was popular – as a prep-school bursar.

'I asked you a question, Colonel Hartley.'

'I know you did. I'm thinking it over.'

Milch sat back and inspected his fingernails. It was a surprisingly feminine habit. Hartley noticed that they were heavily chewed, in some places almost non-existent. Suitably ugly hands for such an ugly man.

'You're not expecting me just to list my networks, are you?'

Milch shrugged. 'Why not?'

'I'd rather die than tell you.'

'I'm not going to let you die, Colonel Hartley. That would be too easy for you.'

Hartley didn't know whether to feel alarmed or relieved. He hadn't expected to get to this point quite so quickly. He had thought it was days away, perhaps weeks. Milch was obviously a man in a hurry, with good reason.

'Your choice, Colonel.'

Hartley stood up warily, watching to see if Milch would order him to sit down again. He didn't, so

Hartley walked to the window that overlooked the courtyard. He looked down, wishing he was casting his eyes over an *Appel* thirty years ago. How innocent that life seemed. Now he had fucked up his life. The best he could do now was not to make it any worse by telling Milch what he knew. He would have to take whatever was coming, and if he had to die, then at least he'd know that others would live. He turned back to Milch. 'I'm sorry, General,' he said calmly. 'I'm not going to tell you what you want to know.'

Milch stood up, his face expressionless. He walked to the door, looked back and shook his head, then stepped out into the corridor.

Chapter Nine

THEY CAME FOR him in the middle of the night. Two men, with moustaches and tinted glasses, hauled him out of the room and made him run naked down the corridor. 'Run, you piece of shit!'

Hartley was terrified. Despite the training he had given and received, nothing could have prepared him for the reality. He prayed for a bullet in the back, anything to spare him the agonies to come.

'Stop!'

Hartley stopped and shivered, from cold and fear. Four strong arms bundled him into another cell, in the middle of which stood a wooden contraption. Whatever it was, whatever it did, it looked sinister in the dim light from the solitary bulb. Hartley felt close to panic, wanted to blurt out everything he knew to rid himself of pain and the expectation of pain. Get a grip, he told himself. You're not going to fall at the first fence. You're going to get out of here. You're going to live. And if you don't live, you can bloody well keep your mouth shut.

Suddenly he felt pain in the soles of his feet, like hot coals. He looked down, and saw that he was walking across spiked ridges, which sent needles of pain up his body. It was agony, and each time he lifted a foot to relieve it, the pain in the other doubled. Hartley did his best to stifle sounds of pain, but he couldn't help groaning and swearing. His torturers laughed, as he had known they would. They always fucking laughed.

He was led to the contraption, which was similar to a stocks on a British village green. The torturers placed his head and hands in three grooves on the crossbar, brought down another bar to secure him and locked it into place. All the time the pain in his feet worsened. Hartley gritted his teeth and told himself to ignore it. Now what would they do? Flog him? Rape crossed his mind.

A stand rather like a bird table was brought in front of him, with a large metal bowl of water on top. This was placed below his chin. Suddenly, from above, a trickle of freezing water splashed over his head, ran into the bowl and down the back of his neck. He kept moving his feet, trying vainly to ease the pain, but it was pointless. It was so bad now that he wanted to pass out, to hang limply and drift off somewhere else. Then he realised what the water was for: if he passed out, his face would fall into the bowl, and he would either revive or drown. He could hear more laughter, and then a door slammed.

Yell. He had to yell. It was the only way he could cope. He screamed as loudly as he could, trying to rid his body of the agony coursing through him. The water trickling from the ceiling ran into his open mouth and he spluttered. Nevertheless, he carried on yelling because that was the only option open to him.

No, it isn't, a small voice told him. Seize control, you fool. Pull yourself together. The pain isn't so bad. You can cope. Just accept it. Accept that it's there and it's going to stay. Keep still, don't move a muscle. Let your feet stay where they are, and they'll grow accustomed to it, hopefully go numb. He took several deep breaths, avoiding the trickle of water by turning his head slightly. His feet burned, but he could manage – or, at least, he hoped he could.

For the next minute, Hartley remained absolutely still. He tried to let his mind wander, and nearly succeeded, although it wandered to interrogations he had carried out. He had never tortured anybody – not like this, anyway. They had used sleep deprivation, the occasional roughing-up, but nothing so medievally barbaric. Who had thought this up? Which twisted Stasi bastard had woken up one day and decided to invent something as unpleasant as this? Perhaps there was an officer whose sole responsibility was to invent and improve torture methods. Or even a whole department.

The pain was increasing and he began to feel light-headed. He fought the dizziness, arguing with his body not to give in but to carry on resisting the urge to let his head loll into the water. He breathed rapidly through his nose, hoping that the sudden rush of oxygen would keep him awake, keep him alive.

Then came the first manifestation of temptation. He could end this hell by telling Milch what he wanted to know. All he had to do was scream out that he would talk, and he would be released, freed from pain. No, he mustn't do that – he couldn't. Think of all the others they would torture and kill, just because he hadn't the strength to face up to this. His failure should not be theirs. There were too many who would die if he talked, far too many. This had nothing to do with the Service or the Cold War, but everything to do with doing the decent thing. He couldn't let other people die because he couldn't take a bit of pain in his bloody feet. 'Fuck Milch'. The image of the graffito swarmed into his head. Fuck Milch.

How long had he been there? Five minutes? An hour? He couldn't tell. Any sense of time passing had been replaced with pain. Count the minutes, set yourself a target. Count out loud, shout out the seconds passing. He started yelling the numbers, the water trickling over his face. Come on, get to sixty, and start again. You can do it. Take each minute at a time, don't plan for any longer than that. They can't keep you here for ever. They're not going to let you die. They want what's inside you, want to get it out. Fuck them, it wasn't going to work.

At around forty-three he felt himself slipping into a faint. He grew woozy, drunk, and the numbers were slurred. He was mumbling and whispering them now. Come on, get to sixty. The pain doubled, trebled, dug into him. Fifty-two, fifty-three, fifty-four . . .

The next thing Hartley knew he was choking on the water. He had fainted, but the water had revived him. He didn't know whether that was a good thing – he just wanted the pain to end. If he died then so be it. At least the torture would be over. But he didn't want to die. Sarah and the boys. Stay alive for Sarah and the boys. He had too much to lose by dying, too much to miss. So what if some of his bloody agents got killed? They knew the risks and, besides, Milch probably already knew who they were. All this was just a way to confirm what he knew, so why don't you just tell him and make all this stop?

Hartley knew that the devil was on his shoulder. He had to resist, send the temptation away. You're never going to give them what they want. Never. He started to count again, rushing through the numbers. Please let me get to sixty, just let me get there. He fainted again, brought round once more by the water.

Please let this stop – just one part of it. Please stop that fucking water pouring on my head. He couldn't think straight: its icy insistence seemed to penetrate his skull.

Although he didn't know it, Hartley remained in that state for nearly two hours. The submersion in the bowl became more frequent, and he hallucinated as he drifted between pain and unconsciousness. He saw Royce, his eyes missing, just sockets, beckoning him on, mouthing, 'Come here.' Hartley shouted 'No,' several times, telling the apparition to go away, to leave him alone. It came as a relief when he finally plunged into watery darkness. This was it. This was the end. There was no coming back now. Wasn't drowning meant to be peaceful?

He came to in his cell. For a few seconds, he was not sure if he was alive or dead. The last thing he remembered was his face dropping into the water, then blackness. His feet were still burning, and he propped himself up on his elbows to look down at his body. He was naked, but that did not concern him. In the gloom, he could make out a crust of blood between his toes. He lay on his side, drew up one of his feet and touched the sole. Even that delicate contact sent pain shooting up his body. He decided to leave his feet alone. There was nothing he could do about them.

With the absence of a window, Hartley had no idea what time it was. He suspected it was early in the morning, but there was nothing to confirm it. He sat up a little, but the movement made him feel faint, and he lay down again. He was nauseous too, and retched a little. He should have been hungry, but he had no appetite. If they brought him any food, he would have to force himself to eat it. He lay still and tried to sleep, but every time his eyes closed, he pictured himself in the torture room, riven by pain. He wanted to sob, but once he did that, he would be lost. Never cry, he had told his recruits. It was the worst thing you could do. Your torturers would see you and comfort you, and that was when you would speak. You would love your torturer for not hurting you.

Hartley heard the key turn in the lock. He flinched and tensed, preparing himself to be dragged away for another session. He looked up. The colonel was standing there. He was smiling, always bloody smiling.

'How are you this fine morning, Colonel Hartley?'

His tone was so friendly that Hartley imagined he would walk in with a cup of tea, draw the curtains, and announce that it was a good day for a walk. He said nothing.

'I gather your night was a little disturbed.'

Hartley grunted.

'The general sends his compliments, and says you

can have a good night's sleep tonight if you have another chat with him. He told me that you did so well yesterday, right until the end, when you ruined it.'

Hartley weighed his options. If he refused, it would be straight back to torture. If he accepted, he would be tempted to tell Milch something, maybe something worth revealing. That would be the start of it, the trickle before the deluge. You couldn't just release one secret because then it was all too easy to let the rest go.

'Tell the general,' he said huskily, 'that I won't be able to speak to him today.'

The grin vanished from the colonel's face. Clearly most people caved in after a session with the stocks and the bucket. 'You do know what this means?'

'I do.'

'You understand that you are only delaying the inevitable? Why put yourself through all this?'

'Sod off.'

That earned Hartley a vicious kick in the stomach. It hurt, but it was worth it. He wasn't going to be pushed around by these people. He wanted them to see that he still had his spirit, that they had not crushed him.

A few hours later the same two men dragged him to his bruised and bloody feet. They forced him to walk, and every step was excruciating. They passed the cell with the stocks, which Hartley would have found a relief if he had not thought he was about to suffer something worse. He limped and hobbled to the cell next to it, and there he saw a metal box, about three feet square. He fought off the panic. He knew what was going to happen because he had heard about it from an agent who had survived it.

A pair of strong hands pushed his head down, and he was forced into the box, where he squatted. The door closed and Hartley experienced an almost overwhelming sense of claustrophobia. He had never felt like this in the tunnel, because he had known there was a way out. This was different: the exit relied on the caprice of his tormentors, and for all he knew that might be never. He was hyperventilating. He was going to go mad, and it hadn't even started.

At first, the ice-cold water came as a relief to his raw feet, but the rising level caused Hartley to cry out: 'No! No!'

Were there any air holes? There had to be, or people would die immediately. But panic took over, and he hit the door of the box as hard as he could. 'Let me out! Please let me out!'

Nothing happened. The water rose slowly, now reaching his waist. It was almost freezing. How high would it go? He attempted to control himself, but continued to struggle and plead to be let out. The water reached his chest, and then it was up to his neck. Oh, God, please let me out.

Hartley tilted his head back as the water rose. He must not scream. He must stay calm. All they're doing is putting you in a box of cold water. It's not so bad, you'll be all right. His head was now almost submerged, and his mouth and nose greedily sucked air from the three inches left. How long would it stay like this? He could hear noises outside the box, laughter, footsteps. Perhaps Milch had come to inspect his catch.

It required immense effort to hold a position in which he could breathe. He had to force himself on to the balls of his feet, which increased the shards of agony in them. It was madness to endure this. What the hell was he trying to prove? All the training was irrelevant. Nothing could prepare you for this. It was hell. There were now only two options: to talk, or to die. He could not endure this any longer. They would continue torturing him for days, weeks, months, keeping him alive and making sure he didn't go mad.

The water level rose and Hartley took a last gasp of air. Bastards, he thought. Indignation came over him - who the hell did these people think they were? What gave them the right to kill him? Fucking savages. Hartley's lungs were bursting. He would have to let go soon, and allow the water into his body, which was a mass of pain, his brain overcrowded with sensations from his feet, his lungs and his frozen skin. He had to let go now.

The water level dropped. He took in vast lungfuls of cold air. Thank God that's over, he thought, and the water level shot up again. No, please, no. He couldn't deal with this, he would have to talk, because the bastards weren't going to kill him.

There was another option, though, and that was to escape. Fat chance. The only escape route he had open was death, the best escape of all.

When they opened the box an hour later, Hartley fell out on to the floor. He was near to sobbing, but somehow he controlled himself.

He heard the colonel's voice: 'How was the bath?'

Hartley wanted to tell him to sod off, but he couldn't face another session in the box. Instead, he just breathed in and out, grateful for the dank cell air.

He was given some food – bread, sausage and water – which he devoured. It tasted foul, but he didn't care. As soon as he had finished, he wanted more, and licked every last crumb off the plastic plate, and even the inside of the cup. In just a few hours he had turned into a savage, desperate for food, water and safety, nothing else. His nakedness exacerbated it, and he felt almost subhuman as he lay in the dark, feet still burning. What did they have lined up for him later? He couldn't take any more, because he knew he would crack. He had to get out. There was nothing else for it. He'd probably be shot if he tried, but anything was preferable to this.

But how? The question dogged his mind. He'd heard that some who had been confined here during the war had managed to pick locks, but he had nothing to pick with. And if he could open the door, how was he to escape without any clothes? He didn't fancy running naked around the Saxon countryside, even in the unlikely event that he got out of the castle. Hartley curled up on the floor.

As he lay there, he realised that the only solution was violence. He was hardly in the best shape for a fight, but if he wanted to live, it was the only way.

Time drifted. He was left to lie there for hours, drifting into and out of consciousness. He did his best to think about anything other than his present circumstances, but found it impossible. He ached for sleep, but he was too cold and uncomfortable. Cruelly, he thought of a vast double bed in a hotel room, complete with huge pillows – the image almost made him scream. At that moment, all he wanted was a bed – and a cigarette. A cigarette would do wonders.

The door swung open. One of the moustachioed men walked in, thumbs resting on his empty belt loops. Doing a bit of overtime, Hartley thought.

'Get up!'

Hartley stood slowly, not just because his body ached but because he did not want to give the man the pleasure of seeing his order obeyed quickly. He was pushed through the door and into the corridor. Would it be the stocks or the water box? Or maybe something new. Hartley was resigned to spending the next two hours in agony.

He was pushed into the room with the water box. Thank God for his feet, he thought. It occurred to Hartley that the man was his executioner, and that he would soon be dead. Well, that was fine too. Nothing to worry about then. He couldn't bear to leave Sarah and the boys, but he was grateful for what he'd had. He'd known too many whose lives had been cut short before they'd had children or, worse, when their children were young. At least he had seen his grow up.

'Get in.'

Hartley looked at the water box. There was no way he was going to get into it willingly. He stood still, waiting for the shove, which came a few seconds later. At that point something in him snapped. When he spun round and smashed his fist into the man's face, it was an act born not of careful planning but of sheer anger. To his surprise, the thug crumpled on to the ground. Hartley pummelled his bleeding face repeatedly.

Then he stopped and caught his breath. He listened. There was no sound from the corridor. He would have to work quickly. His hands trembling, he unbuttoned the man's shirt and removed it. It stank but he didn't care. Then he took off the trousers and put them on, the shoes and socks. His feet still hurt, but he would just have to put up with it. Finally he took the keys, and then, most importantly, the gun. He felt the reassuring weight of the pistol in his hand. He looked down at the thug in his yellowing underpants, urine seeping out of them. There was only one place where he could be sure that the man wouldn't be able to raise the alarm.

Hartley dragged him into the water box and closed the door. His conscience pricked, but he dismissed it. The man should die because he was an embodiment of evil. Hartley turned on the tap.

The corridor was deserted, although Hartley knew there would be a guard outside the cell block. How to deal with him? Hopefully he would be able to startle and knock him out before he could raise the alarm. Shooting him would be fatal to them both. He crept down the corridor, noting the lack of light coming through the door. It was night. Good. His feet were on fire when he reached the door to the block. It was a heavy wooden affair with a small grille at head height. Hartley peered out into the old prisoners' courtyard, and saw nothing. There had to be a guard, perhaps just outside the door. He would have to rush him.

Hands shaking, Hartley brought the keys to the lock. There were three to choose from, and he selected the largest. It had better be the right one – he didn't want to scrabble around, attracting the guard's attention so soon. He inserted the key, and turned. It was the wrong one. He tried to turn it back, but it had jammed and he had to wriggle it free, the noise surely filling the entire courtyard.

'Ah, that bloody lock!'

The voice came from outside.

'You'd have thought they might have replaced it since the war!'

Somehow Hartley laughed.

'Hang on, Erich, I'll do it from this side.'

Hartley stepped back. The key turned in the lock. Although the other man was presumably using the correct one, the lock was clearly reluctant.

Hartley stepped back to allow the door to swing open.

'You were quick–'

The guard never had the opportunity to finish his sentence. Hartley drove his fist into the man's solar plexus, causing him to bend double. Then he brought up his right knee into the guard's face with ferocious force, catching the man beneath his chin and causing his neck to snap back violently. Hartley heard bones break. The guard crumpled. He hadn't meant to kill him, but they were at war and he was the enemy.

Hartley grabbed the corpse under the arms, dragged it into the cell block, his own cell, and let it fall on to the floor, then went out and locked the door behind him. He hobbled down the corridor, stepped out into the courtyard, shut and locked the door behind him.

The night was still. Hartley supposed it must be around midnight, although that was only a guess. Where to now? Down the pathway to the old Kommandantur courtyard? If there were any guards, that was where they would be. Perhaps he should try to get out along the tunnel. He glanced up at the windows of the old Dutch and British quarters, blank and forlorn. He was standing in almost the same spot as he had been when Ings-Chambers had shouted down to him – he was something in the City now.

Royce. He had to get Royce. That was why he had come and he couldn't let him down now. There was no point in any of this unless he saved Royce, or tried to. He had no time to think about whether or not it was a good idea, he had to follow his instinct. He turned right, headed through the arch out of the courtyard and down to the Kommandantur. He stole along the cobblestones, pistol in hand. During the war, he would have been stopped ages ago, but this was different. And he had been lucky so far – but he knew that would change.

He walked under the passageway, waiting for footsteps to clatter down the steps to his right. None came. Now for the dangerous part – crossing the Kommandantur courtyard. He turned left, and hugged the wall of the kitchen block. There were some lights on, but Hartley walked in darkness below window level. A door slammed behind him, and he froze. He turned slowly and saw a man in a white coat walking towards the main gate. A doctor. He watched the figure go through the gate, and heard him say goodnight to someone out of sight.

He waited another minute, then moved on, keeping to the side of the kitchens. He was now only ten yards from the entrance to the spiral staircase and was tempted to run. Instead, he padded slowly across, all the time expecting a searing arc-light to snap on, accompanied with the command to halt.

He paused at the foot of the stairs to listen. He could hear distant conversation, which grew fainter until there was silence. He walked cautiously up the steps. At the first floor he stopped, listening for any noise. All was quiet. It was going well, he thought, too well. Another trap? No, that was paranoia. They wouldn't have allowed him to kill two of their men just to trap him again.

Hartley stopped dead. Footsteps were coming

rapidly down the stairs. He darted into the corridor and pressed himself against the wall.

'. . . prisoner?'

'Bearing up far too well. But it won't be long.'

He recognised the second voice as the colonel's. Hartley would gladly have stepped on to the staircase and shot him, but that would be diabolically foolhardy. His real revenge would be to get away. If that happened, the colonel would be disgraced.

'Who's working on him?'

'Erich and Rolf. They're a couple of real professionals, those two.'

The men were passing the entrance to his corridor. Hartley held his breath. Please let them continue walking. He smelt smoke – he could murder for a bloody cigarette, he thought.

'In fact,' the colonel's voice continued, 'Erich's working on him now.'

'What's he doing?'

'I'm not sure. We like to leave that part of the treatment to the individual professional.'

The voice grew fainter, and Hartley strained to hear it.

'I'm on my way over there now. Who knows? Perhaps he's broken . . .'

Hartley's heart thumped against his ribcage. He had two minutes at most to get Royce. He should leave him, save himself. No, he had already done that when he abandoned Royce thirty years ago. He was not going to do it again. It was either both of them or neither. He leapt up the remaining stairs, ignoring the protests from his feet. He'd worry about them later. He stopped for a couple of seconds at the entrance to the corridor, listened, heard nothing, and ran down it.

He burst into Royce's ward and raced to his bed. 'Royce!'

He shook the man, saw his eyes open in the darkness. 'Royce! Come on! It's time to go!'

'Who are you?'

'It's me, Royce – Hartley! Get up!'

'Time to go where?'

'Home!'

'Home?'

Hartley had no time for this. He pulled Royce out of bed, tossing aside the sheets and blankets. He was dressed, thank God, if only in pyjamas. 'Have you got any slippers?' he asked.

'Slippers?'

'For your feet, man!'

'Oh, yes.'

Royce shuffled around looking for them.

'Hurry! We don't have much time – for Pete's sake!'

Royce put on his slippers as fast as he could. 'You're carrying a gun,' he said.

'Yes.'

'My dressing-gown.'

'Sod that! Let's go!'

Hartley pushed him forward. To an observer, it would have looked as though he was taking Royce hostage rather than rescuing him. Royce almost fell over, but managed to retain his balance. He was like an old man, Hartley thought. But they were both like old men – a couple of old men trying to recover their lost youth and act out one last adventure. Look at them, he thought, doddering down the corridor. And what chance did they have? Almost none, but it was better than they would have had if they had stayed put. Royce would have been dead for sure in a few weeks, having outlived his usefulness.

'Wait here!' hissed Hartley. The easiest exit was to the right, through the small road tunnel that led under the Kommandantur to the park. From there they could cut across country. They stood still for a few seconds and waited, listening for any sign of activity. Nothing. Hartley could imagine the colonel's surprise when he found no guard. He had to assume that he carried a set of keys, and would soon discover that something was wrong. He made Royce turn right and they ran up the small tunnel. At the end there was a pair of massive wooden doors, which Hartley prayed were unlocked.

They were not. This was not a good place to be, he

thought, caught at the end of a tunnel. They would be massacred, cut down by an over-zealous guard.

'Back to the courtyard!'

Royce didn't move.

'Come on, man!'

'No,' he said.

Oh, shit, thought Hartley. It was as if they were back in the Greek camp. 'For fuck's sake!'

'Look,' said Royce. 'We could go under them.'

Hartley looked down. Royce was right – the gates had at least nine inches clearance off the ground.

'You genius!' said Hartley. 'Come on!'

The two men hit the floor, with less nimbleness than they would have displayed three decades ago. It was a squeeze, but Hartley got himself under swiftly, although Royce found it more difficult. Hartley bent down and pulled at his outstretched arms. Royce swore as the rough ground tore into him.

Eventually Royce was through and standing, grinning broadly. 'Here we are again,' he whispered.

'Second time lucky, I hope.' Hartley wanted to tell Royce so much, to ask him so many questions, but now was not the time.

A sudden cacophony of alarms and klaxons filled the air and floodlights burst on, illuminating the castle in brilliant whiteness. For a second, Hartley and Royce remained rooted to the spot, dazzled by the sudden *son et lumière*.

'There!' Royce shouted.

The two men dashed across the broad footpath and down a bank into some thick trees. They had been here before, many years ago. It was where their tunnel come out.

'This way!'

Hartley ran through the trees, turning to see if Royce was keeping up – he was managing gamely. He could hear whistles now, and shouting.

'Quick!'

Hartley looked back frantically at the castle as he ran. He was searching for the old lavatory shaft down which they had escaped. There it was! That meant the tunnel's exit was somewhere round here. He got to the ground and scrabbled around in the mud.

'What are you looking for?'

'The tunnel.'

Royce joined him. They couldn't find it. Had it been filled in? Hartley glanced up. They were not quite in line with the shaft. 'A bit to the right.'

They moved a couple of yards and dug with their hands, scratching through roots.

'It's not here,' said Hartley

'I'm sure it was a little higher up,' said Royce.

'It wasn't so close to the path.'

'It bloody was.'

'All right.'

354

The castle loomed over them, the brightness of the lights shining from it almost dazzling them.

'This is too exposed,' said Hartley.

'I'm sure it's here.'

Royce was on his hands and knees, his pyjamas covered with mud. A few seconds later his right arm plunged into the ground. 'Here!' he said.

Hartley joined him, and the two men removed clumps of mud, opening the hole.

'Get in backwards!' said Hartley.

Royce got halfway, then stopped. 'Roots,' he said.

'Kick them! Anything!'

Hartley could hear voices, and the smack of jackboots ringing against the castle walls. A whole bloody army was looking for them. Royce was still struggling.

'It's no good! It's massive!'

'Just fucking break it!'

Royce had probably spent the best part of thirty years in bed so his leg muscles would have wasted away. 'You can do it, man! Come on!'

Royce gave another kick, and shot backwards. He wriggled into the tunnel, and Hartley followed him. He felt the dark earth close over him, and momentary claustrophobia engulfed him. He thought of the water box, and wanted to get back into the open, but fought the urge, calming himself by taking deep breaths.

He listened to their pursuers. He could hear shouting, although it was impossible to work out what was being said over the noise of the klaxons and the alarms. When a shot rang out, Hartley started. A guard spotting the movement of a branch or a fox perhaps. That caused even more shouting, and Hartley thought he heard the voice of the colonel above the din. He almost allowed himself to smile. Good, he thought. That bastard would live out his life in disgrace, shunned by all his fellow Stasi men, and by those who weren't members of the Stasi. But Hartley wanted more than that. He wanted the man to die horribly. He felt a thirst for revenge he had never thought possible, ugly and brutal. He wanted the same for Milch too.

'Search everywhere!' came a shout.

It was the colonel's voice. He could hear the panic, the desperation. Even if they were caught, Hartley was glad that he would have shown them he hadn't been so easily trapped. That would wipe the swagger out of Milch's gait, he thought. What would he say to his masters at the Praesidium? That he had caught a British spymaster and let him escape? He'd be forced to retire at the very least, his place taken by Grass, his pipsqueak deputy.

The voices were getting louder, and Hartley stopped breathing when he heard footsteps approaching. He clutched the pistol with both hands, pointing it towards the mouth of the tunnel. Whoever stuck his face in here would get it shot off. He would take as many of the bastards with him as he could.

They were running right over the tunnel now, the sound so loud that Hartley thought it might collapse on them. But that wasn't possible – the rock was too strong. Thank God he had never written his memoirs. If he had, they would have known about the tunnel and filled it in. The irony of it – to escape from Colditz twice. That was something he might have been proud of, but Hartley knew he should never have ended up here on either occasion. The first time had been because he was naive, inexperienced, but this time he had been pigheaded – if loyal to Royce.

The footsteps disappeared. Hartley began to relax – surely they wouldn't be found? They returned a minute later.

'What are these men doing?'

It was the colonel again, standing right on top of them.

'They are searching as hard as they can, colonel.'

'Why aren't there any dogs?'

'We don't have dogs here, sir.'

'Idiot!'

'Are they looking in the park?'

'Yes, sir.'

'And the town?'

'Yes, sir. I've telephoned the police too. They're getting as many patrols out as possible, although—'

'Although what?'

'They only have two cars.'

Hartley could have laughed.

'Two cars!' The colonel was apoplectic.

'It's only a small town.'

'Get people from Leipzig! Dresden! Chemnitz! Zwickau! This is a murder hunt! Think, you fool, think!'

A pause.

'Don't just stand there! Get on the phone!'

The sound of footsteps running off. Hartley couldn't be sure if it was two sets or one. The colonel was probably still standing there, fuming. Let him, thought Hartley.

Hartley decided that they would have to wait for a while, and kicked Royce gently to indicate that they should retreat all the way down the tunnel. He did so, and soon they were standing at the bottom of the shaft. Something brushed against Hartley's face, and he flapped at it, thinking it was a bat. But it wasn't. 'I don't believe it,' he said.

'What?'

'Here – touch this.'

He grabbed Royce's hand and guided it.

'Jesus!' Royce exclaimed. 'The rope-ladder.'

'I wouldn't fancy using it now.'

'I didn't fancy using it then.'

'It was all right for you,' said Hartley. 'You never had to use the old one.'

'Fair point.'

'Do you remember all this?' he asked.

'Yes,' said Royce. 'I do.'

Hartley said nothing. There was so much to ask that he didn't know where to begin. Was this the right time? Probably not – but if they were captured, he'd never know what happened.

'Tell me what happened at the border,' said Hartley.

'I got shot,' said Royce.

'I know that, but then what?'

'I was sent to a hospital, I don't remember where. There's a lot I don't remember. Whole years are blank. By the way, what year is it?'

'You really don't know?'

'No. Judging by what I see in the mirror, it must be about 1997.'

'It's 1973, Malcolm.'

'Nineteen seventy-three.' Royce rolled it around his mouth as if it was an incantation. 'Is it a good year?'

'Not really. We don't have good years any more.'

'Why? Who's in charge? The socialists? That man Attlee?'

'No. The Tories.'

'Is Churchill still alive?'

'He died a few years back.'

'Oh. How about the king?'

'We have a queen now. Look, Malcolm, there's too much to tell you. It's clear that you've missed out on half a lifetime and I promise I'll tell you everything when we're free. All right?'

Royce stayed silent. A few seconds later, he began to sob. 'What the hell's happened to me?'

Hartley put his arm round his shoulders. 'Why don't you tell me?'

Royce continued to sob. 'I've been used like some kind of guinea pig. God knows what they've put into my body. Have you seen my arms?'

'I saw them the other night.'

'The other night?'

'When I came to get you with Christa.'

'Christa? You came here with my daughter? Are you sure?'

Hartley felt Royce's hands grab him. 'Where is she? You must know!'

'I don't know, and that's the truth. Look, I'd better tell you what's happened to me. It'll be easier for you.'

Hartley told Royce everything. There was clearly a lot to take in, and because of the circumstances, he told the story quickly and quietly. Royce interrupted with various exclamations of 'Jesus' and 'Good God' and 'I don't believe it'. He seemed most troubled about what would happen to Christa.

'When did you last see her?' asked Hartley. 'If you don't count the other night.'

'Last month,' said Royce.

'What happened?'

Royce spoke slowly and painfully. His voice was very frail, reedy like an old man's.

'A young woman was brought in by some officer,' he said. 'He told me she was my daughter, and that we were to have five minutes together.'

'What did you talk about?'

'There wasn't much we could talk about. We spent most of the time in tears.'

'When had you seen her before that?'

'When she was about two. We were all at home one day when a platoon of Russian soldiers came in and arrested us.'

'Why?'

'They said I was an illegal, which of course I was. I had been living with Rosa for a while, and one of the neighbours informed on us.'

'Then what happened?'

'I was sent to Russia.'

'To a gulag?'

'Yes.'

'How long for?'

'I have no idea. Until after Stalin had died. When was that?'

' 'Fifty-three.'

'So, a good six or seven years, then.'

'But how did you keep sane?'

'I don't think I did.'

The muffled sound of automatic gunfire outside caused the two men's heads to swing towards the mouth of the tunnel.

'I pity the poor thing they're shooting at,' said Hartley.

'Well, it's not us.'

'Whatever happens, we've got to move out before it gets light.'

Royce yawned. 'I think,' he said, 'that I should sleep.'

'What? Now?'

'Yes. I'm very tired.'

He sounded like a child, thought Hartley, reminiscent of one of the boys when they were small. He heard Royce slide to the floor.

'Wake me up when it's time to go.'

Hartley didn't know what to say. The poor man must still have been full of drugs, and no doubt the activity had exhausted him. Hartley, too, was tired, but he couldn't allow himself the same luxury as Royce. If he, too, fell asleep, they would risk waking up in daylight, and would have to spend the day in there. Without food or water, Hartley didn't fancy that, and in daylight the tunnel's exit would be a lot more visible.

He crawled back down the tunnel and stopped a couple of feet before the opening. He could hear voices, barked commands, but they were fainter. They were coming from the woods on the other side of the park. Hartley resolved to move half an hour after he could no longer hear them. In the meantime, he would lie here and thank God they had got this far – some ten to fifteen yards from the castle.

'Come on, it's time to go!' Hartley shook Royce awake in the darkness.

'What?'

'Come on! We can't stay here all night!'

Hartley led the way as they crawled down the tunnel. Gingerly, he stuck his head out into the night air, grateful for its refreshing coolness. He listened hard, and could not hear anything other than the alarm. He was glad it was still ringing, as it would drown any noise they made. Slowly, he emerged from the tunnel, and looked around. There was no one to be seen. They would now be searching the countryside – presumably the last place they expected their quarry to be was in the castle's grounds.

He hauled himself out of the tunnel and helped Royce out. Now where? They had no papers, no money, no food. But they did have a gun, and with it, they could get other things.

'Which way are we going?' Royce asked. 'The same as last time?'

'No,' said Hartley. 'We're not young men any more, and I don't fancy spending the night running around the countryside. We'll find a car.'

'A car?'

'You have heard of cars, haven't you?'

'Of course! But where are you going to get one?'

'In the town. Come on.'

Hartley led the way down the wooded slope and they made their way through the park, hugging the tree line. They climbed another wooded slope, and found themselves in the garden of a small house. They walked through it quietly, then crept down a path and came out on to a lane.

They passed several more houses, none of which had cars parked outside. Hartley did not wish to go too far into the centre of the town, but until they found a car he had little choice. They must look a comic pair, he thought, Royce shuffling along in his pyjamas and slippers, and himself hobbling in his ill-fitting trousers and crumpled shirt. They hardly looked like a couple of crack agents infiltrating enemy lines, fighting at the vanguard of the Cold War. Still, he had struck a blow in killing that torturer, albeit a small one.

'There!'

Royce was pointing at a car, bigger than a Trabant, parked outside a large house. It was a Wartburg 353, a terrible car by Western standards but in East Germany it was almost luxurious.

They walked over to it. Hartley tried the door, but it was locked. 'Damn!'

He looked up at the house, which clearly belonged to a Party official: no ordinary citizen could afford to live in a place like that. There would be some Communist justice then, thought Hartley, if he appropriated the vehicle. And to do that he would have to get the keys, and the only way to get the keys was to get into the house.

'Wait here.' Hartley walked up to the front door and rang the bell. It was crazy, but they had little choice. There was no reply, so he rang the bell again, keeping his finger on the button for at least half a minute. Eventually a gruff voice barked, 'Who is it?'

'Open up! Police!'

The knock in the middle of the night was what every East German feared, even Party men. The door opened to reveal a plump man in his late forties wearing a dressing-gown. Hartley pointed the gun at his chest. 'Your car keys. Where are they?'

The man froze.

'I said, your car keys!' Even in the dim light, Hartley could see the colour draining from his face. 'Get me your fucking car keys!'

'Yes!'

'Come on!'

'They're – they're – they're behind me.'

'Get them!'

'Who is it, Peter?' A woman's voice come from upstairs.

'Stay there, Emmy.'

'Yes, stay there!' Hartley shouted up. He looked past the man into the hall. On a small table he saw a china basket, with the glint of keys in it. He pushed past and grabbed them, then pointed the gun at the man's face. 'If you phone the police, I shall shoot you. Do you understand?'

The man nodded vigorously.

'Now, go back to bed and forget this ever happened.' Hartley ran out of the house to the car. He unlocked the door and got in, then opened the passenger door for Royce. He turned the key in the ignition and the engine started reluctantly. He looked at the petrol gauge – just under a full tank. Good. That should get them to the border at Eisenach. God knew how they would cross it.

Chapter Ten

COMPARED TO THE Trabant, the Wartburg was like a racing-car. Hartley headed westwards out of town, although he had no idea of the route he would take.

'Is there a map in there?' he asked Royce.

Royce opened the glove compartment and scratched around. 'No,' he replied, 'just a packet of cigarettes.'

'That's almost as good. Pass me one, would you?' He pressed in the car's cigarette lighter, hoping he wouldn't reduce the engine power. He lit the cigarette, sucked in a lungful of smoke and coughed it straight out. 'Mother of God! What the hell is that?'

'They're called Glatt.'

'*Glatt*' meant smooth.

'They're anything but bloody *glatt*. They're more like *rauh*.'

Nevertheless, Hartley took another drag. He needed it and, frankly, he felt he deserved it. 'No map on the back seat?' he asked.

Royce turned. 'Nothing,' he said. 'Except a doll.'

He reached for it. As dolls went it was rather a nice one. It was made of wood, had a friendly expression and long dark hair.

'She can be our lucky mascot,' said Hartley, placing it on the dashboard. 'What shall we call her?'

'Christa,' said Royce.

Hartley took a drag on the cigarette. Christa had brought him anything but good luck, but he didn't want to upset Royce. 'Christa it is,' he agreed. 'Do you know what happened to Rosa?' he asked.

'I heard she died when I was in the gulag.'

'I'm sorry.'

'I've got used to it. In fact, I have a small confession to make to you.'

'Oh, yes?'

'I saw you back in 'forty-six, or whenever it was. I'd heard that a British officer was looking for me, so I hid for a few days. One day I had to go back home to get something, I can't remember what, and I saw you sitting in a jeep round the corner from our block. I nearly had a heart-attack. I wanted to run up to you, but I knew that if I did you'd take me away and that I'd never see Rosa again.'

Hartley was astonished.

'I knew you'd be persistent, so I got Rosa to pretend she was seeing some Russki soldier, and soon after that you disappeared. I assumed you'd think I was dead, and it turned out I was right.'

Hartley reminded himself to concentrate on the driving. They were negotiating a narrow road down a valley, and the Wartburg's headlights were not very efficient. He was angry at first, annoyed that he had gone to all that effort all those years ago, and that Royce had decided to repay his efforts by avoiding him. But then anger gave way to laughter. 'You crafty bugger!'

'I know. I'm sorry. And now I'm sorry about this. To have put you to all this trouble.'

'I owe you. I should never have left you at the Swiss border.'

'You had to save yourself,' said Royce. 'Come on, you'd have never managed, carrying me.'

'I might have done.'

'That's unlikely. We'd both have been shot dead.'

'Were you really shot? You weren't pretending so that you could get back to Rosa?'

'Feel my shoulder,' said Royce. 'Here, just below the bone.'

Hartley stretched out his right hand and felt where Royce indicated. Sure enough, there was a slight dent and a ridge of scar tissue.

'It went right through me.' said Royce. He pulled down his pyjama top to reveal the scar left by the exit wound.

'I'm sorry to have doubted you.'

'Not at all. I would have thought the same thing.'

369

For a minute or so they drove in silence. Hartley hoped they were still going west. They should hit a main road soon, and he would be able to get his bearings. He flicked his cigarette out of the window.

'What happened after the gulag?' he asked.

'That was when things went bad for me and I lost my marbles again. Do you know what I've got?'

'I do. Do you?'

'No. Will you tell me?'

'I've heard you're suffering from paranoia and manic depression. You seem all right at the moment.'

'It changes, as you might remember.'

Another silence. They drove under a massive railway arch, on top of which was another railway arch.

'That's quite a construction,' said Royce.

'God knows where we are.'

They drove a little further, and a road sign flashed up in front of them: Göhren.

'Ever heard of it?' asked Royce.

'Yes,' said Hartley. 'We're heading south, which is hardly ideal. We'll need to turn right when we can.'

Göhren was the East German equivalent of a one-horse town, thought Hartley. A few houses, a small church, and then they were out of it. It was probably good that they were going south through these sleepy little places: if any roadblocks had been set up, they wouldn't be here.

'So, what's Christa like?' Royce asked.

'She's very bright. Attractive. She's also one of my agents – or I thought she was.'

'One of your agents?' Royce's voice was filled with incomprehension.

'That's right. She was codenamed Sparrow, but, it would appear that she was loyal to the Stasi rather than us – because of you. They'd blackmailed her. They told her they'd kill you if she didn't entice me over here.'

'But she'd only met me for five minutes!'

'Would you want your father murdered, even if you hardly knew him?'

'Perhaps not. Anyway, I don't know if I have a father still. Or a mother.'

Hartley look a breath. 'I'm afraid they're both dead, Malcolm.'

'When?'

'Your father in 1958, and your mother last December. I'm sorry to be telling you like this.'

Royce didn't say a word. Hartley flashed him a glance, but he was staring blankly at the road. 'I've lost so much,' he said. 'Everything. All because of the war. And my head.'

'Well, you're going to get some of it back now,' said Hartley. 'It's not too late to make a life in Britain.'

'Did you think of all this before you came out here?'

371

'Well, no. I just assumed—'

'Well, maybe you assumed wrong. Think about it. I don't know anything about what you call "home".'

'That's right.'

'If I get to Britain, I doubt I'll recognise it, and I doubt it'll recognise me. I'll be like a woolly mammoth come back to life after years in a glacier – that's where I've been you know. A sodding glacier. And now you think you can just bring me back to life again.'

'Look, I know all this is a lot to take in, but I came because I felt I'd let you down. I wanted to make it up to you. Can't you see that? And, besides, you'll get a hell of a lot better treatment in London than you're getting here, I'll make sure of it.'

'As soon as I've discovered my daughter is alive, you're taking me away. You tried to take me away last time.'

'What are you suggesting?'

Royce raised his hands, then let them fall back into his lap.

'Are you saying you'd rather stay here?' Hartley asked.

'I don't know. I don't know anything.'

They sat in silence as Hartley drove on, the Wartburg's engine pushed to its limit. Jesus Christ, he thought, the biggest obstacle he had to face wasn't outside the car, but in it. This was typical Royce.

'You know they'll kill you if you go back.'

'Thanks to you.'

'That's not true. They would have killed you anyway. As soon as they'd found you were of no use to them, they'd have given you a lethal injection.'

Royce harrumphed. 'So you say.'

'I've been fighting these people since 1939. They're ruthless, barbaric. I've told you what they did to me. And they were only just starting.'

'It would have been nice to get to know my daughter, though.'

'So, what shall we do? Go back to the castle and ask to see her?'

'I could go back on my own. You can drop me off in the next town.'

'I'm not doing that, Royce. I'm not going to let you go. Not this time. Just leave her. She works for them, and she has her own life. Even if they did let you live, which they won't, you'll only be a burden to her.'

Hartley noticed that their route was taking them into a more populated area. They passed houses, the occasional monolith of flats, even a factory. Where the hell was this? Just give me one road sign.

After another mile, they were rewarded with a sign that read 'K-Marx-St (Chemnitz)'.

'Shit,' said Hartley. 'We've gone south.'

Nevertheless, it wasn't so bad. An Autobahn ran from Chemnitz all the way to the border. They could take that. It would be risky, but it would be quicker.

373

By now they would know they had a car, because the official was bound to have reported it – Hartley almost felt sorry for the man, then reminded himself of what that man represented, what he worked for. 'Here we go,' he said. 'Here's our road out of here.'

He navigated the Wartburg over a potholed junction and joined a two-lane Autobahn. A sign told them that Eisenach was two hundred kilometres away. He looked at the fuel tank. It had gone down to just above the three-quarters mark. That should be enough, at least for a normal car. But this was East Germany, and nothing about it was normal.

For the next half-hour, they made good progress, passing the large town of Gera. With each kilometre, Hartley felt more confident, but he was still nervous about the border crossing. He didn't know it, but it would be the usual row upon row of barbed wire, tank traps, watchtowers and more barbed-wire. People spent years trying to plan their way out of East Germany, and they were going to attempt it in a little under two hours. It would make the Swiss border crossing thirty years ago look like a Boy Scouts' outing.

Royce remained silent, for which Hartley was grateful. The atmosphere in the car remained frosty, complemented by smoke from the Glats, which Hartley was now chain-smoking. He left the window open to ensure that he stayed alert. The occasional wave of tiredness surged over him: the monotony of the road, lack of sleep and food were beginning to tell. He estimated that it was around two in the morning, and he wanted to reach the border while it was still dark.

When Hartley saw the roadblock, it was too late to do anything about it. If he had seen it sooner, he would have abandoned the car and dashed into the darkness of the countryside. Instead, he found himself pulling up behind a Trabant and another Wartburg, ahead of which a couple of police cars were parked across the two carriageways, blue lights flashing lazily.

'What now?' asked Royce.

Hartley picked up the gun from the footwell. It was a Makarov, a gun he knew as well as any other. Standard Sovbloc issue, and there were eight rounds in it. He slid down the safety catch.

'You're not going to use it, are you?'

'If I have to. Do you think we should just give ourselves up?'

He could see two policemen, both checking the papers of the driver of the Trabant. He was waved through, and the other Wartburg edged forward. Hartley did the same, noticing that the engine temperature was rising. This was no good, he thought. If they sat here for too long, it would overheat. There was no way he was going to switch off the engine, and he left it in gear, ready to pop up the clutch.

Hartley's eyes flicked between the temperature gauge and the policemen. The needle rose alarmingly high. It was almost a relief when the other Wartburg drove off. He drove forward slowly, and stopped in front of the two policemen. One was looking at his numberplate. They were buggered, thought Hartley.

A policeman came to the window and gestured with his finger that Hartley should wind it down. Hartley did so.

'Your papers.'

'I don't have any.'

For a second the young man looked nonplussed, but his expression changed to shock when Hartley produced the Makarov and pointed it towards his face.

'These are my papers,' said Hartley. 'Now get out of my way.'

The policeman stepped back instinctively. Hartley knew he had to seize the initiative – any delay now would be fatal. The other policeman was still in front of them. Too bad, he thought. He would not allow the man to stand between him and freedom. Hartley pressed hard on the accelerator, lifted the clutch, and the Wartburg surged forward, smashing into the policeman.

'Jesus Christ!' shouted Royce.

The man hit the windscreen. The glass cracked, but stayed in one piece. Hartley could just about make out where he was going, and spun the wheel to the left. There might be enough of a gap between the rear of one of the police cars and the flimsy-looking crash barrier.

The policeman rolled to the right, but did not fall off the bonnet. But Hartley could see better now: he aimed the Wartburg at the gap, which was evidently too small. Here goes, he thought. 'Hold tight!' he shouted, as much for his benefit as for Royce's.

The Wartburg smashed into the police car and the barrier simultaneously. The sudden deceleration caused the policeman to shoot forward off the car. Hartley carried on driving, pushing the police car out of the way. The barrier yielded a little, and with a sickening crunch, they drove over the policeman. Poor bastard, thought Hartley.

'For Christ's sake!' Royce yelled. 'You've killed him! You've bloody killed him!'

Hartley slammed the Wartburg into second gear and accelerated. The sound of scraping metal could be heard, but there seemed to be no diminution in the car's performance, such as it was. The engine temperature was almost at maximum, but still the car drove on.

Hartley looked into his rear-view mirror. The first policeman was running towards his fallen comrade, and a couple more figures were emerging from the cars. Shit, thought Hartley, they'll start shooting.

'I can't believe you did that!'

'Shut up!'

He hadn't wanted to do it, but the man had been standing in the wrong place. If he'd waited for him to get out of the way, both Royce and he would have been shot. It was imperative that he got away. It was hardly the whole fabric of Western civilization that was at stake, but it would be a blow to the Service if he was caught. And many lives would be put at risk. But, then, it was his own stupid bloody fault that he was here in the first place, on this mad mission to rescue a man who seemed singularly ungrateful.

He could still see the blue lights in his mirror. Were they getting any nearer? It was impossible to tell. They would give chase, there was no doubt of that, so he had to put as much distance between them and himself as he could. Hartley resolved to leave the Autobahn – it made more sense to use the back roads.

Another glance into the mirror revealed that they were indeed chasing. 'Shit,' he said. 'They're after us.'

'Why don't we just give up?'

'You've got to be joking! Unless you want to die. For Pete's sake, we're not caught yet.'

Hartley willed the car faster, but the speedometer stuck resolutely at around 110 kilometres an hour. It felt pathetically slow, although the police cars didn't look much faster.

'They're getting closer,' said Royce.

'How many?'

'Just one.'

Hartley knew he could not outrun them. There was only one thing for it.

'Why are you slowing down?'

'Hang on.' Hartley looked in his mirror. The blue lights were no more than two hundred yards away. He jammed on the brakes, opened the door and jumped out on to the road. He ran to the back of the car, leant over it and took careful aim. There was no point in firing until the police car was thirty or forty yards away. He had seen a ballistics report that showed the Makarov's shells dropped off considerably after that distance.

He steadied the gun in his hands. Hold steady, he said to himself. The car was now a hundred yards away. It was tempting to take a shot, but that would only act as a warning. He wanted to put the police car permanently out of action.

He stroked the trigger, ready to squeeze it. The police car was slowing – then there was a screech as the driver violently applied the brakes. Damn, he was a little too far away – fifty yards. Nevertheless Hartley pulled the trigger, aiming at the windscreen. The gun kicked up in his hand. Missed. He took aim and squeezed again. The windscreen shattered.

He ran, the pistol pointing forward. He could make

out a face looking at him. Hartley kept running, waiting for a shot, but none came. He ran right up to the car and saw a single policeman in the front, clutching the steering-wheel, his face the image of terror. Hartley punched him in the face through the open windscreen and he fell back against his seat, unconscious. Hartley opened the door, removed the keys from the ignition and threw them into the ditch at the side of the road. That should do it, he thought. Then he took the policeman's pistol and ran back to the car.

'Right,' he said, as he got in. 'Let's get going.'

There was no Royce.

Hartley looked around, and saw a figure running across to the other side of the Autobahn.

'Come back!' he shouted. 'Royce! Come back!'

The man had snapped again. Hartley opened the door, ran to the crash barrier vaulted it and landed heavily on his feet. Pain ripped through him. 'Royce!'

Hartley ran across the carriageways. He could see Royce stumbling through a field. The bloody idiot! He was tempted to let him disappear into the night. That was what he wanted, after all. Well, leave him, save yourself. Hartley thought of the first time he had met Royce. He had shot at him, in rather the same way as he had just shot at the police car. How much simpler life would have been if he had hit him.

He watched Royce trip and fall. He couldn't just

leave him. It would be like abandoning a child. Royce didn't know what he wanted, and it was up to Hartley to help him find it. He certainly wasn't going to find it in this country. He might have Christa, but they would never be able to enjoy a proper relationship, even if they were allowed to live.

Hartley took a deep breath and hobbled towards Royce's prostrate form. 'Come on, Malcolm,' he said, 'Let's get you back to the car.'

'Leave me!'

'I'm not going to do that.'

'Just leave me alone!'

Hartley ignored him. He bent down and lifted him up under the armpits.

Royce tried weakly to struggle free. 'Let me go!'

Hartley ignored him and pulled him up. 'For heaven's sake, man!' he shouted. 'There's no choice any more!'

Royce's eyes were wide and staring.

'What's got into you?' Hartley shook him. 'Come on!'

'The gun,' said Royce. 'The shooting.'

'What about it?'

'My men. I abandoned them.'

'Which men?'

'In the church. In Greece. I ran away. As soon as I heard the shooting. I ran. I never looked back. They must all have died.'

There were tears in his eyes. 'I'm a coward, Hugh! That's what I'm running from! I'm running from me! Drugged up to the eyeballs in an asylum – that suits me fine! That's why I don't want to go home, don't you see?'

'You're not a coward, Malcolm,' said Hartley. 'You showed that in the escape, and you've shown it tonight.'

'It's no use,' said Royce. 'Leave me with the pistol and I'll do the decent thing.'

'I'm not having that, and I'm not going to leave you. Come on, this is your chance to make something of your life.'

'I don't have a life.'

'Of course you bloody do. Come on! This is the way to find it – with me!'

'I'm not moving.'

Hartley drew up the pistol and pointed it at Royce's chest.

'Are you going to shoot me, Hugh? Well, please do. I won't mind a bit.'

Hartley slid down the safety catch. Royce swallowed.

'I'm going to count to three,' said Hartley.

Royce said nothing.

'One.'

No movement.

'Two.'

Hartley knew he couldn't just shoot the man, but he had to look as though he meant it.

'Three.'

Hartley began to squeeze the trigger slightly.

'Don't!' Royce shouted.

Hartley lowered the gun. Thank God for that. 'Can we go?'

Royce nodded. Hartley ran back up to the carriageway, with Royce a few feet behind. Everything was silent, peaceful, even. They crossed, climbed over the barrier and got back into the car.

'Did you kill him?'

'Who?'

'The policeman in that car. He looked dead.'

'I knocked him out.'

Royce eyed him suspiciously.

'I'm telling you the truth,' said Hartley, as he started the engine. 'I don't like killing people.'

The next junction came up a couple of minutes later, and Hartley turned off. Soon they were travelling along what passed for a main road heading west.

'This must be the old main road,' said Hartley, 'from before they built the Autobahn.'

Royce folded his arms. 'I'm sorry,' he said. 'Would you really have killed me?'

Hartley didn't reply. He might find himself having

to threaten Royce again, and he didn't want to lose the deterrent.

'Would you?'

'Let's just say I came close.'

'Well, thanks for not doing it.'

Hartley laughed a little. 'It would have been rather a wasted trip if I had.'

'Just as you were about to pull the trigger, I knew I wanted to live.'

'Good.'

'Maybe you're right. Maybe I can start again back in Britain.'

'Let's just get there first,' said Hartley.

He looked at the fuel gauge. Quarter of a tank. They should just make it.

They arrived outside Eisenach forty minutes later. They had spent much of the journey in silence, and Hartley finished the rest of the Glatts. Taking roads that ran round the town, he muddled through to Creuzburg, which he had heard of. It was on the river Werra, and the border was on the opposite bank. It was starting to get light.

On the west of the town, just before the bridge, the Wartburg spluttered and died.

'What's wrong with it?' asked Royce.

'We're out of petrol. But we're nearly there.'

They got out of the car and stood in the middle of

the road. The bridge was just in front of them and, as far as Hartley could tell, it was not guarded. They walked towards it cautiously, Hartley clutching the pistol.

'Wait!' hissed Royce. 'I've forgotten something!'

'What?'

'Christa!'

Surely he couldn't be referring to his daughter. Please, God, not now. Let's get it right this time.

'The doll,' said Royce. 'Our lucky mascot.'

Hartley smiled with relief. 'All right. Go and get it.'

Hartley stood still watching the bridge, while Royce went back to get the doll. Thirty seconds later he returned with it. 'We'll be fine now.' He stuffed it into one of the front pockets of his pyjamas. Hartley led the way up to the bridge, a low, stone-built affair. It had a brow, which meant he couldn't see the other side, but they had to chance it. He could see the river now, flowing too swiftly to risk swimming across. The two men crept forward, Hartley ready to hit the ground when he saw movement. They were in luck. No one was on the bridge, and Hartley ran forward, beckoning Royce.

They sped up the road for the next few hundred yards. Hartley was exhausted and ravenous. His feet still hurt like hell. After a couple of minutes they crested the top of the incline, then looked down across the countryside, which was inky blue in the pre-dawn light.

Stretching from left to right, about half a mile away, was the border. Floodlights, watchtowers, glistening wire, tank traps, ditches and machine-gun posts. It was one of the most heavily fortified borders in the world.

'What do you think?' asked Hartley.

'I think,' said Royce, 'that things have changed in the last thirty years.'

For the next five minutes, hidden among a few trees, the two men watched the comings and goings at the border. Lorries disgorged guards, filled up with guards. A helicopter flew overhead. Hartley and Royce froze.

'Do you suppose it's looking for us?' asked Royce.

'I wouldn't bet against it.'

They watched the helicopter fly down the length of the border, then pirouette in the sky and turn back towards them. It flew almost directly overhead, its downwash stirring the tree tops.

'I'd say it's definitely looking for us,' said Hartley, as the noise dissipated.

'All we need now is a tank or two,' said Royce.

'I'm sure there'll be some kicking around.'

'What shall we do?'

Hartley scanned the installations. It would be

almost impossible to cross the fence itself – every section was overlooked by a watchtower, and they would be shot before they attempted to get over or through it. The weakest part was the road crossing, which consisted of the usual low-built grey guardhouse, two barriers, and a grey guardhouse on the West German side. There was at least fifty yards of no man's land, the type of ground Hartley had studied through binoculars on countless occasions while waiting for agents to cross. He estimated that there would be twenty or thirty sentries at the crossing, all of whom would be heavily armed. He thought of stealing another car, then attempting to smash their way through the crossing, but the barriers would be far too strong, and they would be riddled with automatic fire in seconds.

He looked back at the fence. It was their only hope. Maybe there was a place where they could get through, perhaps a piece of dead ground. He noticed a point where the fence had a downwards kink as it crossed a slight depression in the ground. Maybe there. If they crawled along it, there was a small chance they wouldn't be spotted. It had to be worth investigating.

Hartley indicated the spot to Royce. 'There,' he said. 'Do you see?'

Royce nodded.

Hartley could tell by his face that he wasn't convinced. In truth, neither was he. But it looked like the only option, and if they were to try, it had to be now.

'Are you ready?'

Royce nodded nervously.

'Let's go, then.'

Hartley looked left and right, up and down the road, then crossed it. They were heading directly to a small copse some three hundred yards away from their crossing point. He could hear Royce breathing hard behind him; the exertions of the night had proved exhausting for a man who had spent so many years stuck in bed. Hartley held tight to the gun, its presence only partially reassuring. It wouldn't worry a guard up a watchtower, especially one armed with a machine-gun, but a few well-aimed shots might buy them enough time.

A couple of minutes later they reached the copse and caught their breath, leaning against the trees for support.

'This reminds me of when we were trying to get into Switzerland,' said Royce. 'There was a lovely moon that night.'

'They probably wouldn't have seen us if it had been cloudy.'

Hartley walked to the edge of the copse and looked down the field to the border. He studied the watchtower to the right, trying to spot a guard in it. For a moment of ridiculous optimism he thought it might be empty, but the glint of a helmet or buckle checked him. He walked back to Royce. 'Despite what happened earlier,' he said, 'I can't make you do this.'

Royce seemed surprised. 'I'm in your hands, Hugh.'

'It could be suicidal.'

'I know.'

'I want you to be sure you think it's worth it. I don't want to lead you to your death against your will.'

'You're not,' said Royce. 'I'm doing this because I want to.'

'Good.' Hartley looked back at the border. 'We should go,' he said. He held out his hand. 'Good luck, Malcolm.'

'Good luck to you, too.'

Hartley walked off.

'One thing,' said Royce.

'Yes?'

'I forgot to say thank you.'

'Don't thank me just yet. Thank me in ten minutes or so.'

Ten minutes. They might not even be alive in ten minutes.

Hartley wanted to run, to get it over with, but he knew it was best to move slowly. He kept his eye on the watchtower to their right. He suspected that it contained the man who might kill them. Suddenly the brilliant white beam of a searchlight issued from it, stabbing into the half-darkness. Hartley and Royce stopped moving as the light caressed the vast fence.

They moved forward again, and soon they had entered the depression. Hartley dropped on to his front, and Royce did the same. The watchtower disappeared from view, which meant that they were invisible. They crawled forward, Hartley grateful that the ground was not too rough or loose.

It took them five minutes to do the first hundred yards. They paused briefly to rest. Hartley heard the sound of a car engine on the road, but it was too far away to worry about. A telephone rang, just audible, in the low grey building at the road crossing. Probably a warning to watch for two fugitives and shoot them on sight. Or maybe it was the Stasi colonel, wondering if there was any news.

Hartley started crawling again. The watchtower was still out of sight, and he prayed it would remain so. It was getting light far too quickly now, which meant there could be no turning back. The occupants of the watchtower would be bound to spot them if they tried to get back to the wood.

With fifty yards to go, Hartley had a good idea of the construction of the fence. With concrete posts and barbed wire, it looked almost impregnable. The wire would cut them, but Hartley thought they would get through. He was crawling faster now, occasionally twisting his head round to see if Royce was keeping up. He was, but he was clearly having a difficult time. Hartley paused, waiting for him to draw near.

With twenty yards to go, he made out the roof of the watchtower. He cursed inwardly, but moved forward slowly, all the time keeping an eye on the building. Thankfully no more than the roof came into view. It would be close, damned close. After another ten yards, the roof disappeared again. Thank God for that.

A minute later, they were there. Hartley lay still, getting his breath back. He was delighted to see that the watchtower was still obscured by the ground around them. On the other side of the wire was the no man's land, in which the depression continued, then another fence erected by the West Germans, smaller, more negotiable. For the first time in hours, Hartley began to feel optimistic. They were going to make it, and he would get away with this. He thought of the Head Man asking how his holiday in Scotland had gone, and how he would feed him some cock-and-bull about the number of salmon he had caught. The Head Man would tell him there'd been a frightful hoo-hah on his patch while he was away, that signals had picked up a real flurry of traffic around Leipzig, Dresden and Chemnitz. Something about two foreigners escaping from an asylum, and did Hartley have any idea what the devil it might be about?

Royce drew up alongside him. He looked pale.

'Are you all right?' Hartley asked.

Royce nodded, breathless. 'I'll make it.'

'Good.'

'How the hell are we going to get through this?'

Hartley looked at the fence.

'We bend it.'

'Do you think there'll be enough room?'

'Just.'

Hartley grabbed the lowest strand of horizontal wire and bent it upwards. It yielded more than he had expected. Cheap East German wire, he thought.

'That's still not enough to get under,' said Royce.

Hartley knew he'd get a better purchase on it if he stood up and pulled. He would be visible, but it would only be for a few seconds. He pushed himself up a little and looked at the watchtower. Now or never, he thought, and stood up.

He heaved up on the barbed wire, which gave another few inches. The searchlight flashed on. Hartley dropped to the ground and hugged the dip. Once more the beam ran along the fence, passing just a couple of feet above their heads. They were in shadow, thought Hartley. No chance that they'd been seen.

As soon as the light was switched off, Hartley nudged Royce forward.

'Go!'

Royce paused.

'Go!'

He crawled under the wire, which caught on his pyjamas, but Hartley freed the fabric. He was frustratingly slow, and Hartley willed him to speed up. With every second it got lighter, and he could hear birdsong. In ten more minutes, they would be horribly exposed. Eventually, Royce was through. Hartley felt his heart thumping against the ground as he crawled under. The wire caught the back of his shirt, but he carried on and it ripped. They were going to bloody do it, he thought. They were going to get away from one of the most hateful bloody countries in the world.

He followed Royce, who was almost on his hands and knees.

'Keep down!' Hartley whispered.

Royce dropped back to his front, although it meant he travelled more slowly. Nevertheless, they made progress, and after a minute they were nearly at the next fence. Don't count your chickens, Hartley told himself. You've still got a way to go.

A distant throbbing. Where was it coming from? Hartley turned to look. The throbbing got louder, became a clattering. It was the helicopter. With its searchlight it would see them for sure. There was no choice. They had to run for it.

'Come on! Get up!' Hartley stood up, and grabbed Royce by the collar of his pyjamas. 'Up!'

Royce stood up shakily.

'We've got to run!' Hartley said. 'Just bloody run!'

He sprinted forward, and Royce fell in behind them. They had only twenty yards to go, twenty yards to freedom. The helicopter was louder. It was almost on top of them now, the wash from the blades flattening the grass.

White light flooded the ground around them. Hartley put his hand in front of his eyes to shield them from the glare.

'Keep going!' he shouted back at Royce.

The din was tremendous, so loud that neither man heard the cries of 'Halt!' Even if they had, Hartley would not have stopped because they would kill him if they caught him. They were right next to the second fence now. More barbed wire, tough. Hartley lifted a strand and beckoned Royce forward.

'Move it!'

Royce bent to the ground and crawled under the fence. The helicopter was only a few feet above them, and Hartley could barely stand.

'Come on!' he shouted, his words ripped out of his mouth by the turbulence.

He watched Royce crawl through. His head was now in the West, then his back, his legs, his feet. He was a free man, he had made it. Hartley hit the ground, and wriggled furiously.

He never heard the shots. But he felt them briefly.

He looked up and saw Royce, the doll poking out of his pyjama pocket. He had made it. That was good. It had been worth it after all. A great adventure.

Epilogue

SARAH HAD MIXED feelings about seeing him there. Although she couldn't have expected him to stay away, it was still disconcerting to greet the man who had sent her husband to his death. As if he was aware of her feelings, he was particularly gracious and polite, and told her that Hartley's mission really had been important, and that what he had achieved was remarkable. If she wanted someone to blame, she should blame himself, because it was he who had ordered him there. What had he done? she asked. The Head Man smiled, and told her he couldn't tell her, at least not yet, but that it was a matter of utmost importance to national security, and that Hugh's mission had been entirely successful.

The Head Man was the first in a line of numerous well-wishers. They were all exceedingly complimentary about Hugh, calling him 'the last of the old breed', 'an original', 'truly brave', 'the greatest of handlers' and 'a privilege to work with'. Fine words, thought

Sarah, but no one told her what he had actually *done* out there. She wanted badly to know, not just for her sake but for the boys'. Surely that was fair?

There must have been three hundred at the wake, and she had spoken to nearly all of them – distant family members, Colditz veterans, regimental representatives, friends from Cambridge and, of course, Service staff. There were even a few old men who spoke with Russian and German accents; they seemed to be the most effusive in their praise.

After two hours, the hall began to empty, and she was left talking to Christopher, Tom and their girlfriends. A few guests still hovered about catching up on old times, sharing the occasional reminiscence that made them laugh. Good, she thought. Hugh would have wanted some jolliness.

'That went well,' said Christopher, 'don't you think, Mum?'

Sarah smiled. 'Yes. It just seems funny to see all these people without your father being here.'

Tom put his arm round her.

'Later,' she said. 'You'll set me off if you do that.'

She hadn't wanted to cry in public. Emotions were private, and she would have plenty of opportunity to express them. Nevertheless, she brought out a white handkerchief and dabbed it under her right eye. She put it back into her bag, and as she shut it, her eye was caught by an old man in a wheelchair by the door to the hall. He was accompanied by a nurse, and looked serene.

'Who's that?' she asked.

'Who?'

'Him,' she said. 'Over there.'

Christopher and Tom shrugged.

'Haven't a clue.'

'Presumably yet another of Dad's old Colditz cronies.'

'I'd better go and speak to him,' said Sarah.

'Don't worry, Mum,' said Tom. 'You've done enough.'

'No,' she said. 'I really must. He's obviously made a real effort to get here.'

Sarah walked over to him, her heels clicking on the wooden floor. As she approached, she saw that the man wasn't all that old, perhaps no more than in his late fifties. 'Hello,' she said, holding out her hand. 'Thank you so much for coming.'

They shook hands. The man smiled. 'I nearly didn't make it,' he said.

'I'm sorry, I don't know your name.'

'Royce,' he said. 'Malcolm Royce.'

Sarah gasped. 'But I thought you were . . .'

'I was,' he said. 'But Hugh brought me back.'

'Brought you back? From where?'

'Germany.'

'Germany? When?'

'Just a few weeks ago. I was with him when he . . . when he died, Mrs Hartley.'

'Sarah, please.'

'Sorry – Sarah. It's nice to meet you finally.'

Sarah struggled to contain herself. She glanced round the room almost guiltily. The boys and their girlfriends were talking among themselves, and nobody was taking any interest in her and Royce.

'How did it happen?'

'You haven't been told?'

Sarah shook her head. 'They never do tell you.'

Royce smiled weakly. 'I'm afraid he was shot, Sarah. They missed me and got him. In 'forty-one it was the other way round. They got me and Hugh got away.'

The man's eyes were wet, old man's eyes, she thought, grey and weak, yet filled with decency and kindness.

'I don't understand,' said Sarah. 'Was he sent to get you back?'

Royce shook his head. 'Not sent,' he replied. 'He went under his own steam. He told me he owed it to me to get me out.'

For a moment, Sarah felt a surge of intense anger. Hugh had also owed it to his family to stay alive, not risk his life. She felt deceived, a fool, cheated. In the end, Hugh had lied to everybody, to her, to the boys, to the wretched Service. And he had done it all for this frail man in the wheelchair.

'The first time we met,' said Royce, 'Hugh almost shot me.'

Sarah twisted out a smile. 'Yes,' she said absently. 'He once told me about it.'

'It would have been better for you if he'd succeeded.'

'You can't say that!'

'Well, it's true, isn't it? He would never have come to get me if I hadn't been alive, would he?'

'I suppose not.' Sarah paused. 'But . . .' she said.

'And . . .' said Royce simultaneously.

'What?' said Sarah.

'No, you first,' said Royce.

'But,' she continued, 'he'd have gone on some sort of mission, no matter what. An adventure, that's what he would have called it. He would have found an excuse. If it hadn't been you it would have been someone or something else.'

Royce nodded.

'You see, he always wanted to make a difference,' said Sarah. 'Always wanted to do his bit. He lived in fear that he never would, that all his time in the army and the Service was just a game, and that the other side were always going to win, no matter what.' She sighed and her hands fell to her sides. 'And now I'm beginning to wonder whether he did make a difference. I mean, it's not as if the bloody Berlin Wall's coming down, is it?'

She looked back into the room, into the space that had been filled with so many men. 'Cold War warriors' was how they and Hugh described themselves. But what were they fighting for exactly? What difference had men like Hugh made?

She looked at the children. It seemed that Tom had told a joke, and the four of them were laughing. Perhaps they might find out the difference, thought Sarah, but not in my lifetime.

The Occupation

Guy Walters

February 1945. In his bunker in Berlin, Hitler makes a desperate decision. He will deploy the V3 – a weapon so secret that its lethal nature is unclear even to the slave labourers constructing it deep beneath the Channel Island of Alderney.

June 1990. Workmen on Alderney mysteriously start to fall sick. Journalist Robert Lebonneur believes he knows why. But the closer he gets to the truth, the more he realises he is up against the same deadly forces that caused so much upheaval nearly half a century ago . . .

'A classic page-turner' *The Times*

'Masterfully crafted and genuinely frightening' *Daily Express*

'A convincing and intelligent thriller' *Daily Mail*

'This gripping thriller, like the sinister, still visible structures it describes, makes for good reading' *Sunday Telegraph*

'Exciting wartime thriller which illustrates a remarkable degree of research' *Guernsey Press & Star*

0 7553 2066 2

headline

The Leader

Guy Walters

The Treaty of London had been signed, and the future sealed. Today was a good day for Britain, the Leader said, a good day for Germany, a good day for Fascist Europe. The Germans are our friends now, he said, Herr Hitler has brought miracles to his country, and I shall do the same for ours . . .

Great Britain, 1937. Edward VIII and his new bride, Wallis, are preparing for their coronation; Winston Churchill is a prisoner on the Isle of Man; and Prime Minister Oswald Mosley – the Leader, as he is known – consults Adolf Hitler on a 'more permanent' solution to the 'Jewish problem'. In exchange for full bellies, the British population has yielded to a regime of terror, enforced by Mosley's secret police.

James Armstrong, a hero of the Great War, is on the run, wanted by Mosley for organising a resistance movement to the government. The Leader is determined to see Armstrong hang. But Armstrong is every bit as clever as the evil men on his trail . . .

0 7553 0058 0

headline

The Traitor

Guy Walters

There was something powerful about it, something magnetic. He had witnessed the effect of such uniforms in the newsreels; now he was about to wear one. But this SS uniform – the uniform proudly worn by so many maniacs and murderers – bore a Union Jack and the three lions. It was an insult to King and Country.

In November 1943 British SOE agent Captain John Lockhart is in Crete, fighting with the partisans. Captured by the Germans, Lockhart faces a stark choice: betray his country, or die.

Lockhart strikes a bargain with his captors. In return for the life of his imprisoned wife, he will change sides. But he is stunned to learn of his mission: to lead the British Free Corps, a clandestine unit of the Waffen SS made up of British fascists and renegades culled from POW camps. Aware that he, like them, will be branded a traitor, Lockhart seeks to redeem himself by destroying a terrifying secret weapon that threatens to change the course of the war . . .

0 7553 0056 4

headline

ROBERT RYAN

Night Crossing

In 1938, Ulrike Walter, a beautiful young German musician, is engaged to be married to Erich Hinkel, a member of the Hitler Youth. But when she meets Inspector Cameron Ross, a Scotland Yard policeman, whose father is a colonel in British Intelligence, her life will be changed for ever.

When war is declared, Ulrike flees Germany for the safety of England but is instead cruelly imprisoned as an enemy alien. Her only hope of rescue is Cameron, who, despite his better judgement, is falling in love with her.

And then Erich is captured by the British and incarcerated in a prisoner of war camp in England. He faces interrogation by Cameron Ross, the one who stands between him and Ulrike, the woman who means more to Erich than life itself . . .

Robert Ryan has written a mesmerising novel that captures the hardships and humanity of the Second World War and explores whether love and compassion can triumph over murder and betrayal.

Praise for Robert Ryan:

'[It] grips from page one. Part intelligent thriller, part love story, it skilfully mixes real events and characters with fictional dialogue to create a novel that's damn near impossible to put down' *Time Out*

0 7553 0181 1

headline
review

The Eagle's Prey

Simon Scarrow

It is over a year since the mighty Roman army landed on the shores of Britain, anticipating little resistance. Yet the savage warriors of the barbarian leader Caratacus continue to torment the legions. Now, though, the Emperor Claudius needs a victory to make his position safe, and the time has come to silence the enemy permanently.

As the Roman troops gather on the eve of battle, centurions Cato and Macro share the confidence of their comrades. Tomorrow a final, decisive blow will surely annihilate Caratacus.

But the battle does not follow the expected course. Inevitably, blame passes down the line. And the most ruthless army in the known world prepares to inflict dreadful punishment on the very men who could bring the long campaign in Britain to a triumphant conclusion.

Praise for Simon Scarrow's EAGLE novels:

'The engrossing storyline is full of teeth-clenching battles, political machinations, treachery, honour, love and death' Elizabeth Chadwick

'Simon Scarrow's stories of Roman military action in Britain have gathered quite a fan club and it's not hard to see why . . . Scarrow's latest book will prove irresistible' *Living History*

'A good, uncomplicated, rip-roaring read' *Mail on Sunday*

0 7553 0116 1

headline

You can now buy any of these other titles from your book or *direct from the publisher*.

FREE P&P AND UK DELIVERY
(Overseas and Ireland £3.50 per book)

After Midnight	Robert Ryan	£6.99
Early One Morning	Robert Ryan	£6.99
This Thing of Darkness	Harry Thompson	£6.99
The Occupation	Guy Walters	£6.99
Jacquot and the Waterman	Martin O'Brien	£6.99
Deadly Web	Barbara Nadel	£6.99
Thorn	Vena Cork	£6.99
The Eagle and the Wolves	Simon Scarrow	£6.99
Havoc, in its Third Year	Ronan Bennett	£7.99
The Big Bad Wolf	James Patterson	£6.99
Flint	Paul Eddy	£6.99
Lethal Intent	Quintin Jardine	£6.99
The Know	Martina Cole	£6.99
From the Corner of His Eye	Dean Koontz	£7.99
American Gods	Neil Gaiman	£7.99
The Devil's Banker	Christopher Reich	£7.99

TO ORDER SIMPLY CALL THIS NUMBER

01235 400 414

or visit our website:

www.madaboutbooks.com

Prices and availability subject to change without notice.